LIVES
REUNITED

ANNE M. McLOUGHLIN

POOLBEG

AMAZON & GOODREADS reviews for *Lives Apart* and *Lives Without End* (Books 1 & 2 of the LIVES trilogy)

"In spite of being set a hundred years ago, the characters' thoughts, joys and worries are so relatable and global. The dialogue is sparkling and witty, the scenes evocative of a time now lost and the interplay between the characters, and especially between the generations, is rendered wonderfully."

"… a beautiful, free-flowing story of emigration which captured my interest immediately and brought me on a wonderful, emotional journey with the main character, Johanna. The author, having introduced Johanna to us, reels us in masterfully with her beautiful, authentic prose and leads us step by step, thought by thought, through her hopes and dreams. There is a beautiful build-up to the major events and a harrowing account of their consequences. The descriptive passages throughout the book are stunning."

"This book carries the reader along a journey through time and between continents. The writing style brings you easily into the heads of the different characters, and the story paints the drama of individual lives onto a canvas of great historical events. Some of the more contemplative moments are really vividly and finely portrayed – this writer knows how to paint colour pictures!"

"Her writing about nature is superb, beautifully observed and recorded. A description of the waves washing in on the shore made me realise I hadn't really looked properly before."

"From the first sentence of this story, the author had me hooked, captured in a web of beautiful descriptive prose, a delicious assault on my senses, and drew me irrevocably into the lives, the joys, the agonies, the minds and very hearts of the two main characters. The author is wholly in tune with the vagaries of country living and is truly at her best when she writes about events and community interactions in vivid detail. With scenes like the reciting of the rosary at a village wake, the quiet night-time atmosphere of the lambing shed, she manages to bring life in rural Ireland alive. Her authentic dialogue comes from the very heart and soul of her characters.

I found myself enthralled with Mary Ann and Bridie as they each encountered the many complexities of life, the twists and turns, the highs and the lows, at times bearing a silent lonely grief that will move the hardest of hearts.

As each woman walks in her own valley of darkness, we are drawn along with them, moved by their plight. McLoughlin explores and portrays superbly that aching feeling of loss, the abandonment of dreams, the descent from hope to despair, but the book has lots of moments of joy, that serve to sustain the characters as they go through their lives."

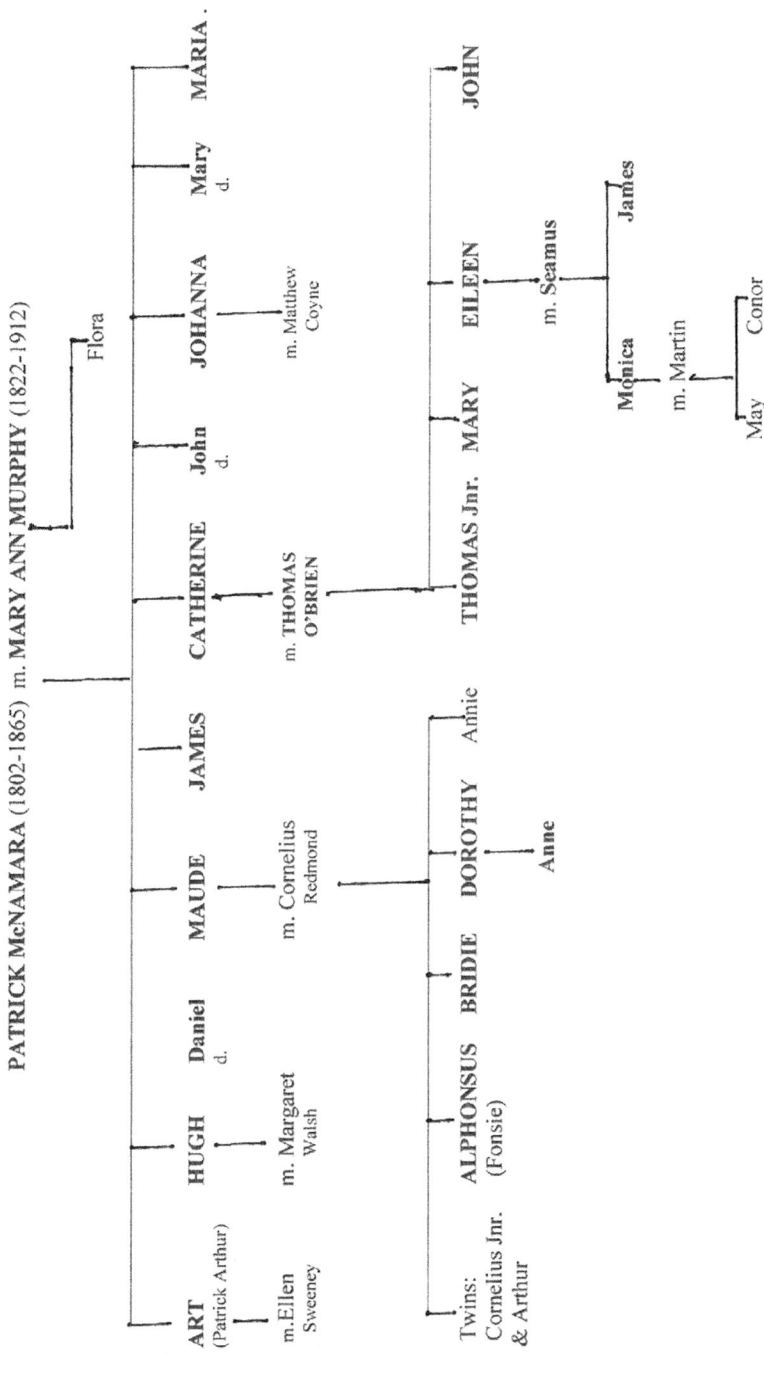

Also by Anne McLoughlin

Lives Apart

Lives Without End

Published by Poolbeg

This book is a work of fiction. References to real people, events, establishments, organisations, or locales are intended only to provide a sense of authenticity, and are used fictitiously. All other characters, and all incidents and dialogue, are drawn from the author's imagination and are not to be construed as real.

Published 2023
by Poolbeg Press Ltd
123 Grange Hill, Baldoyle
Dublin 13, Ireland
E-mail: poolbeg@poolbeg.com
www.poolbeg.com

© Anne McLoughlin 2023

© Poolbeg Press Ltd. 2023, copyright for editing, typesetting, layout, design, ebook

The moral right of the author has been asserted.
A catalogue record for this book is available from the British Library.

ISBN 978-1-78199-454-2

All rights reserved. No part of this publication may be reproduced or transmitted in any form or by any means, electronic or mechanical, including photography, recording, or any information storage or retrieval system, without permission in writing from the publisher. The book is sold subject to the condition that it shall not, by way of trade or otherwise, be lent, resold or otherwise circulated without the publisher's prior consent in any form of binding or cover other than that in which it is published and without a similar condition, including this condition, being imposed on the subsequent purchaser.

www.poolbeg.com

About the Author

Anne McLoughlin was born in Dublin, Ireland, and now divides her time between there and her home in rural Wexford where she does most of her writing.

After spending her working life in television production with RTÉ, Ireland's national broadcaster, she went freelance, working in various capacities programme-making – most recently as originator and Executive Producer of the RTÉ TV series *Page Turners*, a dip into Book Club discussions around Ireland.

In the past she has written stories for RTÉ children's programmes, and also published a series of social history books on the Macamores in County Wexford.

Being highly commended in the Colm Tóibín International Short Story Competition in the Wexford Literary Festival gave her the encouragement to attempt a bigger work and hence the birth of her historical fiction LIVES trilogy.

The inspiration for the family sagas came following the process of researching her own family tree, which led from County Clare to the USA in the late 1800s. So many of the stories she heard provided the ideas, which sent her imagination on a creative journey.

Following the success of *Lives Apart*, her debut novel, published by Poolbeg Press in 2020, the sequel *Lives Without End* followed in May 2021 and achieved Amazon No. 1 New Release in History of US Immigration.

Follow Anne on:

Twitter: @annemcloughlin0

Facebook: http://bit.ly/3EKAEjX

Acknowledgements

I love writing. For me, when the story begins to flow, watching it spill out onto the pages is the most pleasurable part. After that comes the development and polishing of early rough drafts – for me a very satisfying process. Then comes the most difficult bit – as all writers who have been down this road know – getting the work read by a literary agent or publisher. That's an achievement in itself. Unfortunately many great writers slip through the cracks as they don't even get to this stage. With a nation of writers, as the Irish are, there are simply not enough literary agents or publishers to cope with the avalanche of material that comes down the tracks at them each year.

Initially, having failed to make that breakthrough and emerge out of the 'slush' pile that exists in every publishing house, I went the route of competition, and hit the jackpot. Shortlisted in the 'Meet the Publisher' event in the Wexford Literary Festival 2020, I got signed by Poolbeg Press for a 3-book deal for my *LIVES* trilogy. And what a pleasure they have been to work with! Paula Campbell, the publisher, who has a nose for a good story and Gaye Shortland, the wonderful editor who 'gets' the layers of my books and asks all the right questions. Most of the answers are in my head but I've forgotten to put them down on paper. I can't thank them enough. Also thanks also to David Prendergast and Lee Devlin for their Design and IT skills which have brought the look of my books up to such a high standard for the reading public.

Thanks are due to lots of others. The extended O'Keeffe family from County Clare and the USA who steered me through our shared family background many years ago. Some of that information provided me with ideas for development into stories in my fictional historical novels.

Patricia O'Reilly, my former tutor in UCD who encouraged me to plough on and I'm so glad I did.

My extended family, former RTÉ colleagues and friends in Dublin, and my wonderful Wexford friends and neighbours for their excitement and enthusiasm once I got that publishing contract. Unfortunately, while I'd have loved to share the social end of things with them, a halt was put to the book launches, signings, readings and festivals by the Covid pandemic. But, thankfully, we've all came out the other end of it at this stage.

I'd also like to thank the readers of *Lives Apart* and *Lives Without End*. The positive feedback and great Amazon and Goodreads reviews helped keep me going, as did the invitations to Zoom into Book Clubs both in Ireland and America – I really enjoyed those chats.

To all those readers, I hope you enjoy *Lives Reunited*, the final book in the LIVES trilogy as much as you enjoyed the first two in the series.

DEDICATION

For my family and friends, both past and present

CATHERINE

Chapter 1

County Clare, Ireland
1900

Thomas was never in favour of these little breaks. It was the same every time she mentioned an outing. Always an uphill battle with him, but she didn't let the under-the-breath grumble stop her persisting, determined as she was to give her children as happy a childhood as she'd had.

He'd never actually said it but Catherine suspected he considered these outings a waste of time and money. The "*What do you want to do that for?*" was the clue. She didn't need to be a detective to work that one out. The funny thing was that when they did do something out of the ordinary he seemed to enjoy himself, but there was no point in waiting for him to suggest anything. They'd be left waiting a long time. Always something more important to do. If she didn't insist, each year would simply slip into the next, without anything to differentiate one from the other. Today was no different.

"Isn't it well for some people? Nothing to do but go swanning off whenever they feel like it." A light jokiness in the voice to begin with.

"It's important for the children to have something to look back on when they get older. Before we know it, they'll have grown up and we'll have missed the chance."

"*Huh*, it didn't do me any harm to do without."

As she knew, the jokiness wouldn't last. The sharp scraping of the spade on the stone surface at the entrance to the barn, as he shovelled the last of the manure into the barrow, emphasised the change in tone. But this time she was determined to stand her ground.

"Well, I'll take them somewhere myself then, if *you* don't want to come." She turned towards the house and began walking away. Let him suit himself.

"You'll do no such thing." He propped the spade against the barn wall and gripped the handles of the barrow. "If you can take the day off so can I – I can, so I can."

The forced effort to inject a lightness back into the conversation was transparent.

"You hardly think I'm going to stay and do all the work here now, do you?" He paused. "Anyway, I'll tell Tom he can stay and get on with what needs doing here."

"*You'll* do no such thing. Tom will be coming with us. It's a family day out." The firmness in her voice surprised even herself, but she knew that he recognised the shift in power.

"He won't be bothered coming with us. He's sixteen, not exactly 'one of the children' now, is he?"

"As I said, a family day. Leave Tom to me. I'll talk to him." She looked at her husband. "Right so, I'll make a few sandwiches and tell the children."

She caught the look on his face as he turned away, a look that suggested it mightn't form part of *his* plan for the day, but on this occasion he knew better than to argue with her.

She liked to put down a few markers each year. It was really for the children. Important for when they looked back on their childhood that they would remember little highlights dotted through it. Like when they went to the sea at Lahinch on Mary's First Communion day and had tea in the hotel, or young Tom's birthday when they went to the funfair and had rides on the roundabouts. Days out, little parcels of fun, away from the humdrum of their daily lives. She needed them too. A build-up of memories and pleasant thoughts to draw on. Little reminders that life could be good, if they ever needed something to sustain them through the difficult times they'd inevitably encounter as they went through life.

It took a bit of preparation, but afterwards she was always glad she had taken the trouble, even though there were times when she didn't feel she had the energy to deal with the inevitable obstacles placed in her way.

It had always seemed so easy, the way her parents had organised such treats – only now did she appreciate the effort involved – but then her father had always been a willing partner. The trips to Ennis on December 8th to see the Christmas window displays in all the shops and the St. Patrick's Day parades. And the time Pops brought them to see the Cliffs of Moher and pointed out the Hag's Head in the distance. She could see that it looked like a woman's head, but she couldn't follow the story he'd told them. The boys, though, seemed to love the gory details. She preferred the wild flowers and the puffins. Their lovely colours, and what at the time seemed like thousands of them around the cliffs. Then there were the graveyard pattern days. She smiled when she thought of the odd young child she must have been. The only one in the family who liked the pattern. Loved the way her mother always involved them in the preparations that led up to it, how she managed to stretch the pleasure over a couple of days. Kitted them out with the bucket of water, scrubbing brush and rags for washing down the headstones, removing the green marks that had built up over the winter. At the time, some of them, particularly the boys, had whinged at the chore, but it had become part of the valuable treasure trove of memories. She suspected that sending them out to the fields to pick whatever wild flowers they could find had been part of her mother's ploy to keep them occupied for the morning of the pattern, instead of tormenting her as she went about her work. The regular jobs still had to be done, but in half the time.

The picking of the flowers always turned into a bit of a competition to see who could find the widest variety. All her mother had to do on the day was to wait, give them plenty of time to build up their pickings before going out into the garden at the last minute to snip a bunch of big lush hydrangea blooms before they departed for the graveyard Mass. Less than a minute was all that job took her and she always awarded herself last place. Clever mother.

Most of the others preferred the outings that involved being given a few pence to spend. Since those days they'd never discussed it but she imagined that, if they had, those would be the ones best remembered by the lads – well, Hugh anyway. Johanna had often mentioned their conversations in her letters home and the way herself and Hugh would be remembering things.

Apart from the absolutely necessary daily farm tasks, the suspension of work in favour of a treat was always looked forward to, or so it seemed. In truth these occasions only happened a few times a year, but Mary Ann's knack of building the anticipation for a week beforehand made it seem like they were a regular occurrence. Their mother was always a great woman to get the most value out of the smallest of things.

Catherine settled her arms on the wooden table and looked around at the girls eating their toast.

"How would you like a nice surprise, children?"

"I love surprises." Eileen's face lit up.

"Well, hands up if you know what day it is?"

"August 15th." Young Tom appeared in the doorway. "Is there still some tea in the pot, Ma?"

"Just about. It might be a bit stewed."

"Yeah. August 15th, the Feast of the Assumption of the Blessed Virgin Mary into Heaven." Catherine looked at her son in surprise.

"Don't look at me like that, Mother. Think what you may, but I'm not as much of a heathen as you might imagine."

"Oh, I know that, Tom, and yes, that's right." Catherine smiled. The Holy Days were always handy markers.

"Did you know that, Holy Mary?" He smirked at his sister.

Mary, used to his teasing, ignored him. "Yeah, what's the surprise, Mam?" She popped the last crust of her toast into her mouth.

"Well, if I told you, it wouldn't be a surprise now, would it?"

"Ah, Mam!" Mary said. "You can't do that to us. You always do that."

Catherine grinned as the chorus started.

"Well, okay, I'll tell you. We're all going on a picnic to the sea. Daddy is taking us."

"What are we taking to eat?" Tom, as usual, predictable in his focus.

"Well, what would you like?" Glad she didn't have to persuade him to join them, she smiled at him.

"A bit of ham would be nice. I'd better go out and finish in the yard then, before we go." He took a last swig of his tea, picked up a piece of brown bread and left them to plan the picnic.

"*Jam sandwiches, I want jam sandwiches!*" Eileen shouted, her red curls bobbing as she waved her hand in the air, wildly enough to ensure her preference wouldn't go unnoticed.

"Eggs. Egg sandwiches." Mary threw a pained look at her younger sister. "With some scallions chopped in."

"Mammy, she thinks I'm a baby! But I like jam sandwiches!" Eileen protested. "I don't like scallions."

"Well, you don't have to eat them then." Mary looked at her. "Mam can make jam sandwiches as well, can't you, Mam?"

"Let's not have a row about it, girls. Now, hands up for surprise sandwiches!" Shooting up her own hand, Catherine diverted the squabble, knowing that Eileen would quickly mimic her. "Right, I'll make a start so."

Catherine stood up and began clearing the breakfast dishes. She glanced at the door as her husband entered and began washing his hands at the basin.

"We'll go soon now that Daddy has finished his jobs."

"Maybe we'll go on the train. How would you like that, girls?" She avoided his look in order to hold her nerve.

"*Hurray! The train! Choo-choo choo-choo!*" Eileen began racing around the room. "*We want to go on the train! I've never been on a train!*"

"Sit down, Eileen, you don't want to waken the baby." Catherine walked over to the cradle in the corner. Baby John gave a little snuffle and snuggled further into his cocoon, but otherwise gave no sign of wakening.

Catherine had only travelled on the train once since the branch line had opened on the West Clare Railway, so it was still a bit of a novelty. She'd been wanting to take the children on it ever since, but Thomas had always resisted and she couldn't manage them on her own with the beach paraphernalia. Unlikely there'd be any opposition today, not in front of the children anyway, but you could never be sure with him.

"Are we nearly there?" Eileen stirred in her nest under Catherine's arm.

"We are. Not long more." Catherine, her arm dead under the weight, shifted her daughter into an upright position. "You can start getting ready. Pick up the buckets and spades there, so we won't forget them when we get off."

She loved the sea. The way the world seemed to expand to an endless openness filled with salty air. Blue meeting blue on the horizon on a good day, and today was one of those. She'd knelt by the side of her bed and prayed for sunshine and the Lord hadn't disappointed. Shoulders back, she expanding her chest and closed her eyes.

"Can you smell it, children?" She tilted her head back and breathed deeply.

"Smell what, Mammy?" Eileen asked.

"The briny sea. Isn't is lovely?"

"What's briny, Mammy?" Mary said.

"Fresh and salty. Take a deep breath and you'll get the smell." She closed her eyes. "Take a deep breath. Now can you smell the salt on it? Isn't it lovely?"

"Come on, Mammy, we want to get in for a swim!" Mary interest in the salty smell was limited.

"Right girls, hold my hands, one each side." She glanced down at the picnic basket she was carrying and the bag of bathing togs. Thomas was already on the far side of the road with young Tom carrying the cradle with baby John. She could see the rug shoved in on top of the cradle and hoped the child wasn't smothering under it. "Oh, you can't. Right then, Mary, you take the bag of togs." She passed them over. "Now, Eileen, you hold my hand and Mary will hold your other one and we'll all cross together."

She chose a sheltered spot on the beach and waved at Thomas to bring over the rug. She spread it out and once she was settled and the children changed into their togs, she relaxed, content to look on for the moment, while he took them down to the water's edge.

"Don't let them drown, whatever you do!" she called after him.

"I think I'm fairly capable of avoiding that! Give me credit for something, woman!" He laughed back at her. *"Sure, anyway, isn't your big strapping son good at the lifesaving?"*

"Well, let's hope he won't have to put it to the test!" She was glad at the lift in his mood. Hopefully it would last the day.

She envied those who lived in the little houses scattered on the slope overlooking the bay at Kilkee. Eyes looking out at that ever-changing summer view below. The busy comings and goings of visitors in their pony and traps, arriving or leaving after their day of rest. And when they'd gone, the calm of the white surf gently washing the sweeping sands. They could open their windows to hear the gentle swishing and swooshing of the waves below.

The farmland around Ard na Gréine was different. Fields surrounded by trees and hedges. Although the house was located up a slight incline, the main views from it were through the gaps in the hedgerows. Framed pictures of rolling fields, animals grazing on the slopes, or sheltering under the shade of the trees. On a bright day it had its own lovely charm. But no sea.

Catherine picked idly at the woollen balls on the shabby grey rug as she watched the seabirds whirling above. White gulls and black ravens, wings flapping until they found an airflow that allowed them an effortless glide. Every so often, a large bird swooped to retrieve a crust of bread, discarded by picnickers. She watched the small ones engaging in play, wheeling around in a flock, their ragged formation suggestive of juveniles only recently having learned the art. As they jostled and jockeyed for lead, some gave their competitors a wide berth and skirted around the outer edges of the formation. A cloudless sky with the young innocents, like shadow puppets against the flawless backdrop.

A small bird fluttered up from the grassy banks and settled on the tall shoot of seagrass. He hopped down to nibble on seeds and insects on the ground below, before returning to his perch. His plumpness belied the lightness that allowed him rest there, with only the slightest bend in the delicate stalk.

When she'd suggested the lads take the girls for a walk along the shoreline after their swim while she laid out the picnic, Thomas wasn't in a position to object. Once they'd gone, after checking that baby John was still asleep in the cradle beside her, Catherine lay back on the rug. Like the blue cloak of the statue of the Virgin on the landing window at home, the sky above struck her as appropriate for the day that was in it. Hypnotised, the effort of keeping her eyes open became too much, and she allowed herself be enveloped in the blue cape, drifting into the first peace she'd had since making her awful discovery.

Chapter 2

Growing up, Catherine had always felt that she was a plain child, if not bordering on ugly. Unremarkable, others if asked might say, but definitely not ugly. She had no particularly unpleasant features, they were all . . . well . . . just ordinary. If you took each of them individually they were fairly good. Her full lips were her best feature. Brown shiny hair, but dead straight when she'd always wanted curls like her sisters. Her eyes, a deep shade of blue – like cornflowers her mother always said – had straight lashes and their almond shape and wide-apart spacing gave her a slightly oriental look. She envied the girls in her class who had lovely sweeping lashes that curled at the tips, and wished hers didn't resemble so much the straight bristles of their yard brush. When all her features were put together nothing quite matched, so the resultant look was that of a plain girl. At least in her own opinion.

"Have you nothing better to do than be standing in front of that mirror admiring yourself?"

Her mother's gentle reprimand brought her down to earth. Turning, she saw Mary Ann carrying a bundle of bedlinen down the stairs.

"Here, let me help you with those, Mother – you could trip the way you're carrying them." She ran up the stairs and scooped up the trailing sheet. "Anyway, I wasn't admiring myself, I was just thinking that that mirror is getting very spotty with age."

"Well, missy, it's there a long time before you and it'll be there a long time after you, spotty or not. It was my mother's and probably her mother's before her too. It has history."

"I suppose." Catherine grinned at her mother. "And lots of spotty faces looking in it. Like my own."

"Ah, not that spotty. You were lucky – you missed out on the freckles. Nice porcelain skin. Come on now and give me a hand with these sheets. They won't wash themselves."

Catherine's smile when it came often took people by surprise. The way it lit up her face transformed her into a creature bordering on beautiful. That smile and her gentle nature made her a very attractive girl – something she was totally unaware of.

She passed the church on her way home from school each day. Its dark womb, especially when empty, was like a magnet.

"You go ahead." She knew her friends had no interest in going inside and she was glad of that. "I'll catch up with you."

At first, she used to hide the fact that she was going into the chapel, and would wait until they were out of sight before entering. Later she no longer cared that they knew and it became a bit of a joke.

"*Holy Mary, Mother of God!*" they would sing and start a chant. "*We know where you're going! We know where you're going!*"

She guessed they thought her a bit odd but it didn't matter. Their light-hearted teasing was just that. No malice in it. And sure she knew that, if the truth were told, she was a bit odd, but they never actually said it straight to her.

"There's room in the world for all types. Wouldn't it be the boring place if we were all the same?" Her mother's words.

Pushing the heavy wooden door, she stepped inside and held the brass handle firmly as it closed, so that it wouldn't make a bang. For those few seconds, she always harboured a hope that the chapel would be empty inside. Just her and God. A special relationship. Didn't want to share it. The nonsense of her. The Lord surely had enough space in his heart for multiple relationships. The girls were right. Definitely odd.

On sunshiny days, once inside she'd have to pause, to allow her eyes adjust. In the dim interior, the only light was from the sun slanting in through the stained-glass windows, creating patterns on the wooden pews. A gentle glow of warmth in the cool body of the chapel.

The resentment when there were a few people already in occupation was wrong. She knew that. An elderly man, he was often there, so much part of the place he didn't bother her. His brown felt hat always laid on the bench in front, his head bent in silent prayer as he rested it on his hands. Most days it was empty, but often there were a few parishioners dotted around the place and she'd be forced to suppress the niggle of irritation, knowing such feelings weren't right. Against the whole spirit of the visit. Not what the Lord would have approved of.

It was the women in shawls and woollen hats who would be in their usual position, praying in the front pews and passing rosary beads through their fingers, that were the irritant. Letting the beads click against the wood, accompanied by their incessant sibilant whisperings, designed, she was convinced, to emphasise their piety. It was these auld ones that annoyed her. Like it was necessary to have others bear witness in order to add value to their sanctity. First Fridays were the worst. Even selecting a pew halfway down the aisle, to keep away from them, never worked. All she wanted was a quiet conversation with God, but their loud self-righteous mumblings made that impossible. The more aware she became, the more the sounds seemed to increase, until she'd put her fingers in her ears and cast her eyes downwards and pray to God they were nearing an end.

Their rustling and bumping departure was a further annoyance, but at least something of a relief. She'd sometimes glance over her shoulder at the old man, wondering if he too felt the same, but he never lifted his head. Maybe he was mercifully deaf. And just as she thought there was to be a bit of peace, she'd occasionally find a straggler from the group, having bade a noisy farewell to her colleagues at the back of the chapel, headed over to start a round of the Stations of the Cross.

In the depths of winter, a different light enveloped the inside of the chapel. Any sun that might have shone had long disappeared by the time she was passing, leaving the windows a blank grey. The only glow was from the lit candles on the brass votive stand in front of the altar, drawing her forward to a pew at the top of the church.

When she had a coin she would wait until the church was empty before leaving her seat. It wasn't the same when a person came up behind her and stood there waiting for her to finish her business, before stepping forward to light a candle for the Holy Souls. On those occasions she would step aside and smile and usher them ahead. She wanted to savour the slow ritual, hating to be rushed. Sometimes the person would wave their hand to indicate '*after you*'. That was awkward, but she'd developed a technique that worked, one that gave them no opportunity to prolong the debate. She'd shake her head and, withdrawing eye contact, move away to kneel in a pew and wait until they'd gone, squashing the thought that they might think her behaviour strange. Nothing new there, she was used to that. Just another confirmation of her oddness.

Once she was sure they'd finished, she'd return to the shrine and release the coin into the slot. The sound of it falling on the cushion of money already in the box was comforting. The softer the sound the more souls would be released from purgatory that week. A dull clunk on the metallic floor of an empty coin box was always a disappointment.

Taking a candle from the tray underneath, she'd do a survey of the stand. It was important to pick the best position for hers, before embarking on the procedure of lighting it.

The third row was Catherine's favourite. In the centre. If the stand wasn't too full, she would visually select the landing place, one whereby she could stretch in from the side to position the lit candle without any danger. She'd learned that leaning across a row of lighted candles was not the best approach. That lesson came the day she'd seen a woman singe her sleeve doing just that.

Once satisfied, she'd hold the candle sideways and ignite the wick from one of those already lit. Watching the lighted candle, as the flame blackened the wick, had a hypnotic effect as it travelled downwards, burning low enough to allow the wax to start melting. It was a fairly exact science to gauge the moment before the grease began running down the side – just a second or two of opportunity to press the candle into the pronged holder and secure it well before the hot wax burnt her fingers.

There was always the slight anticipation of the candle quenching, just as it was being pressed home. When this happened it had to be removed from the prongs, without the base disintegrating, and be lit again. For Catherine, the expert that she'd become, this rarely happened. The whole procedure was important to her. It formed an important part of the whole spiritual experience.

She'd then go down on the worn kneeler in front of the stand, try to ignore the discomfort of the wood under her kneecaps and concentrate on those dead souls who went before her. With closed eyes, she could see the grace they would receive from her prayers slowly flowing down on them, like a golden waterfall, to soothe their weary souls. Allowing these thoughts drift through her mind uninterrupted, she'd breathe the comforting smell of the melting wax. In and out. Slowly in. Slowly out.

Thomas O'Brien, while not exactly her first, was her only serious suitor. She had despaired of ever having a beau. Boys rarely looked twice at her – at least not in that way. She was aware that they saw her as the good-natured younger sister, the quiet friend, but never as a potential sweetheart. She studied the other girls and how they behaved that made them so attractive to the boys. Tried to figure out what ingredient it was that she was missing. Some of them were even plainer than she was, although she felt bad even thinking this, but it had a legitimate place in her analysis of the situation.

"What is it about me that makes me so dull?" She wasn't sure if she was ready for the truth, but she had to ask the question of someone. Pondering over it by herself for so long hadn't produced any answers. "Am I doing something wrong? Tell me if I am, because I don't know what it is."

"No, you're not doing anything wrong, Kate." Her friend had laughed. "Those lads, they're all just eejits. Surely you recognise that?"

"But I can't even get one of those eejits, as you so eloquently call them." She grinned, but the despair remained in her voice. "Have I a bad habit that I don't realise or something? I don't pick my nose or anything disgusting like that, nor do I smell, at least I don't think I do." She looked at her friend. "I'm sure you'd tell me if I did? Wouldn't you?"

"Well, now that you ask . . . " Peig laughed as she poked Catherine's arm. "No, you don't smell."

"Well, there has to be something lacking then. Can you put a finger on it, because I can't and believe me I've tried."

"It'll happen some day for you." The only comfort her friend could offer.

"Oh, it's alright for you, Peig, it's happening for you already. They have the feet danced off you, but most of the time I'm holding up the walls."

"Ah, there's no rush, Kate. Anyway, you turned down Danny Moloney. He was mad about you. What was wrong with him?"

"Nothing. He's nice but I just wasn't in love with him."

"So it's love you're looking for now? You see, Kate, that's where you and me are different. I see them for practising on. Sure aren't we young yet, not exactly ready for marriage?"

"Yes, but for how long more?"

"Well, I think we can wait," said Peig with a laugh. "Another little while anyway."

As time passed and nothing changed, she wondered if she was destined to go through life never having a man desire her. Not something she was prepared to accept. Not just yet anyway. Hadn't quite given up hope that she might still meet the love of her life. He had to be out there somewhere, surely?

There were times she'd harboured thoughts of entering a convent. Not because she couldn't get a man – that wouldn't have been enough to drive her. No, she'd had dreams that the Lord was calling her. Feelings that tormented her for a year or two. She'd tried to banish them, but they still inched their way back into her head every so often. Not something that she wanted to share with anyone. Particularly Peig. She could hear her . . . *"Ah, Kate, you're not that desperate, are you?"* No, not something to discuss with Peig, for the moment anyway, in case she placed an obligation on herself to follow through into such a life. She didn't want that pressure, especially as she just wasn't sure if it came from a fear of the future, a future that might involve drifting into a lifelong spinsterhood, rather than a genuine 'vocation'. That was something she had to work out for herself.

CORNELIUS

Chapter 3

Knocknageeha, County Clare
1881

The man had almost faded from his memory when they bumped into Thomas on their visit to Clare. Cornelius always enjoyed the annual holiday there, in his wife's home-place. Not just because of the warm welcome from Mary Ann, his mother-in-law, but more especially the boost it gave Maude. It pleased him to see the spring it put in her step throughout the days leading up to the trip. All the preparations and the plans as to what they'd do when they got there, and who they'd have to see. It always seemed like a week would never be enough to fit in all his wife had on her agenda, but he never said a word, just left her to her plans.

As they neared Knocknageeha he knew how the conversation would go. The same as every year since they'd first met.

"Would you ever try calling her Mary Ann? She hates this '*Mrs. McNamara*' formality." Maude shook her head in exasperation. "You know she hates it. How many times does she have to ask you? Maybe this time you'd just try it?" She looked at him. "Cornelius, are you even listening to me?"

"Yes, I'm listening, Maude. I can't. It's just habit." Her persistence amused him, the reminder always the same. "She's my mother-in-law. It's just a respectful thing. Bashed into us in the Force. Very hard to shake off, you know."

"Well, I'll bash it out of you if you don't try." Maude grinned at him.

"Can you just imagine it? It'd be like calling my boss 'Bill'. Where do you think that'd get me?"

"She's hardly your boss. She's my mother, for goodness' sake."

"I know. She's not my boss, Maude. You are."

"Well, at least we've got one thing straight."

"Can we leave it there then?" Cornelius looked sideways at her, his smile half hidden under his handlebar moustache.

The only definite thing he wanted to do during the week was to drop into the police barracks to say hello to anyone who might be there still, anyone who would remember him from his short working term stationed there before he met Maude. Once they married, he'd been moved across the country to his new posting in County Wexford. Not permitted to serve in either your own county or that of your wife. He'd been disappointed at the time, having just got used to the limestone landscape of County Clare. It had taken him a while to become accustomed to the greyness of the rocky terrain, but his regular walks had revealed the beauty of the delicate wild flowers that poked out from every fissure, and there was always the pleasure of an occasional trip out to the cliffs. But the rules were the rules and he understood the reason for the enforced move. Not that he'd ever have crossed the line, but there were those who might succumb to pressure from neighbours to quash their summonses for minor misdemeanours, or God forbid, major ones.

Yes, he'd have been happy to stay stationed in Clare, but there was no point in even asking. Felt bad that he was taking Maude across the country, away from her family and friends, to a place where neither of them had any contacts. However, it had worked out alright once they'd settled in, although the first few years were difficult for her. She hadn't complained much but he was aware of a loneliness for her home-place and her mother. Easier for him as he was out all day working. Once the children arrived, she'd settled into a pattern that included the annual visit to Knocknageeha, and that seemed to satisfy her.

The morning had been grey and overcast. Cornelius arrived into the kitchen, cane in hand, ready for his first walk of the day.

"I'm thinking we might go into Ennis this morning and do a bit of shopping." Maude was glad she'd caught him before he'd had a chance to head out the door and go missing for hours.

"What about the children?"

"They won't be coming with us. The twins and Fonsie are going over to Art's to play with the cousins and Mary Ann says she'll keep an eye on Bridie, so we're free for a few hours. Catherine's going to come with us and we can pick up a few groceries for my mother while we're at it."

"And would a man be allowed to have a walk first?" Cornelius cocked his head to one side, a hint of a smile in his voice.

"Well, so long as a man doesn't take the entire morning," Maude warned. "I'll be ready to leave in half an hour. How about that?"

"I'll make it my business to return in time." He doffed his hat and strode through the door.

"*Be sure you do!*" she called after him, knowing he would be back to the very minute.

The rolls of quality material in the window of the gentlemen's outfitters on Mill Street caught her eye.

"That's a lovely cloth there. Look, they have one already made up in it." Maude pointed to the dark suit on the manikin. "A suit like that would look very smart on you for the wedding. What do you think?"

"While you're looking at that I'll slip into the newsagent's," Catherine interrupted her sister.

"No rush, Catherine – we'll be here for a while." Maude threw her a knowing look.

"I wasn't thinking of getting a new suit made at all." Cornelius looked at her. "It's not as though we're the most important guests, we're only invited because we're neighbours. There's not a soul will even notice what I'm dressed in. Why don't you get a nice frock for yourself?" He knew by her silence that he'd not manage to deflect her from her mission. "Anyway, what's wrong with the suit I have? There's plenty of wear left in that."

"What's wrong with it?" Maude looked at him, eyebrows raised. "What's wrong with it is you have it on you now. That's your everyday suit and at that it's ancient."

"But this isn't every day. We're out on the town, aren't we? Ennis, the metropolis."

"I know you still see it as your good suit, but it's so worn you can nearly see yourself in the shine on the backside of it." She looked at him, a frown on her face. "I'm not having the whole of County Wexford laughing at you, thinking we don't know how to dress up for an occasion."

"But . . ."

"There'll be no 'buts', Cornelius. It high time you invested in a new one." The determination in her tone suggested there was to be no escape. "Unless you want to be buried in that old one?"

"I've no plans to pop off just yet, unless of course you're planning on getting rid of me?" He glanced at her. "No chance, I suppose, that I could go to the wedding in my uniform then? It's fairly smart."

"Absolutely not." She recognised the tease in his tone. "Believe me, it'll be worth the investment. Might even see you out," she joked. "No point in waiting till it's too late, and then it won't be worthwhile buying one."

"Well, if it isn't yourself! My old friend Cornelius Redmond."

Cornelius turned and looked in surprise at the tall man standing on the pavement, both his arms extended outwards, as if he had been appointed to welcome him to County Clare.

"Eh . . . Thomas . . . Thomas O'Brien, isn't it?" He'd like to have forgotten his name but it was indelibly printed on his brain.

"Put it there, Cornelius." The man thrust his arm forward, forcing Cornelius to shake his hand. "Or should I say Head Constable Redmond?"

The mocking tone was unmistakable. Cornelius could see it there under the fake bow.

"And the lovely Mrs. Redmond." He flashed his smile on Maude and reached out to shake her hand. "You haven't changed a bit. Looking splendid as ever."

Maude remembered the name, and the face was vaguely familiar. Nothing more.

"And what is it has you in these parts? A long way from the County Wexford?"

"We're here on our holidays." Maude was happy to engage with him despite her husband's shuffling beside her. "Staying in the old home-place. Visiting the relatives."

"I see. Well, you've had good weather then. Pity about today. Looks a bit like rain."

Outside of the police station, Cornelius rarely talked about work. Not in any detail anyway. Living in a small community, it was easy for gossip to get around. Safer to keep the business of the barracks inside the barracks. So the careers of any officer in the Royal Irish Constabulary was not something he ever shared with Maude, not unless it was general knowledge. Thomas's career had been fairly shortlived. Not a man for being told what to do, he hated the regimentation of the job and didn't make any secret of it. Appeared to wear his disgruntled attitude as a badge of pride, a major factor in ensuring that he never rose up the ranks, unlike Cornelius who, in stark contrast, was ideally suited to the regimentation the force required. Despite the fact that Thomas was responsible for his own stagnation, he harboured a jealousy for anyone who merited recognition and got promotion.

The way he passed himself now as if they had been equals irritated Cornelius. As if Thomas had never ridiculed him for his devotion to duty, or made his life a living nightmare when he was promoted and Thomas assigned to his team. Ah no, more fun to be had mocking and mimicking in front of the other lads when he thought Cornelius was out of earshot, although sometimes he suspected it was intended for him to overhear.

The pull against authority and the begrudging attitude towards people who'd done well within the force had become his hallmarks. Cornelius could never understand why Thomas had continued to hang onto his resentments, like they were a lifeline. How he had never been able to rise above them, but had always managed to continue stoking them, never allowing those flames to quench. He was a fairly clever man, but clearly not smart enough to be aware that these were the very things that would forever be obstacles to his advancement.

"And what are you doing now, Thomas?" Maude asked. "Are you still stationed here?"

Cornelius wished Maude would stop engaging in conversation.

"Oh, did the Head Constable not tell you – I resigned from the force a few years back." Without a pause, he puffed himself up and grinned. "Yeah, I'm a farmer now, a big farm of land a few miles out the road there. I'm just in the town getting a few provisions. Left the hired hands to do the work."

"Oh, a gentleman farmer then?" Maude teased.

"I suppose you could call it that." He smiled back. "I'm sure some might call me worse."

Cornelius had heard about Thomas, how he'd since regaled the locals in the pub with his stories, most of which began with *"When I was in the Constabulary . . ."* as if he had been the greatest policeman in the country.

Cornelius watched his sister-in-law appear from the door of the nearby shop. He wished his wife would end the conversation with

Thomas and let them move on. He could see Catherine busy putting her purchase of the local weekly newspaper into her shopping bag, unaware that they had been joined by someone outside. With no desire to make any introductions, he caught Maude's elbow.

"Well, it was nice meeting you again, Thomas, but we won't delay you. I'm sure you're a busy man, what with milking or other jobs to be getting back to, so we'll say goodbye to you." Cornelius jogged his wife's elbow. "Come now, Maude, we'd better let the man go. Nice to meet you, Thomas." His final dismissal was delivered with a half turn of his head, as he took a step forward in an effort to head Catherine off.

"But sure aren't we going in here to look at the suit material?" Surprised at his abruptness, Maude hesitated, reluctant to walk away from Thomas, for fear he'd consider them rude.

It all happened in a couple of seconds. Catherine arrived alongside and looked at Thomas, leaving Cornelius with no other opportunity, no escape, but to allow whatever was going to happen, happen.

"Catherine, this is Thomas O'Brien, a former work colleague of Cornelius."

Maude's interference had deprived him of any chance to protect his sister-in-law. His concern increased a hundredfold when he saw Catherine's face light up as Thomas used his green eyes to full effect to lamp his prey. An uneasy instinct told Cornelius no good would come of this encounter. He knew with certainty that from then on she was never going to stand a chance. His wife's delaying had ensured that.

With the washing-up done after the supper and the children in bed, peace at last, they were seated by the fire.

"You pair relax there, while I'm out finishing up for the night." Mary Ann slipped a shawl around her shoulders.

"I'll go with you and give you a hand." Maude looked around for her cardigan.

"You'll do no such thing. It's not exactly a two-man job. I've just to lock the hens into the henhouse and then I'll be back to join you in a few minutes."

Maude picked up her knitting. Just a few more rows to finish the sleeve of the child's cardigan.

"Don't let that fire die," said Mary Anne. "It needs a few sods."

Cornelius tended it, coaxing the flames which were reluctant to catch the twigs. Once satisfied that they were in business, he added a sod of turf and sat back in the armchair and told her the full story.

"He left before he was pushed." He paused. "I know you're dying to know. But he's a nasty bag of tricks, always a smart tongue on him. Always the bitter word about everyone. That's why I never liked him."

"Maybe you were just too different." She swapped the knitting needles around and began casting off. "Anyway, what do you mean before he was pushed?"

"He was on his last warning, so he was lucky the bachelor uncle left him the farm. Just at the right time. I heard from a lad that he's going around boasting down here about his great career in the force and, I wouldn't mind, but when he was in it he never gave up bellyaching about the job."

"Oh, just because you didn't get on doesn't mean he's bad." Maude laid down her needles and smoothed the sleeve over the arm of the sofa to admire her handiwork. "He's very handsome, don't you think?"

"I can't deny that, but I know what you're at, Maude. And I'm telling you he's not right for Catherine, so don't go pushing it. She's far too nice for the likes of him. Believe me, I know what I'm talking about. Gentleman farmer indeed! He may be a farmer, but I can assure you he's no gentleman. So if you think anything of your sister you'll leave it alone."

CATHERINE

Chapter 4

Ard na Gréine, County, Clare

Apart from the fact that he'd swept her off her feet, she was never quite sure why she'd married Thomas O'Brien. It was something she did a few years after having made her decision not to enter the convent. She'd toyed with the idea of heading for America when her sister Johanna had told them she was going over to stay with Hugh but, while it was fading, the whole nun thing hadn't quite left her system at that stage. And it came at a time when she'd been offered promotion to housekeeper in Woodbine House when Betsy retired. If she didn't take it, it wasn't a position that was likely to come up again in her lifetime and she loved working there. Even though her sister was a few years younger, there was something about Johanna that made her seem like the older one, more mature or something. Definitely more adventurous. There were times since that she'd wished she'd possessed the same spirit. Her sister had tried to lure her over with the promise of a job in one of Hugh's grocery stores, but something always held her back. Every so often since, and more so in recent times, she mulled over what her life might have been had she had the courage to go, but there was no point in regretting that now.

It wasn't something she'd done on a whim. Marrying him. Flattered by his attentions maybe? Nobody else clamouring for her hand in marriage? If she were honest with herself, there had been brief glimpses of his harder side during their courtship that she'd chosen to ignore. Never directed at her, but the occasional caustic comment about a neighbour or relative, but then was anyone perfect? It might have been nothing more than her naivety that allowed her to slide into it, but she was still asking herself why. There were many times she'd had to admit that it may have been mixed with a fear of a lonely future stretching ahead.

Maude had been no different to other married women. Catherine had seen it all before with female relatives and neighbours. Had she given that more thought, analysed their motives, it might have become evident that most married women, her sister included, felt obliged to fix up their single friends with husbands or the bachelors with wives. No-one was safe from their meddling, regardless of whether they wanted a spouse or not. Not that she didn't, but while she hadn't paid much attention to their manoeuvres, she was aware of their game. No potential opportunity was safe from manipulation. Usually it had nothing to do with marital bliss, more to do with their wanting everyone else to fit neatly into a similar box. To have things orderly. As if by doing so, they would regain some control over their own lives, or would be able to boast about having *'made that match'* at some stage in the future. When she thought about it, none had ever claimed to have been responsible for the matches they all knew had ended in misery, due to drink or fellows being handy with their fists.

The one thing she'd failed to notice was that it usually happened when the initial gloss had worn off their own marriages and they needed a diversion, and she had clearly become Maude's 'project'.

Perhaps she should have paid more attention to Cornelius at the time. He didn't do a lot to hide his aversion to Thomas, even once suggesting that he didn't think he was right for her. She'd never probed as to why. Maybe she should have asked him straight out what it was he had against him, but sure isn't hindsight a great thing? Instead she'd just assumed it had more to do with Cornelius himself. A bit on the stuffy side, old beyond his years. She could never imagine the lightness of youth on him. She was fond enough of him, but he could be very straitlaced, so she hadn't bothered probing. Wouldn't life be wonderful if you could live it backwards and have the wisdom bit early, when you most needed it?

Thomas was not without his qualities, but they were mostly on the surface. He cut quite a dash when she'd first met him, still did, if she were honest. Striking, with his black hair, white teeth and smart tongue. Merits that were not lost on Catherine, well, maybe not so much the smart tongue. In the early days, when she'd questioned what it was about *her* that had attracted *him*, he'd told her that it was her timid smile and gentle nature that had captured his interest. He'd joked that she was the opposite of himself. That, in itself, perhaps should have been a warning. Things had moved fast and within the year Catherine was a farmer's wife.

"I thought they needed someone to live in up in that big place?"

"Where? Where are you talking about?"

"Where do you think? Woodbine House."

"Oh, they'd prefer that, but they're happy for me to continue on a daily basis."

"Well, you're needed here."

"I can do both, Thomas. They've begged me to think about it and you know how much I love working there."

"Well, they'll have to settle for someone else. I'm not going to have any wife of mine going out to work. Can you just hear the gossip?"

She'd backed down too easily. She knew that at the time, but it was hard to go against him, and at his insistence left her job in the big house.

She missed the camaraderie and the preparations for the occasional parties and festivities. A glimpse into another world, but one that she had a hand in servicing and she knew she was good at that. They'd complimented her often enough. She hoped that maybe they'd send for her to assist when there was a special occasion, and they did, but only for a while. With Thomas's objections and the excuses she was forced to make on the first two occasions, they'd stopped asking.

Nothing for it but to launch herself into her own project. With no evidence of a woman's touch for over fifty years, within weeks of being installed in Thomas's crumbling old house, she put all her efforts into creating a home for them both.

The dingy kitchen didn't look much better after a few days' scrubbing. The greenish-black mould spots in the damp corners had faded, but were very little improved after her attempts to clean them off.

"Will you pick up some distemper when you're next in town, Thomas?"

"What's it for?"

"For the kitchen ceiling and walls. And something in pale green for the cupboards and doors while you're at it."

"Sure, it's grand as it is. It's clean. Haven't you been scrubbing it all week?"

She looked at him, surprised. "Indeed, it's far from grand. I have been scrubbing it, but it looks like it's not seen a lick of paint for a hundred years. Now that I've put all that effort into scrubbing, I want to see something for my efforts. It needs freshening up."

The solid look on his face told her he didn't agree. She could see another project on her list. To rid him of his old bachelor ways.

"Would you look at it! All the scouring in the world won't improve that ceiling. And look there." She pointed to the fireplace. "Around the hearth is all blackened from the fire. I can tell you that at home we'd do the whitewashing every couple of years. I'd say here has never been done."

"Well, don't be thinking that I'll have time to do any painting."

"Did I ask you to do it?" She smiled at him. "I'll do it myself if you'll just get the paint – that's all I'm asking. I'm an expert, well used to doing it over in Knocknageeha. I know how busy you are. You've enough to be doing with the farm work."

She sang as she decorated, working around the house, room by room. The paint Thomas had bought home had been just enough to give a facelift to the kitchen, the scullery and hallway.

"I'm running out of paint. I had to give the kitchen several coats. Will you get some more on your travels this afternoon?"

"You'll have us broke, woman, with all these renovations."

"It needs to be done and look at what you're saving – sure you're not paying for any labour." It irked her that his resistance was taking the pleasure out of a task. The novelty was wearing off, and his grumbling didn't make it any easier to muster up the enthusiasm to tackle yet another room. "Anyway, it'll last for years once I have it all done."

"And they're giving the paint away for free, I suppose?"

"You can be sure they're not. Don't be such a miser! And I can tell you they won't be giving away the curtains either when I get to that stage." She continued dabbing a missed corner as she dug her heels in. Without looking, she could feel him turn on his heel and leave the room without a word. She hoped that he would return with the paint without having to bring the subject up again.

The thought of the uphill battle ahead with him dismayed her. His opposition to any changes around the place. It wasn't like she was interfering with the farm or the yard. That was his territory. But the house? It was clear from the state of it that he had no interest, so why the objections? Was everything going to be like this – like a rope tied around her waist and someone, or something, constantly pulling her back? But maybe, when she had the house in order and he saw the improvement, he'd loosen up. She didn't want to think otherwise.

By the time she had worked her way through almost all of the rooms she was exhausted. Not just by the effort. No, that just left a satisfied tiredness. It was the opposition that wore her out. She couldn't understand it. At home, Mary Ann had always been delighted with her daughter's decorating skills, and was only too happy to supply the necessary materials, if she thought she could get a room redecorated.

"Can you give me a hand later to move the table from the parlour?" A good time to ask when he was enjoying his dinner.

"Where do you plan on moving it?" He looked across the table at her as he wiped his mouth with the back of his hand.

"Into the other room. Just while I'm painting." She stood up to get the pot of potatoes and brought it over to the table. "Do you want a couple more of these?"

"Yeah." He put his hand into the pot and took out a handful. "There's only three, I might as well finish them off."

"I said a couple." She laughed as she slapped his hand. "I've a mouth on me too, so I'm having the last one."

He dropped it onto her plate.

"What do you want the table moved out for anyway? Can't you work around it?"

"I could, but I don't intend to. It's easier if it's out of the way. I've emptied the sideboard and we can move that to the middle of the room for the moment."

"Alright. I'll shift it with you after the dinner, before I go back out to the yard."

She was surprised by the sudden change in his resistance. Maybe he was finally accepting defeat in the matter or maybe it was just that he could see an end to it all.

She wiped the side table with a damp cloth before polishing it and returning it to its former place under the window in the parlour. The last piece of furniture back in position. She walked to the doorway and, turning, stood there to check her handiwork.

Noticing a smudge on the mirror above the mantelpiece, she picked up the polish cloth and, folding it, used a clean corner to rub at the mark. It refused to shift. She spat on the cloth and tried again – this time it came off without much further effort. Another one done. All the work was worth it, if only for the freshness of each room as it was finished. Glancing out the open window, she saw that it was beginning to drizzle outside. She went over and closed it down. No point in letting the rain splash onto the newly painted sill if the wind changed direction. It had been whipping up in the last hour or so, but now it looked like it might be down for the rest of the day, the way the clouds had greyed and closed over.

The hydrangea bushes outside the window were at their best. Dotted amongst the pink blooms were a few purple ones trying to turn themselves blue. She loved the blue ones, but the soil wasn't quite right to allow them deepen in colour. She remembered Mary Ann burying a shovelful of rusty nails beside hers, when she read somewhere that it would help to turn hydrangeas blue, and her disappointment when it didn't work.

The curtains had had a wash, and she'd hung them back in place. The edges were faded but they'd do for another year or so. No point in pushing her luck. She was glad she'd cut the bunch of hydrangea blooms before the rain. They now sat in a vase on the windowsill. She was ready to show the room to Thomas. It might help enthuse him. He might even agree to having a few visitors around, now that they'd somewhere to entertain them.

Chapter 5

Despite the fresh paint, the gloom inside the farmhouse remained. She wondered if it had anything to do with the fact that the house faced east, leaving the windowless gable end to catch the lovely southerly sun. A waste. Whoever had built it had clearly not given much thought to its direction, and even less to the naming of the house – Ard na Gréine – 'Height of the Sun'. Never had a house been more inappropriately named.

It took her years to work out that it might have had more to do with Thomas's personality casting a shadow than the orientation of their home. Nothing happened suddenly. It was more of a slow drip-feed, an accumulation over time. Only borne out in little ways, making it difficult to put a finger on. Incidents so minor that it took a long time to realise that the light in his green eyes that had enchanted her in their early days together, was now only reserved for outsiders, or when he wanted something from her.

An absolute charmer to a visiting neighbour until the door

closed behind them.

"What did you let him in for?"

"He came to borrow a shovel."

"Well, don't be lending my things to that lad anymore. They only ever come back in two halves, that's if they come back at all."

"I could hardly say we didn't have one, now could I? What farmer doesn't have a few shovels?"

The lack of generosity on his part annoyed her. After all, she was the one who had moved away from home. How did he expect her to fit into a community where she didn't know anyone, if she couldn't do a good turn for a neighbour?

"Do you not think that someday you'll need a hand with something, or the loan of a bit of equipment? That's how we operated over in Knocknageeha anyway."

"Oh, the perfect family."

"Maybe not, but perhaps it might be something to aspire to, don't you think?" She glanced at him to see how he was taking it. She could tell by the dark look on his face that he was unlikely to take up the challenge. It was rare that she pulled him up on things. She hated confrontation but, if she didn't occasionally challenge him on small issues, how was she going to manage when something important cropped up?

It would take effort, but she was prepared to work at knocking the small, mean-spirited attitude out of him. She knew she could change him.

"Let's celebrate." She smiled at him as he came in the door and sat down in the armchair.

"What's to celebrate?" He pulled off his boots and tapped the dried mud onto the hearth.

"There's lots. That there's a baby on the way for a start. And the fact that I got the decorating done beforehand. I wouldn't be able to tackle that now."

"What do you want to do?"

"Surprise me."

"I'm not good on surprises. You know that."

"Well, here's an opportunity to get some practice."

"Where do you want to go?"

"How about we go out for our dinner on Sunday?" She sighed, some of the pleasure already doused. "Save me cooking."

"I suppose. Sounds alright to me." Thomas stretched out his hand. "Can you pass me that newspaper there, while you're on your feet?"

Occasionally the suggestion of a trip to Ennis, coming from him, gave her hope that perhaps he was mellowing. Until she got there.

Thomas went around with her, a grudging dragging of his feet as he trailed after her while she did the shopping, rarely leaving her side. It was always he who handed over the money to pay the shopkeeper for the purchases. After the first time when he queried several of the items she'd requested, humiliating her in front of the merchant, she never suggested they bought anything that wasn't absolutely essential.

"Well, that's the grocery shopping done. I'm sure you've a few messages to get." She smiled at him, hoping he'd leave her in peace to window-shop. "Why don't you go off and do them and I'll potter around and meet you here in half an hour."

She tried to shake him off, but without success. He stuck rigidly by her side as she wandered up the street looking in the shop windows.

"What are you looking at that for?" His sharp tone had her moving on from where she'd stopped in front of the drapery store.

"I'm not. Can I not just stop for a moment's rest?" She held out one of the bags of shopping towards him. "If you're going to trail after me you may as well carry one of these."

"You can rest in there." Ignoring her outstretched arm, he indicated the doorway of the hotel. "I'll be back in a while."

He walked off before she had time to object. She headed into the entrance of the hotel, the shop windows suddenly having lost their appeal.

She transferred the bags into one hand and pushed the brass fingerplate on the swing door and entered the foyer. She stood for a moment and looked around the slightly shabby but comfortable interior. The wine-red patterned wallpaper above the dark wooden panelling still helped retain the air of its former plushness. The few worn upholstered armchairs were occupied, but two businessmen were standing and one, in the process of buckling his briefcase, was bidding farewell to his colleague. She waited for them to move, not wishing to put pressure on them, before walking towards the vacated seats.

She pulled her coat over her visible bump as she sat in the corner of the foyer, a good spot for people-watching. As she waited, an elderly couple arrive in. The woman, like a little bird, took tiny steps, shuffling her dainty feet along the tiled floor, as he barrelled along beside her with his rolling gait. She watched as he fussed over his wife, helping to take her coat off, before folding it and placing it on an armchair. He held her elbow, guiding her gently as she sat down on the sofa.

"What would you like now, Millie?"

She guessed he didn't even need to ask. They looked to her like people whose order would rarely vary. She watched as he leaned towards the little woman with the silver bobbed hair. Catherine wondered at how his shrunken toothless mouth could show such a wide beam. She couldn't quite hear the woman's answer as she watched her looking up at her husband, her eyes crinkling at the corners as she smiled her answer up at him. He patted her shoulder before going into the bar to order their drinks.

Catherine watched the woman sit back on the sofa, contentment written all over her face as slowly she glanced around at the activity in the foyer, happy in the knowledge that her husband was looking after the business end of things.

He returned in a couple of minutes and, placing a glass of sherry on the stained wooden table, took a sip from his glass of black porter, before sitting in beside her on the sofa. They didn't talk much, just the odd comment passed between them as they watched the world pass by. The woman sat with her hands at rest on her lap, and every so often he would reach across and pat the back of her hand.

At another table a pair of women were drinking tea, their heads nodding as they exchanged news. They looked like a pair who a lot of catching-up to do. She wished she was one of them. China cups and a silver teapot. So civilised. But she had no money on her and anyway Thomas would be back soon.

It was almost an hour later when he returned from wherever he had gone. To meet a man. She never got any more information when he went anywhere than that he was meeting some lad or other, but she couldn't resist putting the question anyway.

"What kept you?"

"Why, were you in a hurry somewhere? Did you need to be anywhere important?"

That almost shut her up. Almost.

"I'd have liked a cup of tea had I known you were going to be so long." She tried to keep the annoyance out of her voice. "You might have left me with some money."

"Maybe it's taking tea in fine hotels you were brought up to."

"It was actually. My mother and I did it regularly on my days off." Satisfied she'd made her point, she withdrew. She could get good at this. At least next time she'd make sure she had money in her pocket.

Chapter 6

Catherine gave birth to Thomas Junior and her husband's delight in his son improved his mood considerably. As soon as the baby started to take notice of activity around him, Thomas began taking him out to the yard in the pram so he could watch whatever jobs he had to do out there. Catherine observed from the window as he chatted to the baby. With the window ajar she could hear him explain about chopping wood for the fire. And whenever the baby gurgled back at him, she had to smile at the *'That's it, you've got the idea. Sure, we'll have you able to do it yourself in no time, Tommy, me lad.'*

Once or twice, careful not to voice her fear, she had to wander out and surreptitiously move the pram a few feet away, to avoid the danger of any chips that might fly off the block taking the eye out of the baby. Her mother had warned her that men were incapable of anticipating danger – something lacking in their make-up. Always seemed surprised *after* the disaster, that such a thing could have happened. She didn't want to draw attention by even making the suggestion that it might be wise to move the baby a bit further away.

"I'll take him out to the yard with me. Come on, Tommy!" Thomas laughed, delighted at his son's first steps. "Let's waddle out together."

"Sure can't he watch you from the window, Thomas?"

"Not at all. I'll keep an eye on him. He might learn something out there."

"What is it you'll be doing?"

"Sawing a few logs."

"I'm not sure it's safe." She couldn't stop herself. "It was different before he could walk. I don't want him distracting you with the saw in your hand. You might end up cutting the fingers off yourself."

Without waiting for an objection, she scooped the child up and, ignoring his struggles, popped him in the pram, reluctant to allow him the freedom of what she could only see as an accident waiting to happen.

"You've got to stay in the pram, Tommy. I'll take you outside so you can watch Daddy."

He kicked against her, his back rigid as she tried to strap him in.

"I know you don't want to, baby, but it's too dangerous for you to be running around. I'll bring you out something to eat in a minute and you can watch your daddy." Hoping her best pacifying voice would calm him, she pushed him out into the sunshine. "Now, there you are, you can see Daddy at work." She angled the pram a distance away but from where he had a good view of the activity before bending down to wedge a block of wood in front of the wheel.

Thomas glanced over his shoulder. "You can move him a bit closer than that, Kate."

"He's near enough, he can see you perfectly."

"How am I ever going to make a farmer out of you, young Tom, with your mother fussing like that?" Thomas winked at his son as he picked up a bough and, laying it across the sawhorse, began his work.

Returning to the kitchen, Catherine picked up a large crust from the breadboard, spread a bit of strawberry jam on it and took it out to Tom.

"There you are, baby. Something to chew on. Nice crust, good for your little teeth."

As the child grabbed the bread and thrust the tail of it into his mouth and sucked on it, she went back to the house and stood there, leaning on the sink, watching from the window.

The ease with which Thomas had adapted to fatherhood and chatted to the baby had surprised her. She'd worried that he might be one of those fathers who had the '*spare the rod and spoil the child*' viewpoint, so to see him involve their son in his activities and laugh at his reactions made her happy. It gave her hope that maybe at last he was beginning to loosen up and shed his tight bachelor ways. Just as well because she suspected she might be expecting again.

Not one to ponder the wonders of pregnancy, as far as he was concerned procreation was a natural process that didn't need any discussion. Not a lot more was said, but the news, coming so soon after Thomas Junior took his first steps, seemed to please him.

"Sure, won't it be grand for young Tommy to have a companion." He paused. "Being an only child isn't all it's cracked up to be. I can tell you that."

It happened in the early hours of the morning. The dull ache in her abdomen had intensified and had come between her and her sleep. Not wanting to disturb him with her tossing and turning, she crept from the bed and, closing the bedroom door behind her went down to the kitchen. She added a handful of twigs to the embers and stood a couple of sods of turf on top, balancing them in a wigwam. Sitting into the rocker, a rug thrown over her shoulders she watched the fire catch alight and waited for the pain to subside.

She could feel the wet between her legs, and even in the dark she knew before she reached the washroom that at three months the pregnancy was about to end in a miscarriage. She sat on the stool and leaned back against the wall. She knew it was red, but the large damp patch on her nightdress was dark as the moonlight streaming in the window made everything appear a navy-grey against a silver background. Its soft light calmed her. The worst had happened and there was nothing she could do to save it. She sat there unable to move as the chill of the early morning seeped into her bones, wishing she'd brought the rug with her. She couldn't stay there much longer, that she knew, but the effort to shift herself, to move from that position, seemed more than she was capable of – but she needed to return to the bed and lie down before she slid to the floor with the weakness. Applying mind over matter and gripping onto the washstand, hoping it wouldn't turn over on her, she managed to stand up. Looking in the mirror she saw a ghostly grey face stare back at her in the dawn light.

The bleeding appeared to have stopped. Washing as best she

could, she threw the stained cloths into the bucket. The clean-up could wait until the morning.

She could hear his snoring through the closed bedroom door. No point in waking him. There was nothing he could do now. It was too late.

Turning the door handle quietly she padded over to the chest of drawers and eased the top one open. It jammed with a dull thud. She looked over at his sleeping figure, but the sound hadn't disturbed him. She listened, hoping that young Tom in the next room hadn't heard the movements, but there wasn't a murmur. The last thing she needed to have to deal with was a fretful baby.

She pressed the drawer back and using her two hands slid it out evenly and took out a clean nightgown and knickers. The freshness of lavender clung to the soft cotton material as she slipped it over her head. Closing her eyes she leaned against the dresser, pausing for a few moments to allow the weakness to pass. Realising if she stood there much longer she'd be unable to move, she took a deep breath before rummaging through the bundle of towels. She padded slowly towards the window and opened a slit in the curtains to let the moonlight through. Not wanting to use the good fluffy ones she'd been saving for the visitors they never had, she'd just enough light to allow her to pick an old one, grey from constant washing, ideal for the job. The dull ache remained, but the blood flow had more or less stopped. Still she wouldn't take a chance. Folding the towel, she settled the pad in place and lifting the eiderdown she crept into the bed.

Lying on her back she envied his snoring. There was no way she was going to be able to sleep now. Her eyes welled and she could feel the slow progress of the tears as they spilled over and travelled from the corners, dripping down onto the pillow. She wanted to wake him. To share the upset. She glanced towards his sleeping body, and even as she reached out her hand to shake his shoulder, she knew she would be unable to bring herself to tell him. Withdrawing, she convinced herself it might be easier in the morning.

Chapter 7

She'd been right not to waken him. She told him as he dressed. After her sleepless night and with the nagging pain in her abdomen, it wouldn't have done any good. She could see that now. His response would only have served to make her feel more miserable.

"That's a pity, but it happens." With his back to her, he continued pulling on his working trousers. "Yeah, that's unfortunate. Sure, why don't you stay in bed for another while and I'll bring young Tom in to you before I go out into the yard."

He paused at the door and looked back at her.

"Don't be upsetting yourself, Kate, sure we can always try again. I'll bring you up a cup of tea when I'm making my own."

For him that was the end of the subject. No more to be said on the matter.

"What's the point in crying about it, sure haven't we got one healthy child to be thankful for?" he said.

She'd thought about dropping the subject but found she couldn't. It was his child too and this was too big a thing to let it go. Whatever about him, she needed to talk about it more. She was going to give it one last try.

She had him now at the kitchen table, with the carving knives in a row before him. He was only starting on the job of sharpening them, so it gave her time before he could use the excuse of another job to get up and go outside – his usual ruse whenever he didn't want to discuss something. She wanted to close off any possibility of him escaping the conversation. It would be more difficult to bring it up again if she let this, possibly her last opportunity, pass.

"I know we have and that's something to be grateful for, but I'd still like to talk about it." She watched him pick up the whetstone and draw the blade of the meat knife across it. "I don't know about you, but I can't just forget about it that easily."

"What's to be said? What's gone is gone, and all the talking about it won't bring it back." Without looking at her he shook his head. "It's a real pity, but as they say . . . no point in crying over spilt milk . . . that's just it. Nothing anyone can do about it. And that's the pity."

"I know it's hard but . . . "

"But what?"

"Well, I need . . . we need to talk about it."

"Why? What is it you want me to say?"

"I've no idea. I haven't been through anything like this before either. But it feels like you are shutting me out." She looked across at him, his defensive reaction making it impossible to read him, impossible to gauge exactly how he felt about their loss.

"Maybe a hug would have been nice?" She hated the pleading in her voice.

He put down the whetstone and stood up.

Maybe she should have left it. Now it looked like he was going to walk out on her. And that definitely would have put an end to it.

She was surprised when she saw him walk around the end of the table, instead of heading for the door, and come to a stop at the back of her chair. It felt good, more than she'd expected, as he wrapped his arms around her and held her there.

"I'm sorry." His words came out in a whisper as she felt his chin rest on her head. "I'm sorry, I just don't know what to say. I'm no good at these things."

She felt his grip loosen and watched him return to the far side of the table. He picked up the knife and, in the silence that followed as he drew the blade across the stone, she felt the door close firmly. She could almost hear it, as, with his face downwards in concentration and the top of his head only visible to her, he continued sharpening the blade. That was as much as he was capable of, but at least it was something and she'd have to settle for that. From that moment she knew there'd be no reopening of the subject. She was doomed to be on her own. No-one to share the pain with. He just couldn't talk about it and there was no point in forcing him. Doing that might have the reverse effect, cause a row, negating what he had just done. No, she would just have to be content with his response and forget about what she herself needed.

"*Children should be seen and not heard.*" How many times had he heard that as a child? He'd often wondered how the other schoolchildren had opinions on everything and no difficulty voicing them, even to the teacher. He'd had the opinions, no shortage there. The problem was, so deep had been the put-downs whenever he'd tried to articulate his ideas at home, he'd never worked out a way to express them without a row. Any childish "*Why?*" was followed by the same stock answer . . . "*Because I say so.*" Or, "*That's the why*". End of discussion.

As a teenager the words changed, but the message remained the same.

"*You've far too much to say for yourself, lad.*" He could still hear his father's voice.

No wonder he'd developed a range of surly looks and sullen silences as alternatives. Enough put-downs had been doled out for him to amass an arsenal of churlish glares. The skill of civilised debating or discussion was not something he'd had any chance to acquire.

In the months and years that followed, he never queried why she failed to get pregnant again. He'd proved himself with siring a son, so it was obviously women's problems. Not something he wanted to delve into. The only time the topic was touched upon was when she brought it up and that had only happened once.

"I wonder why it's not happening?" Her tentative tone sounded as if she'd just voiced the query to herself, until she lifted her head from her embroidery and looked across at him. "Would you like more children?"

"I would if it happens, but what will be, will be." He turned a page of his newspaper.

"Are you not disappointed? Just a bit?" Now that the subject was open, she'd pressed on. "Because I am. And you often said you didn't like being an only child."

"Well, there's not a lot to be done about it, is there? And, anyway, I'm sure not all single children have the same experience as I had. Young Tom has a fairly good life, don't you think?" He'd looked up at her, a look that suggested a hope of putting an end to the conversation. "Anyway, what do you want me to do about it?"

No change there. Always the same curt response. How foolish to even hope for anything different.

"Nothing." She sighed. "You're right. There's nothing we can do. But that's not what I asked. I just wondered how you felt about it."

It was shortly after this conversation that it happened. She was pregnant again.

Her pregnancy proceeded largely uncommented upon. In the early months she'd have liked to talk to Thomas about the fear she felt, the anxiety that history might repeat itself, but was reluctant to bring up the subject. With him anyway. It might have helped had she lived a little closer to Knocknageeha, close enough to be able to just drop in casually. It was just that little bit far to walk without prior planning and she was so tired these days. Seeing her mother on a more regular basis would have helped. When she did talk to Mary Ann it made her wish she possessed more of her mother's nature.

"There are no certainties in this life, Catherine. Sometimes you just have to accept whatever is landed on you, and you never know what that's going to be."

"Yes, but it helps to be able to talk about it." Catherine paused.

"It does. But it's Thomas you really need to talk to."

"Tell me something I don't know."

It was like her mother read her mind.

"He doesn't really understand." Catherine hesitated, unsure if she should say anything further. "Ah, you know what men are like. It helps more to talk to you about my worries, about this anyway. Men don't understand. You've lost a few children so *you* know exactly what it's like."

"It's not easy, Catherine. For me it was all a long time ago. You do get over it. It kind of fades, but you don't forget and you're always worried with the next one. All you can do is take it day by day and hope for the best."

As Mary Ann patted her arm, Catherine noticed the weathered brown skin on the back of her mother's hand, surprised she'd not noticed before how her mother was ageing.

"And look after yourself as best you can. No doing any heavy work. Tell him that."

"Oh, he knows. We've agreed on that."

"Well, it's good to get your worries off your chest every now and again. I'll get Art to drop me over to you when he's going that direction next time."

"That would be great, Mam."

"You're nearly at the seventh month now so you're over the worst. It looks like this time there's a good chance that everything will go alright."

The successful pregnancy reached full term. She was overjoyed. A boy and now a girl. Whatever happened now, she was content with their little family

Chapter 8

Thomas seemed as delighted as his wife when Mary arrived after a straightforward birth. Not that he'd said anything, but it was obvious in the way she'd overheard him chatting to young Tom about his baby sister.

"It's you and me, Tommy. Us men will have to stick together. Can't have two women bossing us around now, can we?" He handed the yard brush to his son.

"What do you want me to do, Daddy?"

"If you sweep all that straw into the corner, I'll get the wheelbarrow and we'll get rid of it, and then we'll go in for the tea and let that young Mary one know who's in charge. Leave her in no doubt just who's the boss. How about that?"

"So am I in charge, Daddy?" Tom looked pleased with himself. "Will I tell her that?"

"You are indeed, Tom." Thomas laughed. "And you better let her know that now while she can't answer back."

The miscarriage following Mary's birth had Catherine carrying the loneliness by herself yet again. She made no attempt to discuss the matter with him. There was no point. He behaved as if the living children were his, but the miscarriages were all hers, and hers alone. She just got on with things as if nothing had happened, as the gap between them widened.

By the time Eileen was born most battles with her husband had all but been abandoned and Catherine buried herself in the lives of her children, the light of her life and a reason to keep going.

With the overwhelming emotion that came with each birth, a throwaway comment by an old woman in the village was something that she'd never forgotten. It came back to her as she filled the water jug in readiness for the last of the evening chores, watering the flowerpots.

"I always thinks that a baby is like a flower." Vera had smiled as she looked into the distance.

Catherine had never forgotten that beatific look on her face, like Vera was remembering something.

"What do you mean, Vera?"

"Well, you know the way when a flower emerges from the ground to find the sun beaming its warmth upon it? Well, sure isn't it the same for a little one. A child can feel the love each time a parent beams it down on them. Just like the sun. That's all it needs. Sure, what more would a little one need to encourage it to blossom?"

Not that she needed to be told, but the image had delighted her. And with lots to smile about with a little one, she couldn't stop herself.

After a long hot summer, the flowers had struggled through the drought. A few had died, but not for the want of care. She loved this time of evening, after the day's work was done, to bask for a few minutes in the last rays of evening sunshine and imagine the pot-bound roots enjoying their drink of water. She could almost see them straightening themselves up again after soaking up the moisture.

The water in the birdbath had evaporated. She wondered how long it had been empty. How had she not noticed? Taking the filled jug, she walked out again into the heat of the early evening sun. She paused a moment in the doorway for her eyes to adjust to the brightness before walking over and filling the birdbath. She scattered the handful of corn she'd taken from the jar before heading back to the bench to sit down and watch. It would take a few minutes for the birds to discover it, but she had the time to sit and wait now that the children were settled.

The log seat that had been placed against the wall was in a great position to catch the evening sun. No sense in leaving it where it had been set long before her time, along the north-facing wall. It was something she'd noticed that first summer after she'd arrived and suspected that no thought had been given to it. She'd asked Thomas to move it.

"Sure, who do you think ever had time to be sitting on it?"

"Well, I'll make time. Would you just move it with me? Here, I'll catch this end."

"And where do you want it moved to?"

"Over there where it'll catch the sun. I've just cleared and swept the area."

"Alright, missus. Your wish is my command." He hefted up his end. "Mind your back, it's heavier than you think."

"Well, maybe I'm stronger than *you* think, mister."

She got her way with fewer objections than she'd expected, and it had been in regular use ever since, even if mostly by herself.

The white glare of the day had disappeared and had now settled to a soft golden shimmer. She could feel it as she held her face up to the sun, resting her head against the wall. A few chirrups alerted her to their presence. Staying totally still, she opened her eyes and watched two small starlings dipping their beaks in and out of the water, before one jumped in and splashed about. His friend stood on the edge watching, as if patiently waiting his turn. As his bathing neared an end, the fledgling seemed almost suspended half out of the water, his fluttering wings and tail sending droplets of water to fan out into the air, diamond-like, as if from a sprinkler. His friend followed the ritual and each had a few mouthfuls of the seed before flying away out of sight into the copse of trees at the far side of the garden.

She sat there a while, enjoying the peace and thinking about the beneficial things in the life she'd chosen. She had a lot to be thankful for. No point on focussing on the negatives.

She had to hand it to him, he was a worker, and knew how to enjoy his children. To her surprise he'd turned out a good teacher and happily took time to show them how to manage little jobs around the farm.

The children liked doing things with him, but seemed to have an inbuilt instinct for danger. Occasionally they pushed him to the limit of his patience, but the darkening shadow on his face or the sharp edge that entered his tone would stop them short of exceeding it.

With her, his behaviour was different. Most of the time she might as well have been one of his chattels. Communication limited to only what was necessary for daily living. Otherwise it was just a grunt from behind the newspaper. Sometimes it felt like she had more communication with the back of the paper than she ever had with her husband. Companionship didn't seem to enter his head, and age seemed to be doing nothing to mellow him. She wondered if most marriages descended to this level after a few years. Basic survival. Was this the best she could expect? Maybe it was the same for others and they just managed to get on with it. So much for not focusing on the negatives. That didn't last long.

She thought of her own parents. Life at home had seemed fun, but then maybe all family life would seem like that to a child. She'd been eight when Pa had died, so all she had were vague memories of lots of laughter and banter. The haziness of them bothered her.

"You couldn't possibly remember that, Kate, you were too young."

Maude's taunt always upset her, although it wasn't intended to hurt, just said more on the grounds of accuracy.

"I do. I do so remember it," she'd insist.

"I doubt that. You probably just remember hearing about it, Kate."

There was one incident that she'd held onto, the pain of which was so strong that it wasn't something she'd heard about. That was certain. Absolutely no doubt about that. She'd definitely felt it, and it was her memory, precious only to her, painful and all as it was.

She'd seen Hugh do it. Flying down the stairs at great speed, barely touching the treads of the steps. She'd always wanted to fly. A run on the landing to the top step. Speed propelled launch. Light as a feather. Her long straight hair floating upwards with the undercurrent of air, as she realised her little feet were not in contact with the steps. The panic of the fast plummeting towards the wall at the end of the stairs. She reached out to grab the banister, but the speed was too great for her little arms to reach it. The crash against the wall as she came to earth stunned her. All she was aware of was a voice from the kitchen.

"*Mother of God, what was that?*"

Pa appearing in the doorway.

"*Oh, child, what's happened to you?*"

She could still remember his look of horror as he rushed to her. Bending down, he scooped her up onto his knee. Her mother's shocked face appeared in the doorway, as she gasped for the air to tell her pa what had happened, but nothing came out.

"Take your time, alannah, no wonder you're winded. Just take your time."

The feeling of him holding her in a bear-hug and rubbing her back as she struggled to catch her breath – she could still feel it.

"You'll be alright, lovey." He snuggled her in under his chin.

"Where did you fall from, Catherine?" Her mother knelt beside them, the worry evident in her voice, as Catherine pointed up towards the top of the stairs. "You couldn't have fallen from the top. You'd be dead."

"I did." The breathy sound came out as she nodded. "From the top."

"Jesus Christ, you could have killed yourself! Did you trip or what?" Her mother sounded annoyed. "Am I not always telling you to hold on to the banister?"

"Ah, Mary Ann, would you leave the child alone? Sure, she's alive. We're lucky she's still alive." The warmth of Pa's hug protected her from any trouble she was in. "Isn't that right, Katie love? But how did it happen, alannah?"

"I saw Hugh do it. He flew down the stairs. Real fast." She began to sob. "But I couldn't touch the steps."

"Ah, baby, sure you're only five. Your little legs aren't long enough. Don't be minding what that fella's doing. Sure he's fifteen and a long lanky lad. He's not someone to be copying. Come on into the kitchen and your mother will get you a nice slice of curranty cake and we'll forget all about flying. How about that?"

She could remember the feel of his warm, rough paw as he led her away from the stairs.

Mary Ann was the disciplinarian and he was the big softie. That's how she remembered him. A vague recollection of the affectionate touches between her parents, while she'd had no real understanding of their relationship, made for a general feeling of warmth about the place.

Things by necessity had toughened up after he died but that was a different story. All she could remember from before then was the relaxed atmosphere around home, something that was missing here in Ard na Gréine. At least for her. But maybe she'd just have to content herself that at least Thomas loved the children, and there was an understanding between them. They seemed to accept that there were no soft ways with him, unlike herself, where, with persistence, they could wear her down to the point she would give in to their requests.

The row she'd had with him a few years back, about young Tom starting school, came back to her.

"He's too babyish, Thomas."

"And whose fault is that?" He'd eyed her, his voice light, but the undercurrent of blame was unmistakeable. "I've been trying to turn him into a man, despite your mollycoddling."

"He's only four. He's not ready," she'd pleaded.

"He won't be four for much longer."

"Let's leave it till next year. When he's five he'll be better able to cope."

"Yeah, five, going on six. He'll need to toughen up if he's to survive this life at all."

She remembered the way he'd paused as he moved towards the door.

"He's going and that's all."

She'd taken a few steps after him but, as he disappeared from view, she'd stopped. No point. The decision had been made. Conversation ended. Had to accept that maybe she'd be better off teaching the child a few coping skills, certainly better off than continuing the argument. There was no way she was going to win that one and, as it turned out, any future ones concerning Mary or Eileen.

Her own first day at school came back to her. The incident with the seating was the main thing she remembered, the standout incident that was indelibly printed on her brain.

"You sit there, Catherine, in that seat beside Doris." The young teacher smiled at her.

Her backside had hardly hit the bench, before a thunder-faced Doris glowered at her.

"*You can't sit there! That's my friend's seat!*"

It came out as a snarl, and had Catherine jump up as if the bench was red-hot.

The teacher had been busy seating the rest of the newcomers, so it took a few minutes before she'd spotted Catherine, finger in her mouth, standing beside the desk.

"What's the matter, Catherine?"

"She says it's her friend's seat, and I can't sit there." She remembered trying to stifle the sobs.

"Oh, don't worry, I'll find you a better seat then." The teacher took her by the hand. "Here, how about that one? Now, Margaret, you look after Catherine for me, won't you?"

She still remembered the sting of rejection, and it wasn't something she wanted her child to experience. No, her own first day at school hadn't been easy, but somehow she had survived. Maybe Thomas had been right.

By the time she found herself with an unanticipated pregnancy, she had long given up hope of another child. With none of the joy of previous pregnancies to sustain her, she felt too old to go down this road again. Her body was no longer up to the job, and it came as no surprise that she felt unwell throughout. Her system was telling her it had had enough, and she was unable to shake the general lethargy that overtook her. How on earth did some women manage ten or twelve pregnancies?

"I can't manage, Thomas. We'll have to get help."

"Sure, am I not doing all the heavy lifting?" he argued. "What more do you want me to do?"

"That's the point, I don't want you to do any more. It's not that. I know you're busy with the farm work. That's not what it's about." She sighed. Not enough energy for this battle with him. "It's help with the children and the housework that I need, and I know that Maude would be happy for Dorothy to lend a hand here."

"So, you've already discussed this with your sister? Sure isn't Mary old enough to help you?"

"She's only a child herself, Thomas, it wouldn't be fair. I need someone more responsible than that." She hoped he wasn't going to dig his heels in on this. She'd already written to Maude to check out the possibility of her daughter coming over from Wexford, for a while anyway. Hadn't told him for fear he'd put up all the arguments as to why it wouldn't work, before she'd even checked out the possibility of her niece wanting to come. She could just hear him … there wouldn't be room, we couldn't afford to pay her, or any of a dozen reasons why it wasn't a good idea.

Maude had seemed overly enthusiastic which made her wonder why her sister was so keen on the idea. Probably just the clash of the teenage years, with the overbearing mother that she suspected Maude might be. If she'd noticed that on their summer visits, no doubt Dorothy, being on the receiving end of her mother's strong personality, might welcome a move to Clare, even if only temporary. Give them both space.

Thomas kept up his protests for a week but, despite them, Catherine sent for her niece to come and stay, to help with the children. It was worth a try anyway. Wouldn't do anyone any harm, and the children would be delighted.

DOROTHY

Chapter 9

County Wexford
1899

Dorothy had just finished school. Not for the day, not for the summer holidays, but finished, finished. For good. It felt as if she'd been dropped off a cliff, with no idea where she might land. Well, maybe not quite so frightening as that, but a bit of a shock all the same.

It wasn't as though it had happened suddenly or anything, so it baffled her that she'd given so little thought to it, until now. And straightaway there were all the questions, ones that she should have been asking herself over the past year or so, but they hadn't occurred to her. And, so, she'd no answers ready and they all seemed to expect her to have it worked out. The truth was that she had absolutely no idea where she was going, or what she wanted to do in the future. Her own empty-headedness astounded even her, and certainly irritated her parents.

A lucky occurrence that the invitation to come over to County Clare had arrived just when the parents, her mother especially, were beginning to get on her nerves, looking for evidence of her plans. She hoped Maude wasn't going to object or put any obstacles in her path. Her one chance, her only chance, to get away from the constant questioning.

"Maybe it would be something useful to occupy you, while you're working out exactly what it is you intend to do with your life, don't you think, Dorothy? Looks like you're not going to manage that, hanging around here?"

"I suppose so." She needn't have worried. Her mother was all for it.

"That's settled then. We'll go into Gorey tomorrow and get you a few bits and pieces." Maude's business-like tone told her there was going to be no shilly-shallying about it. It was all sorted. "Can't have you turning up in my home county letting the side down, with holes in your knickers. And while we're in there we'll get your hair cut."

"But I like my hair like this." Dorothy looked at her mother in surprise.

"Well, you've a good thick head of hair, I'll grant you that. You're lucky you inherited that from me and not from your father. The thin wispy head on him. Although, I suppose you were lucky enough to get your height from him. A bit gawky, but I suppose you'll fill out in time."

"Lucky then I didn't get *stumpy* from you, Mother."

"Less of that now. Petite is the correct term for it, I'll have you know." Maude picked up her daughter's brown locks. "No, you need something done with that. It's too long. Makes you look like a child."

"But I can plait it. I need to keep the length for that."

"No, plaits are for children. A few inches off would improve that mane and make you look more of a grown-up. Like someone who can be relied on to look after their children."

"It's *my* hair!"

"Enough. We'll see what they say in the hairdresser's tomorrow." Maude studied her. "You've a good face, much as it pains me to give you a swollen head, but you have. Pretty. Inherited again from me, of course, but a new hairstyle is needed to frame it. Show you off at your best. Let them in Clare see no dowdy young one, no country bumpkin, is arriving from here. Now upstairs with you and go through your stuff and see what you need."

"You sound like you can't wait to get rid of me?" Secretly delighted with the rare compliment from her mother, it came out sounding more like a question, but one that Dorothy really didn't want an answer to.

"Go on with you! And when you come down you can write to Catherine and tell her you'd love to come. I've already written and told her you'll be coming and she's happy about that, but she needs to hear it from you. Wouldn't want her to think I was pushing you into it."

"See what I mean?" Dorothy stood up from the table and mock-stared accusingly at her mother. "Before Aunt Catherine changes her mind, is that what you're really saying?"

"Go on out of that with you!" Maude laughed. "And start packing. I'm sure you don't want me interfering in that now, do you?"

Dorothy was a worrier. She fretted over all sorts of things. Things that could happen but most probably never would. No shortage of things to torture herself about. She often wondered where she got it from. Her father was like a rock, carried himself with an air of assurance. Someone who, no matter what happened, could be relied upon to deal with it.

"Don't be worrying, child," he'd say. "If it happens, we'll find a way to sort it. Don't fret about it."

Aware of her irritating trait, she tried to keep her anxieties under control, knowing how annoying it was to her mother, whose attitude to life was to just get on with things. But it was her father's line that helped: "Anyway, think about it, what's the worst that can happen?" He'd insist on an answer and that always sorted her out. Her mother's approach was usually less effective.

"What's the point of agonising over it? If you can do something about it, do it. Otherwise forget about it." That was Maude's stock answer when she saw her daughter beginning on one of her concerns. "Out with you, or I'll give you something to worry about."

Now it was the dog. The anxiety about him only started the day before she was due to head off on her adventure. She'd taken him on as the runt of a litter, despite her mother's objections to the pup.

"That lad will eat the same as a good dog, but you'll never make any sort of a decent sheepdog out of him," Maude had said when Dorothy had brought him home.

"But he's the one I liked best. Anyway, we've no sheep and I'm the one who's going to look after him."

Going to the opposite side of the country to mind Aunt Catherine's children sounded exciting and would get her away from the pressure at home. But, when it came to the time, she hadn't realised how hard it was going to be to let go.

"Would you ever stop the nonsense, Dorothy? You're only going over to Clare. It's not like you're leaving the country." Maude sighed in exasperation. "Think of the relatives who went across the Atlantic. It was more than their dog they were leaving."

"But you won't forget to feed him, sure you won't?"

"That's the third time." Maude shook her head and continued sweeping the floor. "He'll not starve, I promise. Patch will get his breakfast when I'm having mine and I'm hardly likely to forget that now, am I? Then he'll have the leftovers after the dinner."

"Don't forget the water. He needs fresh water in his bowl all the time."

"There's always the trough outside full of rainwater. He won't die of the drought, you needn't worry." She looked at Dorothy. "Lord preserve us but where did I ever get such a fusspot of a daughter?"

Hanging her coat on the hook on the back of the kitchen door, Dorothy couldn't resist one last worry. "You'll take him for a walk, won't you?"

"Hasn't he just been for one? With you."

"I don't mean now. When I'm gone."

"Will you go away out o' that! Can't he go for a run in the fields himself if he wants to? He knows his way home."

"But he likes the company. Promise me!"

"Oh, for heaven's sake, talk to your father. He might take him when he goes walking on the beach." Maude turned the brush in Dorothy's direction and proceeded to sweep the crumbs and dust towards her, before handing it over to her. "Here, you can finish up here as you don't seem to have anything better to do. He'll be grand, I tell you. The dog will survive without you. Or, now that I think of it, maybe you'd be best taking him with you?" Maude threw the challenge at her daughter. "No, I thought not. Now will you just give it a rest and give me a bit of peace!"

Chapter 10

Catherine could hear the children early each morning, whispering and giggling on the landing, followed by a light tap-tapping.

"*Who's that knocking on my door?*" the voice would call out before the children's muffled laughter disappeared into Dorothy's room.

Catherine could turn over in the bed and relax into slumber, content that all would be well. The ease with which her niece had settled in had surprised her. She'd been here only a few weeks and already everything on the farm seemed to bubble along happily. The house felt lighter. It was nice to have another woman around and even Thomas seemed to have a bounce in his step. From what Maude had written, it sounded like it might have turned out the opposite.

"*If it doesn't work out, Catherine, don't think twice about sending her home. We won't be insulted. No point in her becoming a passenger. I'm sure you've enough to do without that.*"

Despite her sister's doubts, Maude had trained Dorothy well. Probably just a mother and daughter personality clash. She knew how domineering her sister could be. Catherine smiled at the memory. No time for slackers. That was Maude. Took herself very seriously as the eldest sister in the family. Catherine could remember her having given up trying to boss the boys when they all lived at home. Art and Hugh were well able for her, so she'd turned her attention to the younger sisters as soon as they came to be of a useful age. She remembered Maude teaching her to clean windows.

"No, Maude. I don't want to. Mam told *you* to do them." Young and all as she was, she had the wit to realise when her sister was trying to fool her. She must have been about seven. Remembered her hair tied up in rags to make ringlets for her First Communion.

"You don't want to grow up useless, Catherine. You'll never learn any other way and anyway it for *your* big day tomorrow, not mine. And that's what we're cleaning them for." Maude had put on her strict voice. "You just do the ones you can reach and I'll deal with the others."

Catherine could just imagine her doling out chores to her own children, but smiled at the thought that she was reaping that benefit now, in the loan of Dorothy for a few months. She'd been right about not allowing children to grow up useless.

With young Tom old enough to help his father on the farm, it was mainly to look after Mary and Eileen that Dorothy was needed, and to keep the home ticking over. These were things she was doing very efficiently, even to the point where she was involving the girls in the chores. Definitely a bit of Maude in her, but much more fun and with less of the dictator in her.

The only time Dorothy thought of Patch was when the farm dog joined in their games in the yard. She still asked after him in her letters home. Couldn't resist a little reminder just to make sure they were still remembering to look after him.

"*The dog is still alive.*" That was as much as her mother deemed necessary to tell her about his welfare. After the dog, the rest of the news usually consisted of the death of an ancient neighbour or an addition to some family in the village. The most unusual event was the burning of a thatched roof down the road when a spark from the chimney set it alight. Fortunately a wisp of smoke was spotted early and the neighbours were able to extinguish it, with a ladder and buckets of water passed from one to the other, before it developed into an inferno. Apart from that one-off, almost-disaster, she hadn't missed anything. Same old trudging along from day to day, but she loved getting the weekly letters.

Not that she whined about it to her mother, but she did miss them all at times, even the good-natured squabbling with her brothers. But there was enough happening here with the children, to keep her mind off that.

She could see the tiredness on Catherine's face. This pregnancy was clearly taking its toll. Without waiting to be asked, Dorothy took over most of the household chores.

"Leave that to me, Aunt Kate. I'll wash those sheets, one pair each day until they're all done, so long as the weather holds. There's no urgency on them and, anyway, you can't be lifting them up to the clothesline. They're too heavy when they're wet. I'll get Mary to help me." Dorothy put the lid back on the laundry basket. "Now, go and put your feet up while you have the chance."

She flew through the jobs each morning before joining

Catherine in the kitchen to help prepare the dinner.

"It's nearly ready, Dorothy. You could give the children a shout and tell Thomas to come in. I think he's out in the near field."

Once they had all dispersed after the meal Dorothy cleared the table and began washing the dishes.

"Do you know what I think would work well, Dorothy?"

"What's that, Aunt Catherine?"

"If you help with the housework in the mornings while they're at school, and use the afternoons to go off and have adventures with the children before it gets dark. I know they'd love that and it'll stop them dragging out of you while you're trying to do the chores. And maybe you'd help them with their school homework after tea. How does that sound?"

"Well, if you're happy with that, I certainly am. I love playing with the children. I think there's still a bit of a child in me." Dorothy grinned at her aunt. "At least my mother seems to think so. Always telling me to grow up. And as for no chores in the afternoon? She'd have something to say about that too. 'Skiving off' would be her term for that."

"Sounds like Maude alright." Catherine laughed. "That's settled then. Mornings for work and afternoons for play."

"And maybe you could go for a lie-down after dinner each day, while I have them out of the house?"

"Ah, you've seen through me. That's exactly what I had in mind. Make the most of the peace."

Dorothy had had the feeling that Catherine wasn't overly

particular about the housework once the children were happy and safe. This conversation confirmed that that was the most important thing to her aunt and, as long as the house wasn't in total chaos, she could relax in the knowledge that the children loved spending time with her niece, and the arrangement suited and was working out very well for everyone.

With no more *"What do you intend to do with your life?"* questions to drive her mad, her head began to clear and she could see a possible path to the future. Maybe a job involving children might be her calling. When Catherine was through all this and had settled down with the new baby, she might check out the possibility of training for children's nursing. Yes, there's a career that would satisfy both herself and her parents. She could relax now that she had a plan and in the meantime let the joy and fun of the children fill her life.

Being in charge, the only rules she imposed were ones that kept them from danger. The old worrying Dorothy was never too far away – no wandering off beyond the yard on their own, and no playing down by the pond unless she was with them. She noticed they seemed to have an inbuilt recognition that their cousin was the fun part of their lives, and their mother the soft part, the one that they had to be gentle with. For the moment anyway.

"Mother will be impressed when I get home." Dorothy stirred the chopped onion in the bottom of the saucepan. "She always says she can tell my soup. And it's never a compliment. Tasteless. But she never told me that the trick was to fry the onion first. You should have been a teacher, Aunt Kate."

"Well, I learned a few tips from Betsy – she was the boss up in Woodbine House. She was the housekeeper but she was in charge of the cooking as well. She trained me in. And my mother knew how to make a tasty meal." Catherine handed over the bowl of chopped carrots and potatoes to Dorothy. "Add those next before you pour in the stock. Yeah, I was good at cooking. Probably should have done some formal training, but sure I'd met Thomas by then and here we are. But you could get good at it, Dorothy."

"I've a lot to learn. That's for sure." She laughed. "I'm not sure if my culinary skills are even on the right side of adequate. But I'm a keen learner, you have to credit me with that."

"Well, if you knew it all I'd have nothing to teach you. Anyway, it's nice to have someone to work alongside." Catherine sat down at the table and watched as Dorothy stirred the saucepan.

"What was it like working in the big house?"

"I loved it there, especially after Betsy left." She paused. "Oh, don't get me wrong. Betsy was great to work under, but it was easier in a way when I took over as housekeeper. Well, the physical work anyway. I suppose being the housekeeper I'd more responsibility for the organising of things and less of the physical drudgery. Mainly had to see that the young ones did a good job."

"That can simmer away for a while now." Dorothy put the lid on the saucepan and sat down at the table. "I often wondered what it would be like working in one of those big houses. You hear stories."

"You do, and sometimes they're true. I was lucky, the Westropp family were decent, and I got on great with them. Some of the others though would treat their staff like slaves." Catherine looked into the distance. "Yeah, there were some great times there. Mrs. Westropp was a great woman for parties and, even though it meant more work, we all loved those occasions. They'd a big grand piano in the drawing room and every so often she'd invite the upper crust to a musical evening. One of the daughters was studying music up in Dublin. She'd a lovely voice and she'd be there sometimes, especially during the summer, and she'd bring down a friend or two and they'd sing opera. All those lovely arias and duets. Verdi and Puccini."

Dorothy, reluctant to interrupt, watched her aunt, the dreamy look on her face, like she was back in those days.

"Not something I was familiar with. We didn't have much of that in Knocknageeha, but it was beautiful. The doors onto the lawn would be left open if it was a warm evening, and the staff could listen to the music. Mrs. Westropp knew we'd be out there, but she didn't mind, because she wanted us to become '*cultured*'. So she could have one up on her friends. Refined staff. There was always a bit of competition amongst them and she was a bit of a snob behind it all, but she was good to us."

"Do you miss that?"

"Oh, I do, but I suppose nothing lasts for ever and your life moves on to other things." Catherine stood up and gave the saucepan a stir. "Funny, I'm just thinking, nobody ever asks me about that. But sure, it's nice to have it to look back on."

———

Dorothy took on the herding to bed of the children and the promise of the storytelling once they were safely under the blankets. One was never enough.

"Tell us another, Dorothy! Just one more!"

Now, as the weeks wore on, she realised it might have been wiser to be firm in the beginning and stick to one story per night. She was going to have to make them shorter if two were required or she'd never get them settled for the night. Fast running out of tales, she had to resort to telling the same ones with different names and making up different endings.

"You told us that one before, Dorothy." Mary was suspicious. The familiar pattern might have fooled Eileen, but not her.

"Not quite the same. Wait till we get into it and you'll see the difference." Dorothy found herself, each night, searching frantically for a few new twists and turns to introduce. When that failed she introduced a little trick.

"Well, maybe you're ready for your prayers then?"

"No, no, go on, tell us the rest of it! We're listening!"

Mugs of hot milk were the start of the bedtime ritual, the whole slowing-down process taking about half an hour. By the time Catherine came to the bedroom to sing them to sleep, their eyelids were beginning to droop, and they didn't mind that it was the same lullaby each night. Mary was a bit old but she seemed to like the comfort of it.

With the calm of the children in bed, Dorothy spent what was left of the evening sitting at the fire in the kitchen writing a letter home or with Catherine teaching her how to crochet. Any companionable silences between them were relaxing. No uneasiness that there might be thoughts of sending her home going through her aunt's head. She seemed happy just to have her here. And she herself had needed this break from home more than she'd realised.

Chapter 11

She loved them all, but it must have been the red curls that made Eileen her favourite, just by an edge. The same red curls as little Annie had. Every time she looked at her it brought back the memories of her little sister, the baby of the family.

Apart from the time of the accident, and each year on her anniversary when they all went to the cemetery together and put flowers on her grave, Dorothy didn't think much about it. The memories now were tinged with a little shame. How could she have forgotten her so easily? Well, not exactly forgotten but side-lined her memory during the year. She was aware that her mother visited the grave regularly – the filling of the water bottle and the posy of whatever flowers were in bloom in the garden gave that away. Although Maude didn't always mention where she was going, they all knew. She had a suspicion that when her father told them to go ahead home without him some Sunday mornings after Mass, that he too was doing the same. Once when she'd looked back, she'd spotted him turn into the road that led to the cemetery. That it was located halfway between the village and home made it handy to slip in on a visit, without a special journey being necessary. She didn't say anything at the time. It seemed like a little secret that her parents kept from one another and the child in her couldn't understand it. The only time they all went together was either on the pattern day or Annie's anniversary. It seemed okay to do it openly then and to bring all the children along. It still puzzled her though, but the fact that she felt she'd been the only one to see her father give them the slip that Sunday, made it seem like she held his secret and that was somehow special.

She was only seven when the tragedy happened, so she could never really be sure if she remembered seeing Annie on the day she died or if she just thought she did. She had a memory of seeing some black thing that she didn't recognise lying on the hearth. It must have been Annie, all the lovely red ringlets burnt off her head. Whether she actually witnessed it or if it was overhearing the neighbours talk about that day made her think she had seen her, she could never really be sure.

Whenever it came back, it was in flashes. Not like she had been pondering over it and the thoughts came in sequence, like this was the way it happened. No, it never came like that. More like a sudden bubble bursting and revealing an image. Like the day she was walking through Courtown Woods.

At the forest entrance, she'd felt the sudden change in temperature that always came when leaving the sharp sunlight and entering under the leafy canopy. The sudden chill made her button up her coat in anticipation of the move into this secret earthy world. She closed her eyes and stood for a moment, drawing the peaty smell of the decaying vegetation into her nostrils. Underfoot, the damp bronzed autumn leaves covered the forest floor. The overnight dew had not yet dried enough for the leaves to crisp up, despite the early morning sun filtering through the trees. It was a weekday morning and the forest was empty of people. She'd awoken with a bad headache and surprisingly Maude had agreed that she could take the day off school, suggesting that a good walk in the fresh air might shift it. No children about and the dog-walkers at work so she had the woods to herself. Herself and the birds.

Her walk took her along the riverbank and over the wooden bridge before she came across a clearing where woodsmen had been burning scrub. Like they were tidying up the year's history and leaving the woodland clean and fresh for the next year's new spring growth. The remains of a charred tree stump, some of its branches still attached, like little arms, lay in the grey ash. When she realised she was shaking, only then did she become aware that she'd stopped walking. Hypnotised by the sight before her and unable to take a step past the blackened lump, she turned back and headed along the path out of the woods to where her bicycle rested against the trunk of an oak tree.

Later that evening she sat with her mother at the fireside. They were both making repairs to the linen, Dorothy replacing missing buttons on shirts and skirts while Maude stitched a patch on the knee of Cornelius's gardening trousers.

"A strange thing happened me in the woods today. I saw something and I couldn't go any further. It was like a memory from years back."

"And what was that?"

Dorothy glanced at her mother. The look of total relaxation on her face made her wonder if opening up this conversation had been such a good idea, but it was too late to turn back.

"Well, it made me think of little Annie."

Maude stopped stitching and laid the trousers down on her knee. "Do you remember her?" Maude looked at Dorothy, surprise brightening her face. "I didn't think you would. Well, I know you'd remember her but not very well. You were very young. You never talked about her. No-one ever talks about her now."

Dorothy told her story, pausing between bits of it, trying to work out how she could eliminate most of the horror she'd felt at the likeness. What it might unearth worried her, but a glance across at her mother as she ended reassured her. The mending was forgotten as she watched a faraway look settle on her mother's face. It didn't seem to have caused distress, more a relaxed look that might suggest she was glad the topic had been opened up. Not knowing how to break the silence that followed, and just to be sure she hadn't done the wrong thing, she just sat there looking into the fire until Maude spoke.

"Ah, that was a terrible thing that happened the poor child, a terrible thing altogether. Falling into the fire like that. And me in the hospital at the time. D'yeh know, I remember it like it was yesterday. A neighbour came into the hospital and told me about it, and sure I knew nothing. Your poor father had just arrived and was about to break the bad news, but she got there before him." Maude paused. "Oh, he was right mad with her, the poor man. He was so upset. Always blamed himself." Maude shook her head slowly. "Ah, poor little Annie! She was such a lovely little one. And do you know what the worst part of it was? No-one would talk to me about it at the time. I knew they were all discussing it amongst themselves, but they wouldn't talk about it to me."

"And why was that? They must have sympathised with you at the funeral?"

"Oh, they did that surely, but after the burial they never mentioned her in front of me. And I'd know they'd be talking about it. It was the way they'd stop their conversation when I'd come into the room or the shop or in the church porch."

"Maybe they thought it would upset you?"

"Yes, I'm sure that was it, but I wanted to talk about her, could they not understand that? The way it was, I felt excluded from the conversations. It was alright for them to talk about her, but I wasn't allowed to. And if ever I brought Annie up in conversation, they'd just tell me not to be upsetting myself and change the subject."

"And what about Father?"

"Well, you know what your father's like. He doesn't show his feelings much but he felt it too, I know that. Still feels it. He was very cut up about little Annie. Sure, she was the baby. But he wasn't able to talk about her. And I know he felt responsible because I was in the hospital and he was in charge here at home. That's why he found it so hard. Blamed himself. No, you were just expected to get on with life. That was just the way it was."

Dorothy sat there, unsure what to say. There didn't seem to be anything to say. It was all so long ago although it only seemed like yesterday. And when she thought about it, her mother was right. Her father had never spoken about it since. At least she'd never heard him refer to it. But then she'd seldom heard her mother talk about the accident either. All she could remember from that time was the tears, and the whispers of comfort between the adults, and the long silences when the neighbours had all gone away to their own homes.

The swish of her mother's skirt as she stood up brought her back.

"Wait a minute there, Dorothy. There's something I want to show you."

She could hear her mother pad up the stairs, a slight spring in her step. Placing a sod of turf on the fire, she wiped her hand on the sleeve of her cardigan to remove the peaty dust from her fingers before picking up the button jar and selecting one to suit the missing button from her blouse. As she did so, Maude returned, an unfamiliar small silver tin box in her hand.

"What have you got there, Ma?"

"Patience, Dorothy, that's what I'm going to show you." Sitting down, she made herself comfortable before handing over the tin. "Here, you open it."

Dorothy gave her mother a glance before taking the tin. Opening it slowly she revealed a rectangular piece of cream tissue paper. She paused to give another glance at Maude.

"Go on, open it, but be very careful."

The hint of anticipation in her mother's voice, accompanied by the slight smile, reassured her that it wasn't anything sinister. Gently unfolding the tissue, the two inches of red curling hair inside brought tears to her eyes.

"You've kept it all these years and never showed us?"

"You never asked. Nobody ever did."

"Wait. How did you get it? She was burnt." She had it blurted out before she realised how harsh the word sounded, but she couldn't take it back. Feeling her face redden with the unintended cruelty, she watched for her mother's reaction and was relieved that she didn't seem inclined to take her to task.

"I know, I know." Maude nodded. "You might well wonder. The lucky thing was that about a month before the accident I cut a few inches off her hair. I couldn't get the comb through the curls as they got longer and she used to squeal when I'd hit a knot and wouldn't let me brush it, so I decided to cut a few inches off it and I kept one of the curls. My only regret after what happened was that I didn't keep more of them. But who would have thought . . . I suppose I'm lucky to have the one."

"That's lovely." She could only whisper as she stroked the red lock before folding it inside the tissue and handing it back to Maude. "I'm glad you showed that to me, Ma. I'll always know there's a little bit of her still here."

"I love it when you comb my hair, Dorothy." Eileen was sitting on the chair after her evening bath, a large towel wrapped around her, as Dorothy drew a comb through her hair while it was wet. "You get the tangles out without hurting me. Mary sometimes used to do it but she nearly pulled my hair out. You're much better."

"Well, I try to do it gently, but it's not easy, so stay still and I'll do my best." Dorothy glanced up and smiled at her little cousin in the mirror she'd given her to hold. "I wish I had your lovely red curls."

"Tommy sometimes calls me Carrot Top."

"Don't you mind him, Eileen, he's only jealous." Dorothy laughed. "I'll give him Carrot Top when I next see him."

Chapter 12

At first Dorothy thought she was imagining it. She'd caught his green eyes on her when she'd glanced up on a few occasions. As the weeks went on, it had occurred too often to have been just coincidence. Embarrassed, she'd looked away and pretended she hadn't noticed. When it happened once too many times her embarrassment turned to irritation at the fact that it was she who felt uncomfortable. The way Thomas managed to hold his steady gaze confirmed to her that he was experiencing no such discomfort. If it happened again she decided she'd stare him out and, if he looked away first, she'd put it down to her reading too much into it. She hoped but knew that that wasn't going to be the case and it rattled her.

Shortly after the supper an opportunity presented itself. He made no move to return to the yard to finish the evening chores. Just sat there across the table from her. Catherine had left them and had gone for a lie-down on the sofa and, even though it was dark, the children were having a last run around out on the grass. She could have taken the easy option and stood up and started clearing the dishes, but it was now or never if she was ever to put her theory to the test.

He continued to sit opposite, hands steepled, tapping his fingers against each other in turn as if he was playing a tune.

"I need a hand out in the barn."

"I've things to do here." This was the first time she'd answered him back. She'd said it fast before she lost her nerve.

Silence.

She watched to see the reaction, unsure if she'd pushed it a bit far. The dark look on his face and the increased speed of the finger-tapping confirmed that he'd detected the meaning in her tone and appeared to be considering his response. She needed to get in before him.

"You'll have to ask young Tommy."

"He's busy. He has other things to do too." He stared her straight in the eye. "You'll have to help."

She realised he wasn't going to let it go. Bracing herself, she knew she'd have to try to outstare him. Play him at his own game. What she hadn't bargained for was another possible result, one which was to leave her more uncomfortable than ever. He gave her a wink, clearly sensing her inexperience and using it to his advantage. She hadn't misjudged him. There was no way she was going to be able to put an end to it with a simple staring contest. This was only the start. He'd managed to turn outwitting her into a game, a game she didn't like, but one which he didn't appear to have any difficulty with.

"I'll be busy with the children – I can't help out." She stood up and started clattering the dishes.

"You can leave those dishes till later."

"I've other things to do after this, so whether you like it or not you're going to have to ask Tommy." Turning her back on him, she carried the stack of plates to the basin.

"Like I said, you can leave those till later." His obstinate tone made her uneasy. A sense of danger had crept in somehow. Opposing him wasn't going to do the job. She swung around, giving him the hardest look she could muster and spat it out.

"Right. Tell me exactly what it is you want me to do."

"I won't keep you long. I just need a hand with the sheep."

"Right. Five minutes and then I'll have to come back to start the children on their homework." Adopting a business-like tone, she walked to the open door before looking back at him still at the table. "Well, are you coming or not? Let's get this over and done with."

It annoyed her that Thomas out-manoeuvred her each time, knowing that she couldn't object too much in front of Catherine. After all, she was here to help. And he was cute enough to choose his timing.

It took a while before he moved from looking to touching and, even then, it was only featherlike and nowhere inappropriate. It started with a tap on the shoulder or a hand on the arm, but each time he laid his hand on her she could feel the heat through her cardigan. Whenever he did it, she wanted to slap his hand away but, having tried it once, the innocent *"What?"* out of him made it seem a bit of an overreaction on her part. Somehow she always ended up in the wrong.

After a while, the hand began to linger just that few seconds too long. The only thing she had to compare it to was the odd time her father had put a hand on her shoulder and this certainly didn't feel the same. If she'd had boyfriends it might have been clearer, she'd have had something to judge it by. Might have been able to tell the difference and she wouldn't have had this confusion in her head. This just felt wrong. She knew it, and she knew that he knew it. What he was relying on was that she didn't know how to deal with it, and in that knowledge he knew it was safe to continue. That was clear.

There was no denying it, he was handsome and charming when it suited him. None of this changed the fact that she didn't like him. No, that was too mild. Detested him. Detested him intensely. He was strict with the children, although they seemed to get on with him well enough. It was the way he spoke to Catherine that she hated. The dismissive tone that left everyone else feeling uncomfortable.

Thinking back, she realised she'd never experienced this type of aversion to anyone ever. The only time she'd felt a dislike, although different, but of the same strength, was to the young fellow at school who went around pinching everyone. She could still remember the look of surprise on his face when she'd turned around one day and whacked him across the face in the schoolyard. The silence from the other children reflected back the shock she felt. Years of the pinching, from which they'd all just run away, mostly managing to dodge, each in their own way, but that day she'd had enough.

"You're in big trouble. *Big, big trouble!*" Recovered from the shock, he spat the words at her. "*I'm going to tell the Master on you!*"

"*Go right ahead, you big tell-tale!*" she taunted him, confident as he hadn't the brains to add two and two, there would be no way he'd be able to anticipate her defence of her action. She'd have to spell it out for him. "Right, go ahead and we'll see what the Master will have to say about your pinching. Go on. I'm waiting. He's inside in the classroom."

Giving a big spit at her, he turned and skulked off. The yard full of children watched as he headed in through the open door of the school.

Nancy was the first to approach Dorothy in the silence that followed.

"Do you think he's going to tell on you, Dorothy?" Her pigtailed friend looked worried.

"Not at all. Sure, he'll only get himself into trouble. *Big, big trouble*, as he said himself." She grinned at Nancy and, picking up the ball they'd been playing with, she threw it across the yard. "There you go, it's your turn!"

The reign of the bully was over.

From the time she'd arrived in Ard na Gréine, she sensed an undercurrent of something she couldn't quite define. Evil was too strong. Violence wasn't the right description either – he'd never done anything. It was just an unease she felt when he was around. He frightened her, but again 'frightened' was too forceful a word to put on it. What bothered her even more was that in some strange way she was flattered by his attention, that some man, any man would find her attractive. Aware of the danger of entertaining his attentions, she continued to avoid him and make excuses not to be alone with him.

So when it happened she knew for certain that she had given him no encouragement, no encouragement at all.

Lying in bed, on the edge of sleep, Dorothy pushed the thoughts away and began idly thinking of home. The sound of the doorknob being turned alerted her. One or other of the children sometimes came into her room when they couldn't sleep and snuggled up in the bed beside her, but the large dark shape that filled the frame as the door opened confirmed it wasn't one of them.

"What are you doing in here?" She shot up in the bed, the prickles on the back of her neck sharp.

"Don't pretend you don't want it," he whispered, the thick voice now confirming where he'd been.

The slight slurring in the whisper was barely undetectable, but she smelled the alcohol the minute he came into her room.

"You've been asking for it all along with your flirting."

It was the first time he'd ever entered her room and she recognised a shift. The situation had moved up a notch, to a level she had no idea how to deal with. Panic set in as she saw him move to close the door behind him.

"*Don't close that door! Get out or I'll call Aunt Catherine!*" Her heart thumped as she saw that the threat didn't seem to bother him. She had to stop him fast before this escalated. The girls were in bed in the next room, and so, reluctant to frighten them, she realised she was on her own. Would have to manage this situation as best she could. Catherine hadn't been well all day and was sleeping in the spare room at the far end of the corridor next to Tommy's bedroom.

He put a knee on the side of the bed and pushed her back onto the pillow.

"*Get off me!*" She'd fought him in silence for a few seconds, in the vain hope that he would come to his senses, but it had no effect.

Despite the few punches she'd managed to land, her efforts failed. *"I'm going to scream if you don't stop!"*

By the time he was on top of her, his hand over her mouth, she realised that perhaps it would have been wiser not to have given him the warning, but to have shouted before he smothered her, or maybe the moment she'd sensed danger when he'd first come in through the door. It would have brought the children running and might have focussed his mind and stopped things going any further.

Cursing herself for her misplaced consideration, she struggled, digging her nails in and pulling his hair. But no match for his strength, it didn't take long for him to overpower her, trapping her arm behind her back and leaving her defenceless as he did his worst. All she could remember afterwards was the suffocating, the pain, and him deluding himself.

"Like a calf to new milk, you're loving it." His comments, repeated over and over again as he violated her.

His hand no longer over her mouth it was too late to call out. This was definitely not something she wanted the children to witness.

CATHERINE

Chapter 13

Catherine noticed the sudden change in Dorothy. It was shortly before John's birth and with her own health problems, being so subtle a change, she might have missed it. Hardly noticeable, it was like someone had pricked the air out of her bubbles.

"Are you alright, Dorothy? You don't seem yourself. Is there anything the matter?"

"Oh, I'm grand. There's no problem. No problem at all." Dorothy gave a half smile at her aunt. "You needn't be concerned about me, Aunt Kate. You've enough to be worrying about."

"That sounds like there is something I should be concerned about? Like you don't want to add to my worries?" Catherine looked at her niece. "Come on, Dorothy, you know you can tell me anything." She grinned. "I'm not Maude. Remember?"

"No, no, Aunt Kate. There's really nothing at all. It only came out like that." She smiled back. "Really . . . I'm telling you . . . really. Nothing at all."

That first time Catherine thought it might be her time of the month and let it pass, but Dorothy's smile seemed forced in a way that was hard to describe, just somehow not like her usually sunny-natured self. She was still the same as usual with the children, but there was a strain evident, like she was trying too hard, and even they noticed things in the way children do, without reading anything into the signs.

"Does your bruise hurt?" Mary stroked the purple mark on Dorothy wrist. "Is that why you were crying?"

"No, no, it's not sore."

"What happened? How did you hurt it?"

"I hit it off something, Mary, but it's not sore now." She wished the child would let it go.

As Dorothy pulled her sleeve down and moved her hands onto her lap under the table, Catherine spotted her glancing sideways to see if the surreptitious move had been noticed. Best not to comment, for the moment anyway. With the birth imminent it might be wiser to accept her assurances that all was fine. At least until after the baby.

As she rested between waves of pain, her eye was drawn to the spotted patch of wallpaper in the corner, near the ceiling, the beginnings of a black mould stain. Baby John was born five minutes after midnight on the first day of the bright new twentieth century. Looking down at him, the bloody streaks having been wiped from his red healthy face, an inner voice told her this was definitely going to be her last child. As she watched his little fist nuzzling his nose and mouth she could have convinced herself it was because of her age, but she knew that wasn't the only reason. Through the fog in her brain a voice penetrated, telling her that it was going to be her decision and hers alone. No-one else was going to have a say in the matter.

Two months later and still weak from childbirth, Catherine could only deal with the present, could only cope by pushing aside everything that didn't need immediate attention, like matters of life or death. Everything else would have to wait. At the moment she wasn't been able to allow anything in that wasn't absolutely essential to her life. It was then that Dorothy made, what sounded, at least to Catherine, like an excuse to leave. This pushing-aside had included any signs that Dorothy's sudden departure signalled anything of any significance. She hadn't been in a fit state to even consider the whys, much less analyse any doubts or suspicions she might have.

DOROTHY

Chapter 14

It had been a big mistake, not leaving as soon as it happened the first time. Easy to see that later. What had paralysed her was the confusion in her head at the time and the naive misjudged hope that it wouldn't be repeated.

What to do? It had swirled around in her head for weeks. The fact that the birth of the new baby had been imminent didn't help. The guilt at leaving her aunt at precisely the time she needed her most had her holding on, hoping it would all go away. But it hadn't.

It had snowed. A damp, drizzly flurry of snowflakes had started around lunchtime and, judging by the leaden sky, looked like it would continue for the rest of the day. It was not snowing heavily enough for the children to go outside and make a snowman. Dorothy had lit the fire in the sitting room and was seated at the table with them, piecing together a jigsaw.

Catherine had been feeling well enough to join them. She relaxed back into the armchair, holding a sleeping John against her shoulder and listening as they squabbled over who was forcing pieces into the wrong places.

After a while, Dorothy half turned from the table and readied herself to speak – but Catherine had stood up and was laying the sleeping baby back into his cradle. Dorothy hesitated, wanting to be sure she had her aunt's full attention.

"Here, Eileen, you put that piece in," she said. "Look, it has a straight edge, and it's blue, so it must be that missing piece of the sky."

She watched her aunt sit back in the armchair again and pick up her knitting before continuing with her announcement.

"There's something I need to tell you all. I'm sorry to say I have to leave. I have to go back home."

There was a moment of stunned silence as the news of her departure was digested. It had played around her own mind so much in the last weeks that she hadn't considered how suddenly it would land in their laps.

Eileen was the first to break the silence as she began to cry. "But we'll be good! Please stay!" Her red curls bobbed as she clung to Dorothy's arm.

"Hey, let go, Eileen! I'm not leaving now. And you *are* good." She looked down at the tearful face of the child. "You're all very good. I'm not going because you're not good. Don't think that. I don't want any of you to think that."

"But do you not like us anymore or something?" Mary looked at her cautiously.

"Of course I like you. I love you, but I have to go home to my own house. They need me there. I'm really going to miss you."

"But we want you to stay!" said Mary.

"Did Daddy make you cry?" The innocent face of Eileen turned up towards her.

Dorothy saw Catherine, her knitting already put aside on the arm of the chair, register what she knew was the shock on her own face – shock at how a young child might have detected such a thing. It took a moment before she recovered enough to shoot a laughing glance at Eileen.

"No, no, he didn't. Don't be silly." She could feel the heat of the flush that had started to travel up her neck and hoped it would go unnoticed.

"But why was he in your room?" Eileen wouldn't let it drop.

How often had the child heard and what?

"I heard you crying when he was in your room. I was going to go in but Daddy would have been mad if I got out of my bed."

"Big girls don't cry." Dorothy stood up and gave Eileen a tickle. "Come on now – let's go outside for a while. It's stopped snowing and there might be enough snow to make a small snowman!"

"But what about the jigsaw?" Mary said.

"We can go at it again after the tea. Now, who's coming with me?"

Chapter 15

Catherine buried herself in her knitting, the steel needles splitting the stitches as she forced her trembling hands to continue . . . one plain, one purl . . . but not before she'd noted how her niece had avoided her eyes as she headed out of the room with the children. She needn't have tried to cover. It was all coming clear now. A truth neither of them could escape.

It was the child's questions that did it, piercing through the haze left by childbirth, revealing a stark picture that she couldn't hide from. The incidents individually may not have appeared to be of much consequence, but the warning signs had been obvious. The proprietorial hand placed on Dorothy's shoulder. Her pulling away from the slight brush against her as Thomas passed to take his seat at the top of the table. She'd noticed them at the time, but knew that had she commented he'd just have brushed them off as "That's just your imagination playing tricks on you" or "You're not jealous, are you?" Just like he had when she'd pulled him up a few years ago on how much time he'd spent in one particular neighbour's house – a single woman, nice enough, but with a questionable reputation. The realisation now of the increase in the seriousness of the incidents, or what she was picking up, reading between the lines of the child's comments, shifted everything into a different territory entirely. She'd noticed a cloud pass over Dorothy's face at his request for help in carrying something out of the barn one evening after dark. At the time she thought it could be just a reluctance to face out into the bitterly cold night. She should have paid more attention but, now with the veil lifted, she could no longer ignore the fact that her husband was at best a philanderer. Too much to absorb that in this case, possibly an abuser. She needed to get her head around this. Unfortunately the damage was done with her niece and at this stage it was too late . . . all too late to undo it. She could only do what she could do.

It was only a little lie. She'd had to give some explanation for her decision to leave so suddenly. Much as Dorothy would have liked to expose him as the brute he was, she wasn't sure if she would be believed. Torn between that and having them live the rest of their lives knowing that their father and husband was a rapist, she decided the best thing to do was to keep it to herself and remove herself from the situation. None of them needed know the real reason why she had left and gone home. It wouldn't help anyone.

The same lie was told to all. Her parents didn't need to know either, so in their ignorance were delighted at her decision to go to Dublin, pleased that Dorothy, at last, had sorted her life out with a job in a children's home already lined up. It would keep her going until she could realise her dream. To train as a children's nurse. At least one positive thing had come out of her experience. She'd sorted her head out where a career was concerned. Now if only she could blot out the other horror.

CATHERINE

Chapter 16

Sitting in her kitchen, Catherine had drifted into a reverie. Couldn't motivate herself to do anything. Life was harder now that Dorothy was no longer there. It wasn't just having someone around the place to help with the housework, it was her company she missed most. Only a young girl, she could hardly even call her a woman, but the age gap hadn't made much difference. Hard to put a finger on what it was her niece had brought to the house, but whatever it was it had lifted her spirits. Now, with her gone, the hole she'd left revealed something else, a gap that had probably been developing in the early years of her marriage, something she must have got accustomed to it as the years went on. She had no friends.

She traced back to when that had started. Working in the big house there was plenty of camaraderie amongst the staff and on days off she always had someone to go out with, do things with. At home in Knocknageeha she'd retained her childhood friendships with neighbours and school pals. Always a few ready to go to a dance. So it wasn't a thing that she was incapable of friendship. No, it was something that had just drifted.

She remembered inviting a couple of her school friends to visit when she'd finished the renovations at Ard na Gréine, but there had been something uncomfortable about it. Thomas seemed to have an excuse to keep coming into the kitchen to pick up something or other and interrupting the flow. She'd moved the visitors into the parlour the next time, but she had a recollection of Thomas joining them after a while, with the excuse that the rain had brought an end to the yard work. Trying to include him in the conversation, when he didn't know the people they were talking about, made the light chat awkward and she remembered wishing he'd leave them to their talk, but he'd stayed until they made an excuse to go home.

For a while after that her friends invited her to their homes, but always on the day Thomas conjured up a reason why he couldn't spare her, and on one occasion he'd suggested he might come with her and that clearly wasn't going to work. And so, after a few invitations the visits had dribbled out, and she saw none of her friends and acquaintances, apart from an odd time when she was over at Knocknageeha to see her mother and one of the neighbours would drop in for half an hour to catch up with her. But no further formal invitations. And then, with the children coming along, she had ceased to notice the lack in her life. That was until Dorothy had come and then gone, revealing the chasm and leaving behind her this gap in her life.

She would have to work out a way to address that if she wasn't to stay adrift in a sea of isolation, but at the moment she felt powerless. The daily chores exhausted her, so she had no energy left for anything else. She'd have to shift herself soon to go out and take the washing from the line before the shower that had been threatening for the last few minutes began. Through the window she could see the tea towels dancing in the breeze. Every so often two of the towels wrapped themselves around each other, leaving the red-check-patterned one to do its own dance.

All the while she'd been sitting there looking out through the windowpane, a wasp had been fussing around the kitchen. If she got up from her chair and dealt with him maybe she'd motivate herself. He continued to buzz against the glass, refusing to go out when Catherine opened the window. She picked up a cup and placed it against the glass, capturing him inside, taking care not crush his little legs in the process. The wasp's buzzing increased in speed and volume, panicking as he realised he was trapped. Skilfully she slid a card between the opening of the cup and the glass windowpane, keeping the wasp secure inside, while she headed with the covered trap towards the open door. Having released him into the freedom of the great outdoors, she sat down again at the table.

She could not ignore what she suspected any longer. The easiest thing would be to pretend it never happened and say nothing. Catherine had pondered over it for a few days, rolling it around in her mind. At first she didn't want to let it in, the thought was so obscene, but history couldn't be rewritten and, now that the doubts were there, they couldn't be pushed out again. Each look, every movement, when she thought back, now seemed indicative of what had been his intent.

Dorothy was gone before she'd even started to digest things and now she was left with a guilt over her own silence on the matter. What bothered her was that, after the rushed departure, Dorothy hadn't stayed with her parents, despite her insistence that they needed her. Instead, after a couple of weeks at home in Wexford she had moved to Dublin. Said she had a job there. But there was something about this that didn't sit easy with Catherine. What had not been said in her letters was the something that bothered her.

The embarrassed way that Dorothy had batted away Eileen's awkward questions that had given an indication. With her early doubts, she'd set up a few opportunities for Dorothy to confide in her before she left, but her niece had avoided all conversation openers. Had given no hint as to what had happened. Even now in her letters her niece didn't mention anything. Not an easy thing to admit to having occurred, that's if anything had, but she'd enough imagination to be fairly sure about it. She couldn't be certain just how far it had gone and whether Dorothy's reluctance to talk came from embarrassment or if she felt to blame for what had happened, or what possible combination of reasons might have kept the girl silent on the subject. She was absolutely sure that Dorothy hadn't been the one to instigate anything, whatever had happened. But it was there, like some ghostly presence in the letters, like a shadow, almost, but not quite coming into focus between the lines.

Sitting now with the recent letter in her hand and a clear head, at last she knew it had to be tackled. Replacing it in the white envelope she gazed at the neat handwriting. She'd agonised about this long enough, reading and re-reading it, hoping it might, but knowing that it would never, ever, go away if she remained silent.

She'd asked Dorothy out straight in her last letter. "*Did Thomas do something to you?*" She'd tried out several versions of it. "*Did something happen to upset you, Dorothy?*" or "*You were happy here, so what happened to change that, Dorothy?*" In the end she'd forced herself, however painful, to grasp the nettle and put the question down in black and white: "*Did Thomas do something to you, Dorothy? Please tell me straight. I won't be angry with you. I just need to know.*"

The arrival of Dorothy's response had been the trigger.

"*No, Aunt Catherine, nothing happened.*"

Nothing more, no further reference. Went straight on to asking about the children. Not even a question as to why she would even think that he might have done something. The complete shutdown that confirmed the "nothing happened" was a big fat lie.

If Dorothy wasn't going to open up, there was only one other option.

No more changing her mind as to the way to tackle it, considering which route might be the best one to go. Say something or say nothing, just to save everyone the mortification and a plethora of lies and denials. Saying nothing meant it would never go away, not for her anyway. The doubt, no longer that, would remain sitting inside her, slowly corroding her body and soul and mind. No more indecision. It was now time for action.

She had come to the brink of opening up on him a couple of times, but fear had stopped her. She hadn't been sure if it was fear of the truth or dread of his reaction to the accusation. But now as the fear poked its head in yet again, she gave herself a shake and, fired by the need to overcome her own weakness, built herself into a state of fury that overrode any trepidation. The children had left for school and young Tom was away, giving a hand to a farmer up the lane who needed an extra man for the day.

Thomas was alone at the table, having finished his early-morning milking. No better time. No asking if, or what, or why and giving him an opportunity to bluster his way out of it. A direct accusation was the way she intended to go with this.

She turned around from the sink to face him.

"*What the hell did you think you were at?*" Catherine's anger exploded in his face.

The force of it surprised her as much as it did him. The spray from the sudsy water landed on his toast as she stretched out to grab the towel.

"*For Christ's sake, will you watch what you're doing, woman!*" With a quick movement of his thumb he swept the glob of bubbles onto the plate before they seeped through the butter into the slice of bread. "What are you on about?"

He didn't look up from the task of pouring another cup of tea for himself, and it was just that simple lack of acknowledgement when she had thrown the accusation at him that told her that he really had no idea what was coming. His lack of awareness almost disarmed her for a second before she swept that aside.

Up to now she may have been afraid to mention it, fearful of his reaction, but it was something in the lack of consciousness of his own power to dominate that infuriated her, spurring her on. The very power that had dogged their relationship from the beginning, and here it was again. And in that second she identified that lack of awareness for what it was. His weak point.

That recognition gave her the advantage – the opportunity to take control, for the first time in their marriage. Just a tiny window of opportunity when she realised she had the upper hand and she had to use it before that power evaporated.

"*Dorothy.*"

She watched closely and in that moment, in the slight pause after she mentioned the name, she detected a jolt of unease in him.

"What about her?"

She knew she wasn't imagining the deliberate casualness that had crept into his voice, and there was something in the look he gave her, a definite wariness in the slow way he raised his eyes to meet hers.

"*If you've laid a finger on her, I'll kill you. I swear it. God forgive me but I'll kill you.*" She didn't recognise her own low voice.

"I don't know what you're talking about." A startled expression replaced the caution, telling her that this time she had hit the nail on the head. There was nowhere for him to hide. "What did she say?"

"What would you expect her to say? Come on. You tell me."

"I told you I've no idea what you're talking about, Catherine."

"Oh, I think you do. Would you expect her to say that you interfered with her?"

"Ah, go away! Interfere with her? I did not interfere with her. It was only a bit of messing. There was no harm in it. A bit of innocent fun and she –"

"*Don't even try that one.*" Catherine could see the blame game starting. Always someone else's fault. "She's only seventeen, my niece, and an innocent."

"*Huh*, that's what you might think!"

She could almost see him grasp his opportunity, regaining a little of his confidence. With Dorothy well gone, she wasn't in a position to dispute this.

"Makes no difference what I think." The returning cockiness in his demeanour infuriated her further.

"Sure, you don't know the lads she was with over there in Wexford."

"You shouldn't know anything about that either, one way or the other. I'm sure she didn't choose you to discuss her love life with. But we've talked, so I know what an innocent she is. Or should I say *was*? And I'm sure she wouldn't have chosen you, a married man, or have you forgotten that, to introduce her to the ways of the world – *those* ways."

"Don't delude yourself, woman. Well, all I know is that she was asking for it." He smirked. "Well then, she's gone so let that be an end to it." Pushing away his plate, Thomas stood up. "And let me get on with my work." He lifted his jacket from the back of the chair and headed out of the kitchen.

She stood there, back to the sink, watching him stoop slightly as he went out through the door into the white sunshine. Enraged at how easily he tried to brush aside his offensive behaviour and with a reluctance to let her advantage pass, Catherine follow him out to the yard.

"Oh, don't think that's an end to it at all, Thomas. You're not off the hook that easily."

"What do you mean?"

"Well, the children noticed something. They heard you. And more than once."

"How do you know?"

"They said it to Dorothy. I was there. And they were asking a lot of questions, very awkward ones."

"You're not going to tell them surely?"

"Well, if it was only a bit of fun, why not? *Go on, why not, you tell me?*"

He glared at her in silence.

"So? I'm waiting." She paused. "So, not a bit of fun then? Maybe they need to know what sort of a monster they have for a father."

She looked at him challengingly. "Yes. Why not?"

"*You wouldn't dare.*"

"No, I won't say anything to the children. They loved having Dorothy around, but you've spoiled that on them. No, I won't say anything to them, but not to protect you. The only reason being that I don't want to taint that memory for them. And she could have stayed a lot longer only for you. Maybe you'd like to go and explain to them why she had to go – the girls are still crying after her."

"But you're not going to say anything?"

"Not to the children. No, not for the moment anyway. But as I said, not to protect you. To protect them."

Catherine turned back to the house and something made her look over her shoulder, expecting to see Thomas's back retreating into the barn. She was surprised to see him standing there, still looking at her. A chance for one last shot.

"What about Cornelius?" She had him rattled. She was surprised at the pleasure it gave her to see the dart of fear on his face.

"What about him?"

She watched the uncertainty settle on her husband, unsure where this was leading.

"Well, he's Dorothy's father. He might need to know. What do you think?"

"You never would."

"*Hmmh* ..." She couldn't resist planting one last seed of doubt in his mind. "Leave that with me. I'll have to think about that one."

Chapter 17

After the confrontation, once the trembling passed, a calm settled on Catherine. Certain now that she had done the right thing. There was no doubt now in her mind. Thomas's changed attitude confirmed her worst fears. The possibility of his former superior getting to hear had achieved that. Despite the awfulness of the discovery, it was better to know for definite rather than live the rest of her life wondering if it had just been a figment of her imagination. The uncertainty would be bad enough, but to have to tolerate his bullying on top of it would have been worse. Her threat had put a stop to that and now that she had the upper hand she intended to keep it.

While still with no idea how far it had gone and Dorothy not inclined to tell her, she knew enough. She wasn't even sure she wanted to know more, to know the details. No, she didn't need access to quite that level of information. Her only worry now was the damage to her niece and about that she could do little. The harm done was irreversible. There was little chance now that Dorothy would ever bring it up. But she'd have to leave a door open, in case Dorothy ever wanted to talk to her about it sometime in the future. How best to reply to the letter was the dilemma now and not something to be rushed into.

She fretted over it. This might possibly be the most important letter she would ever have to write. She tested a few possible replies. Would it be better to say nothing at all about Thomas and let everyone get on with their lives? No, that was the coward's way out. Definitely not. She could mention something about her husband's somewhat difficult personality and say that she hoped that this had nothing to do with her departure. She might slip in a hint that she'd gleaned from the children that he hadn't been very nice to Dorothy and she was sorry that she hadn't picked up on this and intervened. This might leave an opportunity in case she ever wanted to bring it up. Or maybe not. Maybe the poor girl just wanted to forget all about the whole thing. She'd make a start on the letter and consider when she got to this part whether or not it would be a good idea to refer to his behaviour.

The opening was easy. Stories of the children and baby John's toddling around the place. After the news of Mary Ann's recent recovery from her fall in the yard and the letters from America, she had to go for it. This one and only time she'd refer to it.

"I'm sorry you had to suffer at the hands of my husband. It was very wrong what he did to you and I tackled him on this. Be in no doubt, the blame is entirely his. I know you probably don't want to talk about it, would prefer to forget it ever happened, but I can assure you it will never happen again. You will always be welcome and safe in this house, should you wish to visit. I have to apologise that I didn't realise what

was going on at the time. I should have paid more attention and stopped it, but I cannot fix that now, only to say I am so sorry that you had to suffer like that."

She couldn't leave it so bald. Tapping the pen on the table, she considered how to end the letter. What might Dorothy want to hear?

"I won't refer to this again, Dorothy. I don't know if you've told your parents. That is up to you. I'll leave it up to you also to decide if you want to talk about it to me or anyone else.

The children all send their love and they miss you."

Out in the yard she gave the baked clay a few seconds to absorb the water before pouring more into the flower tub. While she waited, she stroked the velvety leaves of the shrub and wondered what it was. It had just appeared from nowhere the year Eileen was born. A stray seedling under the bay window, it had bloomed with exotic flowers each summer since. But not this year. She had planted it up in a large tub to protect it from getting weeded out in error, but this year the buds which normally clothed the shrub in purple satin blooms had failed to open. Strange how the pale-green buds had showed such promise, but had stopped short of unfurling. They'd just sat there for months on the tips of the branches, alive and promising all, but delivering nothing. She wondered what had caused the buds to shut down? As she poured some more water into the tub, an old song went through her head.

'*For love is teasing and love is pleasing*
And love is a pleasure when first it's new

*But love grows older and love grows colder
And fades away like the morning dew.'*

She hadn't realised that she had been humming the tune. The scene from her childhood returned. The old neighbour whose party piece it was, singing it on evenings when she visited their house. The woman's wrinkled, lived-in face, eyes closed as she sang the words to her small audience seated around the fire on a winter's night. She loved the tune, but as a child had never understood the meaning of the words. She did now. Whatever shred of feeling she might have left for Thomas now lay stone cold in the pit of her stomach.

Years of being persuaded that everything was her fault, her shortcomings, making excuses for his behaviour had run their course. It was her fault that she'd not challenged him sufficiently in the early days, that she'd allowed the pattern develop. Regret for the time spent with anxiety and wasted emotions and trying to please him, she felt oddly at peace now. There would be no going back to that. No-one else might be able to see the change in her, but she could see it, could feel it, and she'd make sure he did too. Her loyalty now lay with her niece. She went into the kitchen and picked up the envelope. Stepping out into the sunshine again, she gave a shout to Thomas to keep an eye on the children.

"Where are you going?"

She considered saying "Out". No further explanation, but maybe she'd get more mileage teasing it out a bit longer. "Down to the village."

"For what? What do you want down there?"

"I'm going to post a letter."

"*Huh*, important business then." He paused. "Who are you writing to anyway?"

She started walking, knowing he was looking after her as she remained silent.

"Well, don't be long then."

Not much change there, but maybe he was beginning to get an inkling and perhaps, when he got used to the new Catherine, he might get the complete message, that his reign was well and truly over. Without answering, she headed off down the lane to walk to the village post box. She would take all the time she wanted.

DOROTHY

Chapter 18

County Wexford
1901

She'd kept in touch with Nancy when her friend left school early. The story at the time was that Nancy was going to live with an aunt in Dublin, but the whispers around the village suggested that there had been more to it than that.

"I don't know why you want to keep up with that one Nancy Dunne, Dorothy." Maude held out the envelope to her daughter, the disapproving tone confirming that she believed the rumours, even before she added the confirmation. "She's bad news."

"How do you know who the letter is from, unless you opened it?" Dorothy challenged her mother.

"I certainly did not open it. I wouldn't stoop so low." She glanced at the envelope as she passed it over. "I'd know that uneducated scrawl anywhere."

"She's not 'bad news' as you so eloquently put it. She's a good friend." Dorothy wasn't going to be drawn into any speculation with her mother. "Anyway, I think I'm capable of choosing my own friends, but thank you very much for your input."

The panic of her friend at the time had never left her.

"What am I going to do, Dorothy? I'll be shown the road when I tell them I'm preggers."

Without any answers it was a relief when Nancy told her that she'd confided in her aunt in Dublin. She didn't want to be the one to shoulder the burden of this great secret alone. The aunt's husband had just died and glad of the company. She'd offered to give Nancy a home with her, for the moment.

"And will you go, Nancy?" Dorothy was going to miss her. "But what will you do when the baby's born?"

"Of course I'm going to go. What other option do I have? I'll have to see after that. One step at a time." A relieved Nancy was happy to grab the opportunity to hide in the anonymity of the city.

After Nancy had departed, Dorothy often wondered how her own parents would react in the same situation. Not well, that was for sure. It hadn't been difficult to keep Nancy's secret. Her baby was a toddler now, over a year old, and despite the whispers in the village nothing had been confirmed locally. Dorothy kept her letters locked away in her 'treasure box', well away from Maude's prying eyes. Wouldn't want her mother discovering that Nancy had had a baby, much less that she'd kept her daughter and that they were both living happily enough with the aunt. Whatever was suspected locally was vaguely batted away by her family, saying that Nancy had a grand job up there in Dublin looking after her aunt's little girl. So sad that the woman's husband had died before the baby was born. A possible paving of the way for the future when Nancy might want to bring the little girl down on a visit.

Dublin

It had never occurred to Dorothy then that '*keeping up with that one*' was to play such a big part in her own life. The only person she'd been able to confide in. The only one who could offer help in her dilemma. There was no way she could go to her own aunt for assistance!

Nancy had it all worked out when Dorothy took the train to Dublin to meet up with her in O'Connell Street to discuss the situation. The immediate bit anyway.

"Come on, I'm taking you to a new place that's opened for fish and chips. You must be starving – seeing that you're eating for two." Nancy linked her.

"Not funny, Nancy." Dorothy looked at her friend. "I'm in a right panic."

"Well, panic over. I've spoken to the aunt and persuaded her to allow you to lodge with her, with us. It'll only be for a few weeks until we've worked out what to do with you for the next part."

"Are you sure?"

"Certain. I told her you'd get a job and be able to pay rent. She liked the sound of that cos she's a bit strapped for cash. And that you'd mind my young one in between. Give the aunt a bit of freedom. So she was easily persuaded."

"Well, I hope I'm able to get a job. Sure what am I good for?" Dorothy made a face at her friend. "What my own mother would say is '*good for nothing*', and can you imagine what she'd say if she discovered?" She paused. "It doesn't bear thinking about. And what am I going to do when I can't work?"

"Stop it, Dorothy. Stop looking too far into the future and worrying about what might never happen."

"Well, this is going to happen whether we like it or not."

"Look, there's a children's home not too far away and my aunt knows someone working there. They're always looking for staff. I'm sure she'll put a word in for you. She'll be anxious for you to get fixed up fast, start the rent rolling in."

"Well, let's hope that plan works. At least I've a bit of experience at that. And I'm good with children. For whatever reason, they seem to like me." Her face hardened. "And I'd have had a lot more experience if that bastard hadn't done what he did."

"Well, you're going to have to put that behind you for the moment." Nancy searched her face. "Unless you've decided to do something about it? Expose him for what he is. Is that what you're thinking?"

"I can't do that. Sure, who'd believe me? And, even if they did, it would tear the family apart." She shook her head. "Not that I haven't given it thought. I know Aunt Catherine knows. She told me in a letter. But I can't do it to her. And, anyway, I know she'd believe me, but I doubt that anyone else would."

"Maybe you're right. Knowing your mother." Nancy attempted to lighten the mood. "Anyway, the good thing is that the orphanage is only ten minutes' walk away so you'll be able to save money."

"I'm sure as soon as they see the bump developing I'll be needing the savings. I'll only be able to keep it hidden for so long." Dorothy looked worried. "What I'm going to do then I'm not sure. I don't suppose your aunt . . . "

"*Whoa, whoa there!* There you go again. Let's just take it slowly. You're only up here for the day. We'll worry about that later, when you're up for good and settled in. I know, though, she's not going to take on another child, so we'll have to come up with a plan. But we don't have to concern ourselves about that yet. There's still a long way to go. Believe me. Let's just deal with today's problem."

"And what's that? There are so many of them."

"Securing the job, you dope!" Nancy laughed. "Here, around the corner – some Italian fella opened it and I hear the fish and chips are great."

County Wexford

Within a week Dorothy had her bags packed for Dublin.

"That Nancy one is planting ideas in your head." Maude didn't seem pleased.

"But you told me to get a job and now I have one."

"I didn't mean for you to be going away again so soon."

"Well, it's only a stepping stone before I go for my nursing training. I'm trying it out before I apply. See how I like it." Dorothy looked at her mother. "I thought you'd be pleased that I'm taking steps to better myself."

"I am but you need to take care of yourself. You've no experience of a city."

"I'm a fast learner, Mother. Don't worry. I take after you." She grinned at Maude before heading into the hallway. "Well, I'm ready. I just have to bring down the bags. Will you give Da a shout? He promised to drop me to Courtown so I can get the Long Car in to Gorey. I don't want to miss it."

"Oh, he's out in the yard, ready and waiting. Sure, don't you know your father?"

Dublin

"You seem to be full of ideas, Nan. What's this latest one?" Dorothy sat on the side of the bed, the open case still half full, wedged into the nook between the dark oak wardrobe and matching dressing table.

"Well, someone has to be." Nancy leaned against the windowsill.

"I suppose. But I can see you're not going to give me time to catch my breath." She'd hung up her clothes, but the bits and pieces were still awaiting a decision as to where best to store them. She glanced over at the case. "I need to finish unpacking."

"That can wait. My idea is good. We'll walk up to the Home first so you can see where you'll be working and then I'm going to take you on the tram up to the Phoenix Park and we'll go into the zoo. While you can still walk!" Nancy gave her a grin. "Come on then. Let's get a move on. Make the most of me while you have me on my day off. And sure it'll give you a bit of practice for what's ahead."

"What do you mean?"

"Well, you don't think I'm leaving Maisie at home, do you? It'll give you a chance to see what it's like pushing a babby around!" Nancy said, laughing.

"This is just gorgeous." Dorothy stopped and looked around her at the expanse of green. "I feel like I'm back in the countryside. I never expected anything like this in Dublin. A park this big. Sure it's so much bigger than the biggest field at home."

"No cows though." Nancy grinned. "It's supposed to be the biggest city park in Europe – or maybe in the world. I can't remember.

"Look! Look over there in the forest." Dorothy pointed towards the trees. "I think they're deer? Are we in the zoo already?"

"No, you dope!" Nancy threw her eyes to heaven. "They're wild. They roam around the park. You've led a very sheltered life. Just as well you had a reason to leave Wexford. All I ever remember seeing was herds of cattle and sheep. Oh, and I forgot hens and an auld cock. Just wait till we get into the zoo and you'll think you're in the wilds of Africa."

"Will they ate us?"

"Well, I don't think the giraffes or elephants will. I think they prefer grass and vegetation – I doubt you'd be to their taste." Nancy glanced at her sideways. "Having said that, maybe the lions would find you tasty."

"Can they get at you? They're hardly loose, are they?" Dorothy raised her eyebrows.

"No. They're in cages. Pacing up and down." Nancy screwed up her nose. "It's a bit sad really to see them shut in like that when they'd be used to roaming free. They can't even go for a decent walk. Here, shove over, I'll push her for a bit." She took over the handle of the pram and pushed up the slight incline. "Come on, let's step on it or it'll be closed before we get there. It's over this way. Of course, if someone were to accidentally open one of the cages . . ."

"Stop it, Nan."

"But, then again, we could always run. Oh, I forgot – you're not able to run." Nancy laughed. "Silly me."

"Oh, I can still run. I'm not that big . . . yet. But let's hope I won't have to."

"Here, I'll pay for you. Just this once, mind you." Nancy shuffled in her pocket and took out some money. "Once you get fixed up in the job you can treat me."

As her friend handed over the money at the entrance, Dorothy stood back and admired the little lodge.

"D'ye know, this thatched cottage reminds me of home. They're like the ones in the village, only they're not so ornate. This one's gorgeous."

"I told you it's well you came to Dublin. There's more to life than where we come from. I'll show you plenty."

"That's what I'm afraid of." Dorothy laughed.

Chapter 19

"Would you stop jumping ahead, Dorothy. You're an awful woman for worrying. If they don't believe you, we'll come up with another plan."

"But at least I need to be prepared, to have something figured out. Just in case."

"You don't. Let's just cross that bridge when we come to it. If you're stuck just pretend you're feeling faint and ask for a glass of water. I'll be with you. I'm good at thinking on my feet. Don't worry, we'll come up with something. Well, I will anyway." Nancy gave her arm a nudge. "You were always a bit slow in that department."

In the end she had lied about her name.

The nun hadn't been keen to allow Nancy to stay as she'd checked into the Home, but Dorothy had insisted.

"Just while I'm filling in any forms. I need her." She didn't care if the nun presumed she was illiterate. Once she had Nancy there, that was all that mattered.

Sitting across the mahogany table from the nun, she wondered if it had been such a good idea after all. Worried now that Nancy might smirk or roll her eyes or do something that might suggest her story was all made up.

"And where are you from?"

"County Clare."

"And where in County Clare. I need an address. And I'll need proof." The nun looked hard at her.

"I don't have an address anymore. Our home was burnt down a couple of months ago and my parents perished, and all the contents and papers were destroyed." She hadn't intended for it to come out all together in such a rush. She'd have to calm down. "The thatch caught fire." She glanced at the nun to see if there was any indication on her face that she recognised the rehearsed speech, but was relieved to see her concentrating on filling in her date of birth and ticking a few boxes on the page. She put her hand in her pocket and drew out a document. "The only thing I have is an invoice from a drapery shop in Ennis, if that's any help. Look, my mother's name is on it. Mrs. Catherine O'Brien. Alterations to a coat." Luckily she had stuffed the receipt in her pocket the day she'd collected the coat for her aunt. It came in handy now: safe evidence with no address on it. She passed it across the table to the nun.

"That isn't enough. It won't do. I need an address." The nun held her with a steely gaze.

"Well, she's staying with me and my aunt here in Dublin for the moment. Will that do?" Nancy chimed in and, ignoring the nun, she nodded over at Dorothy. "That's your address from now on, Dorothy."

"I suppose it'll have to do then, if that's all you have."

The two glanced at each other as the nun, head bent, began writing it into the big ledger. Not sure if she believed their story, but hoping that with the large bump on Dorothy she could hardly turn her away.

She could see the reflection of the two heads in the dark wood of the sideboard in the hallway as they admired the sheen.

"Great job, Dorothy." Daisy swung her blonde plait over her shoulder and standing up straight looked at her and grinned. "Best mirror here."

"Only mirror here." Dorothy laughed, giving the surface a final rub with the stained polish-cloth.

"You're right. Not too many of them around. Might give us notions."

"Little fear of that. Do you think that'll pass the good Sisters?"

"Oh, I'm sure it will."

"D'yeh know, I thought it would be worse." Dorothy stepped back from the sideboard and replaced the lid on the polish tin.

"What d'ya mean?" The Dublin accent was distinctive.

"Well, you hear all sorts of stories about how cruel the nuns are in these places."

"Oh, they are. In some of them. But, sure, we don't have many choices, do we? There aren't too many of these sort of places, so we're lucky to get into this one." Daisy rolled her eyes. "It isn't so bad though, so long as you keep your eyes down, pretend you're sorry, and don't give any guff, they're not too hard on you."

"I heard some of the others saying that in some places they have your hands red-raw in laundries and nearly starve you." Dorothy had wondered if there was truth in the story. "Or scrubbing floors every day on your hands and knees. Here they give you work to do, but polishing the furniture and cleaning the kitchen and preparing the meals isn't too bad. Sure I've been doing that at home since I was a child."

"Well, we should be paid here." Daisy leaned over and admired herself in the polished surface.

"Well, I can tell you my mother wasn't one for paying either."

"You were lucky that you didn't come in here until late – that you didn't show much and you could keep a job until a couple of months before the baby." The girl looked young, but the trace of a few lines at the outer edges of her eyes suggested she had experience of this world. "You'd have been put doing heavier work had you come in earlier."

"How do you know? How early did you come in?"

"Oh, this time I came in late. Smart enough, that's me." Daisy laughed. "With some things anyway."

"Oh, you've been here before?" Dorothy's eyes widened.

"I have." She glanced sideways at Dorothy. "Don't look at me like that."

"I'm not . . ."

"You were. I know you're thinking, 'Now here's a right skanky one, used to spreading it around'. Well, you're wrong." Her mild tone suggested she recognised a lack of any intended insult.

"I wasn't thinking that at all. Believe me, I wasn't."

"I know, I know. Don't be worrying. I don't take offence that easily." She laughed. "I know a country bumpkin when I see one. Sure what would you know about the ways of the world? But, you're right – it's not too bad here – they only give you work that you'd be able for, coming towards the end and when you're recovering. That's why I didn't come in too soon this time. Like I said – smart, me."

Dorothy stroked the downy head of the baby with her free hand as she held the bottle of milk in position. There were already hints of a reddish gold in the little fuzz of hair. Definitely from her side of the family. At least there was some comfort in that.

"Aren't you just beautiful?"

She worried about the little blister forming on her baby's upper lip. One of the girls in the home assured her that it wasn't serious, just the delicate skin not used to the friction of the bottle.

It hadn't happened while she'd been breastfeeding. The closeness between them made up for the initial biting pain when the baby first latched on and for the first couple of weeks she enjoyed it. To her ears the snuffling and gurgling noises coming from her daughter were like music, making her smile as they cuddled together. She memorised every sound in a frantic effort to store a treasury of memories to comfort her in the years to come.

The burning of the mastitis was a pain like she'd never experienced before, forcing her to accept that she could no longer feed her baby. The only time she'd even heard of it was when the cattle at home got it but she'd never given it another thought when she heard farmers talking about it. It came as a surprise that new mothers could also be afflicted and only now did she appreciate what the poor beasts had to put up with.

When she'd mentioned it to one of the other young mothers, all the comfort she got was a "Welcome to the milking parlour!"

She had to laugh. At least it was the relief that there wasn't something awful wrong with her. That she wasn't alone.

"You better tell the nun about it before it gets any worse. You won't get sympathy but she might give you something to ease it." The young woman paused before continuing with a grin. "Well, if you're lucky."

"There's always a price to be paid for wrongdoing."

The sniff that accompanied the comment made her wish she'd chosen one of the other Sisters to ask about changing to bottle-feeding. This hard-faced one's views were well-known.

"The child has to be fed, one way or the other. And, anyway, it's for the best. I don't agree with letting you lot breastfeed. There's no point in getting too attached." Said in a tone that confirmed she enjoyed flaunting her disapproval. "Not good for you and it's not good for the baby. Because it won't be for long. "

No point in arguing. It would get her nowhere. In one way she was right. The days were short and passing all too fast. She knew from the talk around her that the nun would soon come and take her child. Couldn't think about it. Just savour every second with her daughter Anne . . . little Annie.

Now when it came to filling in the form for the baby, she wondered if she should tell the truth. Each time they asked for it she said she hadn't quite finished, that she needed more time. In the end she found she couldn't completely break the connection. She had to leave a thread – an invisible one. Well, almost invisible.

A single string, as delicate as a cobweb. No-one but she would be able to see it, and she'd already set the first weave. If it ever did come to light, Thomas O'Brien would recognise that little trace of evidence and forever live in fear of his secret being disclosed. So she could live with half a lie. Annie O'Brien, that's what her baby was to be named.

She knew it was against the rules but she'd done it anyway. She'd written a letter to her daughter. There was no point in asking the nun to deliver it to the new parents. The other girls had warned her not to waste her time.

"It won't even get to them. It'll go straight into the bin."

She took their advice. Didn't hand it to the nun. Instead she pinned it into the inside back of the little matinee coat she'd knitted for Annie, before wrapping her in the white crocheted shawl. The day was cold so she hoped the wrap might conceal any rustling of the paper when the nun took the baby from her. It was important that her baby knew how much she was loved by her, and she hoped the new mother would have heart enough to keep the letter safe until she was old enough to understand.

Her tears began to trickle down her cheeks as she watched the black habit and veil of the Sister head for the door, her precious baby in the nun's arms. She managed to hold back the loud sobs until the door had closed behind her. She wished Maude was here. Despite everything, she'd have been comforted by her practicality. Or better still, her grandmother. Mary Ann would have been softer. She now understood them both. The huge hole left by the loss of a child. The circumstances totally different, but neither being able to talk about it. She was glad she'd given her mother that chance, even though it was years after, a chance she herself would never have.

She wept at the realisation that no-one who'd lost a child could give her that opportunity. Ever. Not even Nancy. The difference there – she still had her daughter. She'd passed on the opportunity to confide in Aunt Catherine and now there was no going back.

She folded the little matinee coat, an exact replica of the one she'd sent Annie to her new home in, glad she'd the foresight to knit two identical ones. White with a shell-patterned yoke and trim around the bottom. She'd threaded a pink ribbon through the loops at the neck for tying in a bow, but had had second thoughts about that in case the baby strangled herself with it. Leaving the ribbon in place she had cut it short and stitched each end securely so that it was purely decorative. No dangerous tails.

The only difference with this coat, the one she was keeping, was that it held the smell of her baby and she had no intention of ever washing it.

MARIA

Chapter 20

County Clare
1912

The hypnotic rhythm of the waves breaking on the far side were calming as she walked along in the shelter of the dunes. A faint blue-green haze on the sandy surface, heralding the promise of wild gentians, made Maria wish she could stay the few weeks longer that it would take them to carpet the place. The weak sun had clouded over, but she wanted to make some final sketches in her diary before leaving. She looked around for the gap they'd used as children to get onto the beach, but it was nowhere to be seen. It had all changed.

The woman from the village had been missing for about a week. Despite the best efforts of the local constabulary nothing of Emily had been found except for a pair of brown ankle boots resting on the sand, toes pointing out to sea. Her terriers had been found seated there, one on either side of the boots, ears on alert.

The last few sightings of her had been as she heading down the road to the beach. A cyclist had to dismount to avoid falling off his bike when one of her dogs ran into his path. A young mother washing breakfast dishes at her kitchen sink waved and Emily had waved back. A youth, coming back from his run on the beach claimed to have seen her, but hadn't noticed anything unusual about her appearance or behaviour.

Her disappearance was the main topic of conversation in the area, but then Maria supposed not much happens in a small place, at least nothing so dramatic. Had the woman been depressed? Taken off her boots, waded into the waves and kept going? Maybe she'd simply walked away from her life and left the boots on the sand to suggest drowning, wanting the concentration to be focussed on finding a body rather than following her? At this stage she might well be off in another part of the country setting up a whole new life for herself. She wondered if it had entered Emily's head that people might think she'd been murdered? No strangers had been seen in the area that day and no local held a grudge against her. A quiet woman, shy but friendly, described as *"very nice, never did harm to anyone"*.

Her husband knew nothing of her disappearance until half past six the evening she went missing, when he arrived home to their cottage to find no dinner bubbling in the pot over the fire. The routine was almost always the same, timed perfectly. She'd always mention if there was to be any change and she'd said nothing different that morning when he was leaving. But that day, just the cold grey ashes of the previous night remained and all was quiet. Her coat was missing and that puzzled him, set him wondering why she'd gone out at that late hour when normally she walked the dogs in the mornings. Maybe, now with the lengthening evenings she'd just gone for another walk to make the best of the day. Although it wasn't like her. A woman of habit, she was not someone to break from the normal routine without leaving a note, so the absence of one was a bit of a worry. Maybe she'd just done something different for a change? Bored with the fact that they were both such predictable creatures? He got himself something to eat, and when she hadn't returned by the time he'd finished, he found he couldn't ignore the prickles of anxiety any longer. Taking his coat from its hook he cycled to the beach, the only place she ever took the dogs. As soon as he climbed to the top of the dunes, they spotted him and began barking and running towards the waves.

The husband had been the first to be questioned by the police, but witnesses confirmed he had been at work all day and she had been spotted by a neighbour in her yard after her husband had left that morning. Several local men were questioned too. Each time it was heard that a new person was helping with enquiries the case took on a fresh energy, only to sink into a trough when nothing came of it. Until the next man was called.

Neighbours rallied around, forming groups to take turns patrolling beaches, in the hope of finding her, alive or dead. They took the coastline in sections and each group was assigned a stretch of a mile. Every so often a shout would go up as something was spotted.

Maria had joined in the search on a few occasions and saw things in the distance herself, but invariably they turned out to be jetsam from passing ships, a piece of driftwood, a marker for a lobster pot or the occasional seal bobbing his head up above the water, curious to see what was going on. As the days wore on with no sign of Emily, the groups got smaller. A few still walked the ridge looking out towards the sea, but the vigour seemed to have drained from the exercise. It was like those last few searchers just felt a need to continue, didn't want the husband to think they'd abandoned all hope.

Someone had placed a log in a sheltered spot behind the dunes. Maria sat there for a while, leafing through the red leather book in which she'd recorded the highlights of her visit home, her first since sailing for America twenty-odd years ago. The little events were important to her, the sort of things one would be inclined to forget unless a note had been made of them. The thrill of the starling formations, like swarms of bees, or the badgers at the quarry pond. She hoped the sketches and notes would remain as a memory of her travels and take her back to her roots when later she sat by her fireside in New Jersey.

Sitting daydreaming, it wasn't until the sun reappeared that Maria realised she'd become quite chilled. The warmth of its emergence lulled her, making her reluctant to rouse herself, but she wanted to fill those last pages. She'd be glad later.

She sketched fast and loose, the figures silhouetted against the sky, hands shading their eyes as they scanned the horizon. After adding a footnote '*Searchers on the dunes*', she began a quick drawing of a cow and her calf drinking from a trough a short distance away, and included the man digging the earth beside them. She'd seen him a few days previously, laying foundations for what looked like a house, smoothing over the surface with an unusual sensuality before stepping back to admire his handiwork.

The sun disappeared behind a cloud again so Maria closed her diary and, slipping it into her pocket, headed off. The late spring weather hadn't yet turned warm enough to sit outdoors for too long. A mist from the sea had just started coming over the dunes, the sort that would wet you fast with its dampness.

Engrossed in his digging, he didn't lift his head as she neared. She wasn't sure if he'd not noticed her or was just an unfriendly type, so she was surprised when he looked up as she approached. Now that she had a better look at him she could see his skin, darkened from years in the elements, gave him a foreign look. Like the locals would say, probably a descendant from the shipwrecked Spanish Armada. He straightened, rolled his shoulders and leaning on his spade looked towards the ridge. Maria wasn't sure if he was going to speak, but thought it might be rude if she didn't acknowledge him.

"You'd wonder if they'll ever find her." With Emily's disappearance the only topic of the moment, Maria's comment was more a statement than a question.

"Well, they'll not be finding her out there anyway."

Something in the man's tone suggested he'd never been one of the volunteers. Picking up his rake, he began smoothing over the earthy surface.

Chapter 21

When Maria went out that evening to post the cards, the misty air of the afternoon had changed to a persistent soft drizzle, its moist freshness gentle on her face. By the time she arrived at the shop, the trickle had turned to a downpour.

She'd written her last two postcards to her brother and sister in Boston. Dropping them into the post box sunk into the wall of the shop, she wondered if Hugh and Johanna would receive them before or after she returned to America. But she liked the idea of this little test to check the efficiency of the postal service.

Shaking herself off in the porch of the shop that doubled as the local pub, she watched the drops darken as they spattered the floor, spreading out in perfect circles, before seeping into the limestone slabs. Inside, the wooden counter, its brown sheen stained from a century of custom, stretched to the back of the long narrow shop. A frosted glass divider half-way down provided a partial screen for the men who congregated at the far end of the room for their evening pint. Drinkers who preferred that the world didn't observe them. An ineffective privacy when the entire population of the village knew exactly who these creatures of habit were, who it was seated behind the screen, at what time they arrived, and what time they left.

In the shop section of the premises, a customer, in no hurry to end his conversation with the shopkeeper, was settling his weekly bill.

"Be with you shortly, Maria." The shopkeeper smiled and winked at her.

"Take your time, Dermot. I'm in no hurry to go out in that deluge again."

The first time she'd come to the shop during her visit she'd noticed that he'd thickened, very unlike the sporty lad she'd gone to school with. He'd told her that he'd taken over the running of the business from his father whose health wasn't the best. She watched him now as he dealt with the garrulous customer, glad to see that he seemed to be enjoying the banter, not just a case of feeling obliged to step into his father's shoes.

She glanced at the newspaper on the counter. An article caught her eye reporting the *Titanic* sea trials prior to the ship's maiden voyage. Maria picked up the paper and checked her pocket for the correct money.

It was early. Only a few men yet in the pub end of the shop. She could see the shadow of one, hidden behind the screen. A couple of others sat on bar stools, in view, at the opposite wall, their pints settled on a ledge. She recognised one as the swarthy man she'd met earlier and beside him was a youth. No mistaking the relationship – the dour look of his father was echoed on the young man's face.

Their silence differed from that of two elderly men seated on a bench by the fire. With identical cloth caps, they looked like twins but may just have been brothers. They stared into space, drinks in front of them, in the companionable silence of acceptance, the sort that comes from familiarity with an unchanging pattern of life through the generations. Maria noted there was none of this contentment shared in the auras of the man and his son.

A vaguely familiar face at the fireside glanced up from his newspaper as he reached for his pint on the mantelpiece. With the full view, she recognised him as the musician she'd met on the Cliffs of Moher a few days ago.

Wild and windy that day, it hadn't been easy to face the elements, but she'd needed to feel the Atlantic spray on her face. Notes of music could be heard in the distance, bending in the wind, as faint as a banshee's song. He'd been sitting close to the edge of the cliff, a rock sheltering him from the worst of the wind, so she didn't see him until nearly upon him. It was only as she drew close that she spotted the tin whistle, half hidden by the woollen scarf he'd wrapped around his head and neck. He hadn't yet seen her and with no wish to intrude she slowed, approaching only as the last slow notes drifted on the wind and disappeared into the ocean. She'd hoped for a chat but he didn't seem inclined, so she settled on asking if he'd mind her doing a sketch. She'd taken the half smile and raised eyebrow as permission and he went back to his playing. Maria wondered as he played and she drew, if the lonesome lament was for some lost love, but as he seemed content in his solitude they didn't speak again. She had just given him a smile and a raised hand before she moved onwards along the cliffs and he had disappeared from his place behind the rock on her return. Now, from his seat at the back of the shop his eye caught hers as she waited at the counter, and he gave a nod before returning to his paper.

"That's turned out a wet one." Having settled his bill, the customer in front turned to include Maria in his conversation.

"It certainly has and it's getting heavier." She felt a cold rush behind her and turned to see the door opening and a man with a mop of grey hair and a sheepdog entered. The dog shook himself, showering the cold spray on them.

"Sorry about that." The man nudged the dog out of the way.

"Search called off, Colm? Too dark, I suppose." The customer put the last of his messages into his bag as Colm began to take his coat off.

As the dog gave himself another shake Maria moved out of his way.

"Hey, stop that, you're drowning the woman! Sorry, ma'am."

"Oh, don't worry, I'm fairly wet as it is." Maria smiled at him and patted the dog.

"Ah, there's not many going out now. Too long. I'd say she's gone at this stage. Sure there's been no account of her since that young fellow saw her with the dogs – he was the last to see her." With a half swivel of his head for Maria's benefit, Colm indicated the pair further down the room.

"Oh, his was the last sighting then? That must be his father beside him. They're very alike?" Maria wasn't sure why she asked but there was something about the man and his son that had her curious. "I passed the father on the dunes earlier."

"Yeah, that's Dan. I met him meself, burying the calf." Colm gave a nod to the shopkeeper. "A bottle of stout there when you're ready, Dermot." He headed down towards the fire and pulled up a stool beside the father and son.

Leaning on the ship's rail looking at the Queenstown docks disappearing into the distance, Maria realised it had been a mistake to leave packing until the last minute. She'd left several things behind at the farmhouse in the rush, not just the jacket. Her mother could use that. No, it was the sketchpad diary, still in the drawer of the bedside locker, that annoyed her the most. She'd been looking forward to reading it on the voyage home. She'd have to wait until she arrived back in the States to write home and ask them to post it to her.

The missing woman had been on her mind. Hadn't been able to shake off the slight worries she had about it.

"You were always fanciful, Maria." Mary Ann had dismissed them completely. "Whatever put that into your head? A fella filling in the foundations of his house, and then it's him burying a calf, and now you think he was burying a body. Have you lost your reason?"

"Well, there was something about the way he was smoothing over the foundations and then his remark that they'd not find her out there in the sea that I thought odd."

"And do you think he'd say that if he was after murdering her? Well, down to the police station with you, if you're that suspicious. But I can tell you that they'll have you locked up as a madwoman." Mary Ann laughed. "For sure he'd be burying a body in full daylight and all those searchers around – and you looking on. For sure."

But the feeling persisted. The notes of her unease and some questions it raised, jotted down in the diary, was as far as she'd got.

DOROTHY

Chapter 22

County Wexford
1912

Despite being aunt and niece, Maria and Dorothy had never met until recent times, at least not that Dorothy could remember. Originating as they did, on opposite sides of the country, there was no reason for their paths to cross on any regular basis, and anyway with Maria already emigrated to America by the time Dorothy could talk, becoming part of each other's lives wasn't something that would ever have been on either of their horizons. Growing up, for her, Maria had only ever been a disembodied name, like some of the other relatives. The same that could be said of her mother's old neighbours over in County Clare that she'd never met, but would be referred to in letters from Mary Ann.

It was only when the nagging started about the choice of a career that this Aunt Maria, occasionally referred to in adult conversation, had become much more interesting. The postcards arriving from different parts of the world, travelling with a wealthy American widow sounded exciting. Exotic sunlit scenes with palm trees or ornate churches in cities all over the continent of Europe.

The months she'd spent in Clare minding Aunt Catherine's children had been a time when she'd toyed with the idea of following in her aunt's footsteps. She'd talked about it to Catherine the day the postcard arrived from California. It had been drizzling outside and the grey day had the children squabbling over a card game at the kitchen table. The blue sea on the coast of Santa Barbara and the whitewashed buildings looked exotic.

"Oh, wouldn't you just love to be there!" Dorothy gazed dreamily at the scene. "All that lovely sunshine!"

"Maybe you should think about it, Dorothy." Catherine took the card and turned it over.

"Did you ever think of following your sister, Aunt Kate?"

"A bit too late now, but if I had my time again maybe I would do a bit of travelling. I may have missed my chance. No, I *have* missed my chance." She looked across at her niece. "Don't you do the same. You should give it some thought, some serious thought. You've been talking about training in children's nursing. That might open a door for you to take a similar road to Maria and cross the Atlantic."

But that was then. A time of innocence when she thought she had control of her future. After all that had happened, not something that she cared to dwell on, as it only served to remind her how such dreams could, in a short space of time, be rendered completely unrealistic. She'd mostly forgotten that she'd even considered such possibilities, the act of another had such an profound effect. Her plans for a glamorous future had dissolved like a snowflake, even before they'd settled. Had sent her life lurching off in a different direction altogether, burying her dreams under a veil of secrecy.

The annual long letter from Maria that arrived each Christmas provided more information with exciting tales of her life working as a lady's maid.

"She's no maid, I'll have you know, missy." Maude's eyes widened, her eyebrows raised, disapproving. "A lady's companion, that's what she is."

"Maybe that's what I might be. Sounds like a great life." Dorothy gazing dreamily into the distance, ignored her mother's snobbery.

"Might you then? You seem to think it's easy, but you'd need to think again. Maria is a very cultured woman. You'd have to smarten yourself up a bit." Her mother continued ironing at the kitchen table. "You speak French? Or any other language?"

Dorothy threw a puzzled look at her mother.

"No, I didn't think so." Maude paused. "Come to think of it, all that talk of training to be a children's nurse. Whatever became of that?"

"I don't know." Dorothy's brow furrowed as she looked out the window. "I suppose I liked working in the children's home and I stuck with that and never bothered to do the training and sure then I came home."

"And what have you done since then?"

"Well, I haven't exactly been idle, Mother. I've worked in the hotel."

"You have, but not trained for anything. You can never go up the ladder that way." Maude looked at her daughter. "You've still time, but not much. You'll be missing the boat before you know it, so you'd be needing to get a move on."

"I suppose."

"Well, your aunt learned French and has a smattering of Italian, and she didn't learn that sitting on her behind at home in Clare." Maude paused. "No, you're right in one way. She didn't start in America as a lady's companion. She did start off as a maid but she soon realised that that was no way to spend her life and she did something about it. Yeah, our Maria was ambitious. Always had a lot of go in her."

"Go on." Dorothy hoped she'd pick up a few tips from the story and at the same time it might deflect from her own lack of direction.

"She was very bright, my sister, you know. Didn't sit around watching the grass grow." A touch of envy crept into her voice as she warmed to her theme. "No, she pushed herself and began to build on her education. And I can tell you she didn't have much, just the same as the rest of us, left after the national school."

"And how did she do that?"

"Well, she didn't have the money to go to any fancy college, but over there in New York she found a native Frenchwoman to teach her French in exchange for conversations in English and went to the art gallery to learn about art on her days off. And the rest she taught herself from books and maps."

Dorothy could hear the pride in her mother's voice as she described her younger sister and wondered if Maude would ever talk about her own daughter with the same admiration.

"Yes, she did well for herself, but it wasn't as easy as you might think." Maude rested the iron on the table. "And the lesson you could learn from your Aunt Maria is not to think you've arrived when you land your first job, as you seem to have done. You need to be thinking – is this all there is? You need to see it only as a foundation, and then work on building on it."

"Do you ever wish you'd done something like that?" As soon as the question was out she regretted it. She hadn't meant it to sound like it did and Maude was sharp enough to pick up on it.

"Ah, sometimes. When the postcards arrive." Maude stopped in her folding of the clothes. "But I don't dwell on it."

Dorothy relaxed.

"When you think about it, I have something Maria hasn't. A husband and children." She shot a glance at her daughter and grinned. "You can't have everything, I suppose."

"And aren't you blessed you have us!" Dorothy gave a mock smile at her mother.

"Oh, sometimes I wonder . . ." Maude smiled as she stacked the last of the pillowcases on the pile. "But, to be serious, you only have one life and you have to make choices and I probably wouldn't have had the same vision as her. And I met your father and that was the choice I had to make. Maria could probably have had both, because she was young when she got the job with the wealthy woman. There was nothing to stop her getting a husband and having a family after she'd got the travelling out of her system, but that was her choice, not to."

"Wouldn't you wonder about that?" Dorothy pondered the thought how someone might forgo romance for adventure. "Did she ever tell you about any romances?"

"I never really asked her. It's not exactly something you'd enquire about in a letter – it'd seem a bit nosey."

"When did that ever stop *you*, Mother?"

"Less of that." Maude thought about it. "I suspect she must have had. She was very good-looking. Dark curly hair and big brown eyes and she could look very elegant when she was done up. She went out a lot. To theatres and functions and I know it wasn't always with her rich mistress. I know she didn't go alone because she'd often mention it was with a friend." She paused, her arms full with the bundle of ironing. "Come to think of it, she often mentioned the friends by name, but it was always female friends, so I'd guess the times she just said '*with a friend*' and no mention of a name, it was probably with a gentleman friend. Kept us guessing."

"Yeah, I know the photo that Granny has of her on the wall in the sitting room. The one taken in a studio in America. All the fine clothes, she looks so glamorous." Dorothy could feel the seeds of great possibilities setting. Maybe something she could consider but as her mother reminded her she didn't have much time to ponder.

County Clare

The most surprising thing then was that at the age of almost thirty, when Dorothy finally met Maria for that first time during a trip to her grandmother in Clare, that in the space of a week they became such close friends. The age gap had all but closed.

"I can't call you 'aunt', it doesn't feel right."

"I'll kill you if you do. Makes me feel ancient."

"Right . . . Maria . . . let's see how youthful you are. C'mon, up on the bikes."

"Oh, let me tell you, you won't be able to keep up with me where I'm about to take you . . . *child*. Plenty of hills to test you." Maria passed the oilcan to Dorothy and wiped her hands on a rag. "I don't know when these were last used, but they're rusty as hell. Put that can back in the shed and we'll be off."

Up and down the laneways of Clare, revisiting childhood haunts, added an unexpected dimension as Maria pedalled ahead as Dorothy's guide.

On the day Maria left it was as if the sun had gone in for Dorothy. There are people who drain the life out of everyone they meet and there are others who energise the very air around them. Maria was in the latter category.

For the first time, Dorothy now saw her life as if it were divided in two parts, well, maybe three if she were to count the unmentionable. She'd settle for two – a before and after Maria. A new beginning. Revitalised. Ready to kick start herself into the next phase of her life. She didn't quite know what that new life was, but it was bright. Unlike the previous 'before' and 'after' Thomas.

In *that* 'after', for a few years, she'd decided to stay on working at the children's home. It was safe and comfortable and she'd grown attached to most of her little charges, none of whom were true orphans, but had come from some difficult background or other. Waifs and strays in need of mothering and that she was good at. Not good. Excellent. And for years it had given her what her soul needed. As Maria had advised her, love what you are doing. The wrench when the children moved on broke her heart but she'd come to see it as an occupational hazard. What she got from her job more than made up for that and a few of the children had stayed in touch, for a few years anyway, until they arrived into adulthood and then it was just the Christmas card. But it was good to know that they still remembered her, even after she'd left the home and moved back to Wexford to work in the hotel in Courtown.

Her tears of parting with Maria were a strange mixture of sadness and relief. There had been something about Maria that drew confidences. Strange that, because apart from tales of her exciting travels, Maria didn't give much away about her own life in America. It wasn't until after she'd gone that Dorothy realised she knew hardly anything of Maria's romantic life. Was there one? She was single. She was fun. That was clear. But had she ever loved, or loved and lost? Did she regret not having had children? These questions would all have to wait for another time. She'd been so wrapped up in her own past that she'd forgotten to ask.

She didn't know what it was that had prompted her to tell Maria about her torment at the hands of Thomas O'Brien. To tell her that the consequences of that torment had forced her to disappear to Dublin and hide the results, ripping the heart out of her. Told in a weak moment. Until then it was something she'd never drawn breath on, apart from Nancy and Nancy's aunt.

"You have to promise, Maria – promise me that you'll never tell anyone what I've told you." She was already having regrets. Revealing her secret now, so many years after, might not have been the wisest thing, but somehow she felt drawn to disclose this one part of her life that had been cocooned inside her for so long. "I've never, ever mentioned it and they've no idea. My mother would probably have dumped me out had she known."

"But it wasn't your fault, Dorothy." Maria looked at her, understanding written in her eyes. "He's a dark horse. I could never work him out. Always felt a bit uncomfortable with him although he never messed with me."

"He probably wouldn't have dared, Maria. You'd have been well able for him. But I was only young and hadn't a clue how to handle it."

"Yeah, I can understand how you had to keep it to yourself. Knowing Maude . . . although she might have killed him had you confided in her, but maybe . . ."

"I don't know if she'd ever have believed that I did nothing to encourage him. But I know it wasn't my fault, Maria." Dorothy looked at her aunt, sensing a danger. "No, Maria, you're not to even *think* about it. It's not just my mother. It's Aunt Catherine and her family too. She's the only one who has any clue of what he did, although I've never discussed it with her. But she has no idea about the baby. It's all too late now so please, please keep it to yourself. Think what it would do to Granny if she discovered it. Now you're to promise me!" She was almost crying now. "I should never have told you."

"Okay, okay. I promise. I'm glad you did. You've kept that bottled up inside you for far too long. Look," Maria drew her finger across her lips, "satisfied? Not a word. Not to anyone. I'll keep it to myself, just between you and me. Okay?"

For twelve years she'd imagined a little girl with reddish gold in her hair and green eyes, dancing in the sunshine somewhere. A child, happy in her innocence. At least that was what she hoped. Trusted she'd been placed with a good family, a kind one. Hopes that she'd shared with Maria.

Before her departure, Dorothy repeated the reminder never to speak of it, but it was with mixed feelings that she waved goodbye to her. There was always that lurking fear that it might just slip out in an unthinking moment in conversation, or a clue, however unintentional, might creep into a letter. All it might take would be a vague hint, picked up by someone with a probing mind who would chase after an explanation for the reference.

Chapter 23

To fill the void on the afternoon of Maria's departure, Dorothy had taken Mary Ann for an afternoon tea treat in the hotel in Ennis. It turned out to have been one of her better ideas. In the foyer of the hotel they'd bumped into a couple of acquaintances that her grandmother hadn't seen for a long time. An ideal distraction to take Mary Ann's mind from her loss. Dorothy hadn't ever met the women, but was glad when they'd suggested they all join up for the chat. It took the full responsibility for cheering up her grandmother from her shoulders. They were both feeling lonely and it was hard to know what to say to each other.

The women sat down, full of enthusiasm to hear all Mary Ann's news.

"My granddaughter Dorothy is Maude's daughter. You remember Maude, although she was a lot older than you pair." Mary Ann made the introductions once they were all seated. "And, Dorothy, these are the Murphy sisters. Josie and Philomena. They used to live in the house at the crossroads near us – you know, the one with the lovely red roses over the wall. They live in Ennis now. Went to school with Maria."

It always surprised Dorothy how great her grandmother was with the potted histories – gave you an image of the family tree to follow. Knew exactly how to whet your interest in the stranger from the offset and include you in the conversation. She'd been wondering how Mary Ann was so familiar with the women, they being so much younger, but now it all fitted together.

"How many years is it now you're in Ennis?"

"Nearly thirty years now, Mary Ann. You wouldn't feel the time passing. Sure, I suppose you could nearly call us 'townies' at this stage." Philomena laughed. "And to think those same roses are still out there in the old garden. My father must be looking down on them and minding them. God rest him. And how is Maria?"

"She's just gone back to America. Went off on the boat today. She was here on a holiday."

"Isn't it a pity that we didn't know she was here on a visit." Josie, who appeared to be the older of the women, a few strands of grey hair showing through her dark waves, looked disappointedly at her sister. "It would have been so nice to meet up with her again, wouldn't it, Philomena?"

Their fascination at hearing details of Maria's exciting life in America had them both agog and it was clear they'd have liked to stay longer only their ride home was imminent.

"Wouldn't it be the one day you'd hope she get delayed." Josie laughed as a young woman appeared in the doorway and waved. "My daughter. We'd better be off. Jane's not renowned for her patience."

"Well, it was lovely to meet you again, Mary Ann, after all this time." Philomena stood up, taking her cue from her sister and they shook hands. "Sure, maybe we'll get Jane to drop us out to see you some afternoon."

"That would be lovely. I'm nearly always there. And we can have a proper catch-up and you can see those lovely red roses." Mary Ann smiled. "I'll tell Maria I met you both. She'll be delighted to hear that. I'll be writing to her shortly."

"Granny, she's only just left." Dorothy laughed. "She'll hardly be out of Cork Harbour yet."

"Well, I've a bit of news for her now, haven't I?" Mary Ann laughed back as she waved. "Goodbye, ladies."

Heavy raindrops had started to fall by the time they arrived home, so Dorothy busied herself doing jobs around the house. The outdoor work could wait, although it looked like the rain might be down for the day. Taking the sheets and pillow cases from the bed in Maria's room, she put them in the laundry basket, ready for washing when the rain passed.

She moved a few half-empty bottles and jars of cosmetics onto the bed and taking the lid off the tin of bee's-wax gave the surface a quick dusting before polishing the wood to a shine. A drip from one of the bottles had left a mark, a perfect ring on the dark wood.

"Grandmother will not be best pleased with you, Maria!" She rubbed the stain with an increasing vigour, but the stubborn mark refused to disappear. Smiling to herself she gave up. Sure, maybe it's no harm to leave a trace that her aunt had been there.

Having wiped the mirror with a clean cloth, she pulled open the empty top drawer and gave it a cursory wipe. The second drawer still held a few items that Maria had missed in her rushed packing. Amongst the pieces of jewellery she found a pair of earrings. Delicate filigree silver droplets with a milky bluish moonstone set into each. The necklace was a match, a chain with the same delicate lacy design and a moonstone set into each flower shaped disk. She held the necklace against her and admired how it sat just below her neckline. How could Maria have forgotten these gorgeous treasures!

There were a few books on the bedside locker and a leather-covered book in its drawer. Recognising it immediately – it was Maria's sketchpad diary which had always accompanied them on their bicycle trips – Dorothy picked it up and ran her hand over the satin-smooth dark-red leather cover. Gazing out the window her mind reran the images of her days with her aunt as if they had been memories from a distant past, instead of her life in recent days.

She found an empty shoebox in the bottom of the wardrobe and began gathering the toiletries and forgotten items, placing them, along with the diary into it.

"Granny, I've cleaned out Maria's room."

Mary Ann was already topping up the water in the kettle. She must have heard her granddaughter coming down the stairs.

"Good girl. I'll make us a cup of tea now. Maybe while the water's boiling you'd go out and lock the hens in for the night." She tapped the ill-fitting lid in place. "You'll need a jacket on you, it's still raining out there."

Dorothy placed the box on the table as Mary Ann hung the kettle over the fire.

"Can I borrow this coat that's hanging on the back of the door?"

"Yes, do that." Mary Ann nodded across at the box. "What's that you have there?"

"Just a few things that Maria left in the room. I'd say she probably intended to leave the jars. The other stuff, the jewellery and diary were in the drawer and there was a jacket and a lace blouse. She mustn't have done much of a check." Dorothy slipped her arms into the raincoat. "What do you want me to do with them, Granny? Do you think she'll need the books? They were on top of the bedside locker. They're very heavy to be posting. Maybe she's already read them?"

"Well, you needn't worry about the books. They belong here. She took them from the bookcase in the parlour."

"Would you like me to take the other things back home when I'm going and post them over to the States?"

"That would be great help. Save me having to find wrapping paper and lugging them to the post office. You can keep the lotions and potions for yourself. I'm sure she left them on purpose. Before you send anything though, write to her and ask. She'll want the diary with her drawings, but maybe she intended to leave the bits of jewellery and any clothes for you, Dorothy. I'd say the diary's probably the only thing she'll want."

"I feel bad leaving you so soon, Gran." She hugged Mary Ann. "You'll have an empty house now that we're all gone."

"Well, at least you're not too far away, child. Only across the country. You'll be back." Mary Ann smiled at her granddaughter. "And sure you might persuade your mother to come back here with you and stay a bit longer next time. I don't know what Maude was in such a rush to get home for. She's always the same. You'd think the world was waiting for her over there in Wexford. I can understand Maria, she has to get back to work, but I know she'd have loved if Maude had stayed longer, especially after her coming so far."

"Ah, Gran, sure that's my mother. You know what she's like." Dorothy threw her eyes to heaven. "Thinks the place can't manage without her. Acts like my father is useless. She should have stayed here and given him a bit of peace over there at home."

TRAGEDY

Chapter 24

County Wexford

The white face of her father as he burst into the kitchen told her it was bad news.

"*The ship went down!*"

"What are you on about, Cornelius?"

"*It's in the newspaper. They had it up in Duffy's. Maria's ship, it went down!*" An unfamiliar hysterical note had entered her father's voice.

"It can't have. They said it couldn't sink. The greatest ship in the world? You must have it wrong, Cornelius."

The note of irritation in her mother's voice was false. An effort to will away the truth of what he was saying.

Dorothy stood, frozen to the spot, looking at her father waving the newspaper.

"I wish I had it wrong, Maude. It is the truth. Look, the *Titanic*. There's something like two thousand missing."

The stubborn look on her mother's face, the effort to hide her disbelief fell away.

"What about survivors? There must be some?"

"There are, but there's chaos. It's too early to say how many. They're searching as we speak. They just don't know yet."

Dorothy went upstairs and lay on the bed, stunned. She'd sat in the kitchen for a little while after her father had made the announcement, listening to the meaningless comments and questions, unable to speak.

She didn't know how the neighbours had got to know so quickly, but suddenly they were all there, before they themselves had time to digest the news. They sat there watching their faces as if searching for further updates and none having the courage to ask the question outright.

"Sure, maybe Maria will be one of the survivors. Didn't you always say she was a great swimmer?"

But it has gone down, Dorothy thought. The ship's gone down. And, anyway, where exactly would you expect her to swim to? She felt like screaming at them, but fought the urge and remained silent. It wasn't their fault.

The international nature of the tragedy, with so many bodies missing and from so many countries, added a dimension that no-one had encountered before. There was nothing to hold on to. Nothing to be done. The rituals that normally provided stability and comfort at times of death and loss were absent. Like a roadmap that had blown away in the wind. Nobody had any idea how they might deal with these strange circumstances. People who'd hardly spoken to them before, now wanted to be part of the drama, wanted to touch someone who knew someone who went down in the disaster. The air of frantic excitement seemed wrong, but it was palpable in the air.

She'd slipped out of the kitchen unnoticed as the room filled up. Several women were making cups of tea. It was as if the wake had already started. She couldn't stand it. Most of these people filling the house were people who didn't even know Maria, had never met her. All wanting to be part of the drama. It might give some comfort to her mother, but it was no help to her. Her head told her that they were well-meaning, but her heart said that all she wanted to do was to go back to her grandmother in Clare. Her fortnight's holiday from work was almost up. The first thing she'd have to do was contact the hotel and tell them she wouldn't be back for a few more weeks. Then she'd have to tackle her mother.

Halifax, Nova Scotia

Hugh and Johanna had spent several days trying to locate the body of their sister, hoping she was amongst those recovered following the sinking of the ship.

One survivor testified that he'd tried to revive a woman who lay freezing in the bottom of a lifeboat, but she'd slipped away before the rescue ship arrived. He'd recognised her as a fellow passenger who'd said she was from New Jersey. They hoped it had been Maria, unless by some miracle she had survived. It was just too terrible to imagine her dying alone and terrified in the freezing waters. Better to imagine her surrounded by others in the lifeboat.

Ireland

Hugh sent several telegrams to Art during the awful days of waiting, and Art did his best to keep them all informed. It had taken some time to establish if Maria's body was one of those recovered from the *Titanic* and in the end the worst was confirmed. As soon as the news came through, relatives who never visited each other's homes came together from all quarters, the way families do in times of crisis. Dorothy couldn't talk about it, always finding something urgent to do whenever the conversation turned to what might have happened to Maria. They'd gone over it and over it. She was gone. They would never know the circumstances. All the talking and speculating about what she might have suffered was helping no-one, just adding horror upon horror on top of the grief.

When she could take no more she found herself taking to lying on the bed. Fully dressed, on top of the eiderdown. She couldn't bear to go downstairs when they were in, sitting around the table, drinking the endless pots of tea and talking. One of the days it was a bit chilly and she slipped under the quilt and lay there listening to the hum of voices below. Without realising that she'd dozed off for a few minutes, she came to, drifting back into the present. In her half-alert, cocooned state the thoughts slowly seeped back. Left her thinking she'd had a nightmare and for a few merciful seconds allowed her the relief that the whole awful thing had been but a dream.

A certain guilt had attached itself to her following Maria's death. Something that in her worst moments seemed to appear and peck away at her. Try as hard as she did to drown the thought, it bobbed up every so often to torment her. A faint relief had somehow got tangled in her anguish. She didn't want to entertain the thought that it might be all mixed up with the knowledge that her own secret was safe at the bottom of the ocean.

Things were upside-down. With no wake or funeral to organise the familiar procedures were missing, leaving a big hole in their lives. No-one knew where they should be. It was her father who seemed to have the clearest head and that was how the decision was made to travel to Clare, to Mary Ann.

"You need to be there with your mother, Maude. There's nothing to be done here." He'd been surprised at his wife's dithering. Unusual for her. "Nothing to be done anywhere. But we'll travel down tomorrow and stay for a few days. It might give her a bit of comfort."

"I'll come with you," said Dorothy.

"You've a job to go to, Dorothy. And so has Bridie – and the lads need to keep things going here while we're away." Cornelius was firm. "No, there's no need. It's not as though there is a funeral or anything you can do. Leave it to your mother and myself."

They'd continued to come to the house for a few evenings, but the frequency of the neighbours' visits began to taper off as the shock faded, and with Maude and Cornelius absent there wasn't the same mileage to be had. Added to that, with the reports in the newspapers petering out, each began to get on with their own lives and the disaster no longer the main topic of conversation as the reports of survivors began to thin out.

DOROTHY

Chapter 25

County Wexford

Dorothy unfurled the eiderdown and stepped out of the bed. With her stockinged feet padding across the wooden floor, she hoped her footsteps wouldn't be heard below. Any sound might have her mother calling her and she wasn't in the mood to be asked to join the visitors who'd be dropping in to get the news from Clare. Not that there was anything further to be added.

"My mother has taken it very badly as you'd expect, so I'm worried about her," Maude had told them on her return. "We thought it might help with your father and myself going over to Clare, but it made no difference. Art is going out of his mind. There's nothing himself or Ellen seem to be able to do. Catherine is spending a lot of time there also, but there's no comforting her at all."

She could hear the faint clatter of dishes below and felt a bit guilty. Bridie was downstairs making the tea – maybe she should go down and give a hand. No, she'd go down later and do the washing-up, less talking with that. In the meantime there was no need for her to present herself and sit there mute with a face on her.

She went to the wardrobe and took the diary from the shoebox inside. She'd had no intention of reading it. Had previously only flicked through the pages to look at the sketches. Had all gone according to plan, she'd never have read it before posting it back to Maria. Not until this happened. Stroking the leather cover, she wondered about it being one of the last things that held Maria's fingerprints. Now in her hands, it was the closest she would ever come to touching her aunt again. It suddenly became a precious thing, to be returned to Mary Ann. She would possibly feel the same – the last link with her daughter.

There would be no posting it to America now, so it wouldn't really matter if she read it before she handed it over to her grandmother.

Climbing back into bed she plumped up the pillows and, wrapping the eiderdown around her, settled herself comfortably and began to read.

The expertly done drawings had notes added by Maria, giving an additional insight into her encounters. The blacksmith working in the forge and the note she'd made about the stray horse he'd rescued and homed. The Honey Man at his hives. Underneath the sketch was a story about his rescuing a hive that had set up a colony under the slates of a house. The owners had been prepared to live with the buzzing – it was only when the liquid honey began to drip down the walls inside the cottage that they sent for the local Honey Man to remove the hive.

The pictures collected during their cycles were ones she had watched her aunt draw, and envied the total peace and concentration that settled on Maria's face. The drawings were good. Their quality suggested Maria could have made a career of it.

"Did you ever think of becoming an artist, Maria? You've a great talent for capturing things."

"Oh, I thought about it when I was young, indeed I did, Dorothy, but my mother soon disabused me of that notion."

"What do you mean?"

"Well, she asked me one question."

"And what was that?"

"What do you intend to live on in the meantime? Until you become famous?" Maria laughed. "My mother was no dreamer. A bit like your own. Must have been where Maude got it. Practical to the last. Told me to keep drawing and when I'd sold my first ten paintings that might be a good time to reconsider."

"And did you ever sell any?"

"Oh I did, but not for much more than would cover the cost of the materials." Maria nodded at her niece. "Sometimes you have to be realistic, Dorothy, but it doesn't mean you have to give up something completely, even though you need a real job to pay the bills. It can always be a pastime and that might just be enough to keep you satisfied."

She could still hear Maria's voice and looking at the sketches and reading the notes brought back the days for her. She could once again feel the breeze in her hair as they freewheeled down hills, unsure how she was going to save herself at the bottom.

As she came towards the end of the journal, a newspaper cutting wedged between the pages fluttered out and landed on the bed. '**Woman Missing from Clare Beach.**' She'd heard the talk and recognised the drawing of the group of volunteers on the dunes. It had all happened before her own visit to Clare, but Dorothy knew exactly where Maria had sketched the man digging the earth. A site she'd passed a few times on her travels. But it was Maria's note underneath that made her scalp prickle. It was clearly written at a later date than the sketch. An afterthought. At right angles to the drawing and in blue ink.

The Burrow. What makes him so certain they won't find her at sea? What does he know? Under the foundation or in the grave? Report it or what? Will they think I am mad?

Why had Maria said nothing? Hadn't mentioned a thing.

Snapping the diary shut, it suddenly felt like a hot coal in her hand. To think the diary had been there, like an unexploded landmine lying in the wardrobe, waiting to be posted to America.

Heart pounding, the note had her mind racing so fast she could feel the blood thundering in her ears. Taking a deep breath, she struggled to compose herself. In an effort to regain control, she tried telling herself that two minutes ago she didn't know anything about this. Life had been calm. Tragic, but calm. Nothing had changed. What's done was done, or mightn't have been done at all, for all she knew. But it was up to her now to decide what to do with this bombshell. She took another deep breath. She didn't have to decide this instant. No, she could take her time. No point in rushing into anything. Nobody else knew about the diary. Whatever happened the woman has happened. Too late now to save her. Take time to think what best to do. Don't have to do anything immediately. Like Maria had written – would they think she too was mad? Anyway, maybe Maria had reported it. But surely she'd have said something if she had?

She closed her eyes and thought. There would be no point in

talking to her mother about her suspicions. She'd have dismissed them as fanciful.

"Oh, that's you all over, Dorothy, always imagining a drama. You'll find there's most likely a simple explanation for that poor woman's disappearance."

Her father, maybe, but not until she'd thought about it a bit more. She was glad he was home. Yes, she could hand it over to him for advice. With his background he would know what to do. The complication was that she knew once she embarked on that course of action there was no stopping what might happen or where it would lead. There would be no going back. A former policeman, her father would be obliged to follow through on the information, whether it was relevant or not.

For the rest of the evening she moved the diary around her bedroom. When she left it on the bed, she worried it might burn a hole in the eiderdown, so she moved it to the drawer of the bedside locker. It wasn't long before she began to imagine opening it to find the book had smouldered and fallen through into the cabinet below, leaving a burnt charcoal rectangular shape in the base of the drawer. Fanciful. Yes, her mother had the measure of her.

That night, unable to sleep with the weight of the responsibility, she wished she'd spoken to her father before she'd gone to bed. Might have been able to get some rest had she passed the burden to him. She couldn't deal with another secret – she'd enough on her own plate. The trace of evidence, the single clue that she herself had left eleven years ago, in the hope that at some time in the future, when she had well and truly departed this world, someone might make sense of it. But that was her own secret. Maria's was different. She'd done much the same, but not intentionally. She too had probably felt that she needed time to think, to work it out . . . but time was not something she'd had as the waters closed slowly over her head.

So yet again, faced with the possibility that it would change someone's life forever, like her own secret, hidden to protect everyone else, this was one she wasn't going to carry, not alone anyway.

The east wind blew in from the sea, whispering through the cracks of the partially open window. Lying back against the headboard, unable to move, she heard a change in the sound of the wind, like a voice developing an urgency. A voice, increasingly angry that she couldn't understand its message. She'd always hated the wind and this one had blown since yesterday. Now that she'd read the diary, she took it as a sign. The only way to quieten the voice on that wind was to make a decision. To make a decision and act upon it.

She could hear her father padding up the stairs. She swung her legs over the side of the bed and ran towards to door. She wanted to intercept him before he went into the bedroom. Didn't want her mother to wonder why she was calling him.

"Pa, can you come in a moment?"

He glanced in surprise at her half-open door.

"Did I waken you, Dorothy?"

"No, Pa, I wasn't asleep. There's something I want to ask you. Can you come in for a minute?"

"You've done the right thing, Dorothy. Sleep well now."

That was her father's only comment after she explained and handed him the diary. She could still feel the soft worn leather on the tips of her fingers long after it was gone, but it no longer burned her hands.

END OF AN ERA

Chapter 26

Maude had been against it but Dorothy had insisted it was for the best.

"Look, Mother, I know you feel you need me here but think of Granny – she's living on her own down there." Dorothy eyes were sympathetic as she told Maude of her plan. "You have Pa and Bridie and the lads here and the neighbours are very good."

"Of course, I know what you mean, Dorothy. It must be unbearable for my mother, but she does have Art and Catherine and their families nearby." Maude's eyes were red. "Maria, she was my little sister, the baby of the family. It's just not right. And what an awful way to go!"

"Look, Mother, I won't stay too long in Clare." A niggle of guilt made her make the promise. A slight shame that she wanted to be with someone else, someone who had so recently spent a lot of time with Maria rather than comforting her own mother. "I'll be back before you know it and I'll be more use to you then, when all the fuss has died down. I'll have to come back to work anyway. They've only given me a little bit of leave and I won't last long with no wages."

Clare

Her arrival at Mary Ann's was not what she expected – her grandmother watching out the window for her, the smile and big hug as she arrived into the kitchen where the stove threw its warmth around the room. Instead, all was quiet, only the dog nosing around her ankles as she approached the door. She pushed it open and he followed her into the cold silent kitchen, rubbing his body against her legs as if glad of the company.

"Gran? Granny, are you here?" Opening the inner door to the hallway, she listened for an answer. "Granny, are you up there?"

"*Hello? Hello, I'm up here!*" The answering voice sounded weak, not at all like Mary Ann.

"Back there, dog, go back into the kitchen." She nudged the reluctant dog backwards and shut the door on his disappointed face, before heading up the stairs.

Mary Ann lay in bed, her head turned towards the door. She gave a slight smile as her granddaughter entered the bedroom.

"Gran, are you alright?"

"Yes, I'm alright. As alright as I'll ever be, child."

A note of resignation that Dorothy had never heard before had entered her grandmother's voice. She wasn't quite sure, but she detected what seemed like a faint sour smell in the room. She went over and, parting the curtains, opened the window.

"Are you well enough to get up, Gran?"

"I'm not ill, Dorothy, just heartsick." She gave a long sigh. "I suppose I'd better get up now that you're here. I could lie here all day . . . but sure what's the point in that? I'll only feel worse."

"Is that what you've been doing?" Alarmed, Dorothy moved to help her turn back the covers, with a suspicion that she hadn't roused herself from the bed or washed herself for days.

"Sure what's to get up for?" Mary Ann allowed Dorothy to help her put her legs over the side of the bed.

"Do you want to get dressed or would you like me to help you have a wash first?"

"Pass me the dressing gown there and we'll go down and have a cup of tea first and we'll see after that."

Shocked at what she'd found, Dorothy was glad she'd made the decision to come but knew she was out of her depth with this. The plate and teacup on the bedside locker were evidence perhaps that Uncle Art or his wife Ellen had been taking food up to her. She'd need to talk to them. See how long this had been going on.

The pain of losing another child to America, but this time losing her daughter permanently, was clearly a step beyond what her grandmother was capable of enduring.

"I'm so glad you're here, Dorothy. She'll be so glad to see you and at least you'll be staying in the house with her." Catherine sat across the table, a look of exhaustion on her face. "She didn't want us sleeping over at night. Some of the grandchildren took turns but it only annoyed her."

"Do you think it might annoy her with me staying? I don't want to add to her problems."

"No, Dorothy, I think it was the chopping and changing that did it, but if you could stay a while it would be less disruptive for her. And sure if nothing else it will relieve us a bit. It's an awful worry the way she is. Not like her at all."

"I know. Not at all like herself. She was always so strong. The matriarch of the family. I can see some of her in my own mother." Dorothy smiled. "But Gran's not so irritating."

"You might have better luck with her. No amount of cajoling from us was working. She sees it as fussing and I know it's driving her crazy and I suppose we're all beginning to panic. You might be a bit more calming and better able to keep a lid on the fussing." Catherine grinned at her niece. "Art and Ellen did their best, and the neighbours, but nothing has succeeded so far, so we're all at a loss to know what to do."

"Well, I doubt that I'll have any bright ideas. But I'll give it a go."

They sat in silence for a while as Dorothy pondered on how she might manage.

"She's carried so many crosses over the years and always seemed to cope. I suppose when we were young we didn't give it much thought as she never shared her worries with us." Catherine looked worried. "This time, though, it's different. Like this is one cross too many and she's now lost the will to live."

"It's understandable, I suppose." Realising she too had never thought much about her grandmother's past until now, Dorothy gazed over her aunt's shoulder, out through the window. "To have been left a widow so young with all those children must have been frightening. And then to lose so many of them . . . sure you'd want to be an ox to shoulder all that."

Tired of being strong. Had been resilient all her life and what had it all been for? What use had it been? It was as if this was what people expected of her. But no more, she'd had enough. She'd put too many of her children in the earth. There was no fairness in all this. You were meant to go before them. And now Maria, her youngest, to meet her end, all alone in the cold seas of the north Atlantic. It should have been a comfort that at least her body was found, but it wasn't. If she'd gone to a watery grave it couldn't have felt any more desolate.

The nightmares were the worst. Seeing her walking into the bedroom, her hair plastered to her head, looking like it was growing down her back with the wet seaweed that hung from it. Her lovely daughter, like a sad mermaid, reaching out a blue-white arm towards her mother, mouthing the words '*Save me!*'.

Apart from the panic at not being able to save her, the terror she experienced during and immediately following the nightmare, she felt nothing. Total emptiness. She couldn't bear the talk any more. The what-ifs. She had started to take to her bed whenever she heard footsteps on the gravel in the yard. There weren't so many now, but she was glad that Dorothy was there to entertain the last of the sympathisers. It had become a habit now, stopping in the bed. Nothing to get up for. It might have been different if there had been a body to bury here at home. The healing interval of a wake, the cleansing purge of the tears that followed behind the coffin out of the church and into the ground. None of that had been available to her, none of the normal opportunities to aid with the recovery or whatever little recovery there might have been. All of that had been stolen from her. Unlike her granddaughter Bridie, all those years ago when she lost her lovely young husband to the sea. A body, a burial and Joseph's grave nearby to visit. Tragic as it was, and at such a young age. But none of that for her with poor Maria's drowning.

She lay in the bed that herself and Patrick had shared, the one they all wanted her to get rid of.

"It's ancient, Ma. Let us just buy you a new one. How do you even sleep on it? It's full of lumps and bumps."

"And how would you know?" Her stock answer when they put on the pressure. "You haven't been in it since you were a baby."

It was there that she made her decision. Her life had been as good as it had been hard. Very hard. If she had been strong enough to survive this lifetime of hardship she was strong enough to will herself to die. She would join her husband and her dead children. Her work here on this earth was done, her purpose fulfilled. No-one was dependent on her now. She had no more to give. She was free. Free as a bird and of one thing she was absolutely certain: she was not prepared to live any longer in this emptiness.

It took time. Dorothy's presence hadn't changed her mind. All efforts to help her met with a gentle refusal. They all knew it wouldn't happen immediately, so they paced themselves, taking turns at doing the necessary chores and keeping an eye on her. Maude came over for a couple of weeks to help out when Dorothy had had to return to work. Someone was needed to sit with Mary Ann each night while she slept. Just in case. She didn't object, seeming to take comfort in knowing someone was close by. As time passed they roped those grandchildren who lived nearby back into the rota again when it became clear that she'd gone beyond caring who it was sat by her bedside.

She appeared to be sleeping. Maude tip-toed from the room when the question came.

"Where's Bridie?" Mary Ann's voice was suddenly alert.

"I thought you were asleep, Mama." Maude swung around, surprised at the sudden interest in her granddaughter.

"I'd like to see her."

"But she was here, Mama, a couple of weeks ago." Maude's response was sharper than intended, worried that this slippage might be the start of the end. "Do you not remember? Two of your grandchildren came over from Wexford. Dorothy was here and then she had to go back to work and Bridie came over."

"Was she here?" She paused, a puzzled frown settling over the faraway stare. "Oh, you're right, she was. And Dorothy too." Mary Ann relaxed against the pillows. "Of course they were here. Don't mind me, I forget the days. It just seems so long ago."

Aware it was difficult for the family to ride this out – the barely eating, just enough to allow them feel they were helping, but not enough to sustain a body – saw Mary Ann fade off into the next world. She exited as she wished, without fuss, a resigned look on her face that suggested a body happy to be at the end of its journey.

―――

It was while they were all gathered in Clare for Mary Ann's funeral that the body washed up on the beach became the talk of the place.

"I feel stupid now." Dorothy avoided looking at her father.

"What do you mean, Dorothy?" Cornelius glanced down at his daughter in surprise. "What reason have you to feel stupid?"

"The way I let my imagination run away with me. Thinking that woman had been murdered. I even had a suspect."

"No. That was Maria. She was the one who pointed the finger. But it's better to report these things even if you're wrong."

"Did you go to the police with the diary? I didn't want to ask you before, but now that she's found it doesn't really make a difference."

"I did. And they followed it up. But there was more to the story than we knew. It seems it wasn't the first time she tried it." Cornelius shook his head slowly. "Her mental state wasn't the best. A sad situation but now it's over and at least the family know what happened and they can bury her and set her to rest now."

"And what about the diary?"

"The guards will give it back to me later. I rang one of my colleagues in the barracks and it will be arranged. It's no use to them now." He paused. "Would you like to keep it? Now that Mary Ann is gone, maybe you're the right one to have it."

"I'd like that." With a faint smile Dorothy nodded up at her father.

DOROTHY

Chapter 27

County Wexford
1913

She wandered over the footbridge, stopping to watch the gulls gather on the railings along the harbour wall, remembering her fear as a child that they would shit down on her head as they flew above her. She could remember the scene as if it had happened yesterday and not twenty-five years ago.

"Don't be ridiculous, Dorothy." Maude was pulling on her daughter's hand. "Why do you think that in the whole of the big wide world they are going to single you out for special attention. Oh, there's Dorothy Redmond. Let's fly over her and drop our plop on her head."

She smiled at the memory.

"But why can't we stay on this side of the harbour?" she whined. "The gulls don't come over here."

"And if we do, how do you think you're going to be able to get into the sea for a swim? Now stop the nonsense and come along." Maude gave another tug. "Look, the others have gone ahead and they're safe enough."

"Well, I saw a nun in town once and there was white bird poo all down the back of her black veil." Dorothy began to giggle. "And she didn't know it was there."

"Well, there you are. She must have done something very bad to deserve that." Maude still held the grudge. Had often told them about the bad-tempered nun at school who'd mocked her when she couldn't explain big words in their religion class, terms like *'consubstantiation'* or *'a mess of pottage'*. Not exactly stuff you'd be dropping into conversation at home.

Yes, Maude was a great one for holding onto a resentment, especially when she knew the criticism was born out of something ridiculous, like that one had been.

Dorothy watched a father and toddler walk down the steps which led to the low walkway that ran along one side of the harbour. The father, releasing the child's hand as they reached the bottom, began studying the boats that bobbed about beside their moorings. The child continued walking along, rummaging in his bag for bread for the swans and gulls, unaware of the big drop into the water. She fought the urge to shout down to the man to watch the toddler. Oblivious as he was to the danger, he only just caught the back of his son's cardigan in time, as the child wandered too close to the edge.

"*Would you stop it!*" She could imagine her mother's admonition. "*You can't save the world. It's his child, his responsibility. If the child falls in, the da will just have to jump in after him.*

Unable to watch, she took herself off the footbridge and walked over to the sea wall. With her view of the perilous pair below blocked, she perched herself on the wall and, looking across the harbour towards the roadway, she watched for Nancy.

She didn't have to wait long before she saw her, two hands in the air in a big enthusiastic wave. The tall willowy girl beside her, Maisie, her daughter, all grown up. What a difference the year had made!

"Oh, how gorgeous you are, Maisie!" Her voice was muffled through the hug. "Quite the young woman now. You'll have to watch her, Nancy."

"I know. Who're you telling?"

Maisie sent a withering look in the direction of the two women. "I'll leave you two to have your chat." She pointed to the wall. "I'll meet you somewhere here later."

"Where are you off to, young lady?" Nancy was immediately on the alert.

"Just for a walk in the woods. You needn't worry. I'm just meeting up with a couple of my pals."

"Which pals? Anyone I know? You can't have too many down here, a Dub like yourself."

"None that you know." Maisie tapped on her nose and grinned. "Keep it out of my business, Nancy. Oh, don't worry. I wouldn't be that lucky. It's only a girl."

"Well, don't be too long then."

Maisie laughed and left.

"She's lovely, Nancy. Where did you get her at all? She's really blossomed in the year." Dorothy looked after Maisie as she headed down the sandy track towards the woodland. "Do you think they suspect?"

"I'm sure they do suspect," said Nancy. "Sure isn't she the image of me, the same platter face?"

They walked down onto the beach where Nancy settled herself on the sand and leaned her back against a flat rock.

"What are you talking about? She's not a bit like you! She's growing up a right beauty."

"And what's that supposed to mean?" Nancy feigned indignation. "Anyway, I'd say there's plenty of chawing over it in the village, but I just stick to the same story every time I come down here on a visit. The aunt's daughter. I tell them we're very close, almost like my own daughter. They're hardly going to challenge me to my face now, are they?"

"And has Maisie never let it slip?"

"I was always a bit worried that she might when she was small, because she's known since she was old enough to ask questions."

"Did you think it was wise telling her so young?"

"Maybe not wise, but I didn't want it to be a shock maybe discovering it when she was older and she'd probably never forgive me for lying to her. No, it's better that she knew and I know there's no way now she'll say anything. She only too well acquainted with my mother's opinions on such subjects."

"Yes, no doubt. But what about your mother?"

"Oh, it's never brought up. I know she knows and she knows that I know she knows, but it's never aired. Sure, bringing it up would mean she has to admit her daughter is a harlot and that's a fact that she wouldn't want to accept. So no, she knows better than to open up that subject."

"God you're priceless. I just wish I had the same brazenness as you." Dorothy laughed. "Is there nothing you're afraid of?"

"Not a thing." Nancy puffed herself up. "Go on, up to the shop and get us a couple of ice creams. I'll stay here and mind our valuables. Go on, you owe me."

"When am I ever going to finish repaying the debt?"

"Never probably. Two ice cream cones a year? Cheap at the price, don't you think? No, it'll never be cleared."

"D'ye know, I look forward to this every year." Dorothy licked a drip from the back of her hand.

"Ah, that's sad. The highlight of your year and it's eating an ice cream in Courtown with me." Nancy gave a lick to her cone. "Tragic."

"Not that. Meeting up with you, you dope."

"Tragic that too. If it's all you have to look forward to."

"Can you never take anything seriously, Nancy?" Dorothy looked at her friend. "You know what I mean. You're the only one I can talk to about it."

"I suppose. It's a bit late to be asking you now, but do you ever regret your decision? To give her away, I mean."

"Every day of my life, but I'd no other option. You know the circumstances." Dorothy turned and looked at her friend. "I feel really guilty though."

"About giving her away?"

"Well, no, not really that. I just hope she's had a good life and has loving parents." Dorothy paused. "No, I feel guilty about the fact . . . I don't know if I should even say this . . . "

"Oh, would you spit it out, woman!"

"Well, when I first found I was pregnant . . . "

"You what? You hoped you'd lose it?"

Dorothy jerked her head towards Nancy. "How did you know I was going to say that?"

"We all felt like that at the time. It's normal. In the panic."

"So you felt the same?"

"Of course I did. Anyone who says otherwise – well, anyone who finds themselves in our position who says otherwise is lying."

"I don't know . . . " Dorothy trailed off. "I still feel guilty about that. Even after all these years."

"Well, you needn't, because, like I say, it's the first thought that comes into your mind when you realise you're up the spout. When you shouldn't be. Like us." Nancy gave her a nudge. "Now, enough of that. Put that guilt to bed or you'll torment yourself for the rest of your life. How do you think I survive?"

"Ah, you'd survive anything!"

"Did you ever think about trying to trace her?"

"Often. But where would I start? The nuns would hardly give me a lead. And maybe they'd be right. Anyway, what would I tell her? That she was the result of a rape?" Dorothy gazed out at the far horizon.

"Are you mad? Surely you wouldn't think of telling her that?" Nancy stared at her. "You'd have to come up with a different story."

"Yeah, come to think of it, I suppose you're right."

They sat in silence for a while until Dorothy broke it.

"You're going to think I'm crazy . . . "

"That's not exactly something new."

"No, seriously, Nancy. Every year I used to go to the Home on her birthday and walk up and down the road, remembering the few weeks I had with her."

"You what? You're right. I do think you're crazy. Did you think she was suddenly going to appear?" Nancy stared at her. "Why torment yourself like that?"

"I don't know, Nancy. I don't know. It's just something I had to do, but you're right I was tormenting myself. I suppose I was so lonely for her that I thought I couldn't be more miserable than I was, but it would just upset me all over again for weeks, so I stopped it. After that, I just went into a church and prayed for her."

"And what exactly were you praying for?"

"That she'd have a happy life."

"Jesus, Dorothy, that's awful." Nancy shook her head. "I know I'm not strong on the whole empathy thing, but I never realised it was quite so hard on you. And to think it went on for years? At least I can bake a birthday cake."

"It never leaves you, Nancy. You're always left wondering – what's she like, what's she doing, would she ever give me a thought? I wonder if she even knows I exist or if she was ever told they weren't her natural parents?"

"You really know how to torture yourself, don't you?"

"Well, when I tell you the next bit you're definitely going to have me certified."

"And what's that? Ah, this just gets better."

"When I came back here to live, I went up to Dublin each year and took the tram over to the Phoenix Park."

"And you never let me know? I'd have joined you."

"No, it was something I had to do myself." Dorothy shook her head. "Remember the first time you took me there when I was pregnant. I thought it was the most gorgeous place and I was really happy that day with you. I don't know if you realised it but you were my saviour."

"Of course I do. Sure that's me, Nancy, Patron Saint of Damsels in Distress. But yeah, amazing to have such a huge big space in the city. A great place to leave your troubles behind if only for a few hours."

"Well, that's where I went after that. Each year on her birthday. Spent the day wandering around thinking of her and I'd sit on the grass and have a picnic and watch the deer wandering through the trees in the distance."

"And do you still do it?"

"No. I missed one year. Couldn't get the day off from work and then I began to ask myself why I was doing it and I stopped. Now I just go down to the sea here and wallow in nostalgia for a bit."

"Now, let's leave that depressing stuff behind. Romance. Where are you on that? Anything to tell me?"

"Well, you'll find that subject even more depressing." Dorothy laughed. "Not a lot on the horizon there. Although there is this waiter . . ."

"Go on. Don't keep me in suspense."

"Hold your horses, Nancy, there's not much to tell. It's only a possibility. Nothing has happened yet, except we get on really well."

"What do you mean nothing has happened? Have you been out with him yet?"

"We've gone out for a drink a few times after work."

"And . . . ?" Nancy popped the last of her cone into her mouth. "Don't be milking it!"

"And dancing the odd weekend."

"And?"

"And nothing. Just as pals. Nothing more. As yet." Dorothy grinned at her friend. "But he's gorgeous. He's from Kerry and has this lovely lilting accent."

"Ah, forget the lilting . . . is he a good kisser?"

"Oh God, Nancy, why do you always have to turn it into a steamy bodice-ripper?" Dorothy rolled her eyes to heaven. "We haven't even got that far yet. I don't know if he sees me that way. Let me enjoy the fantasy of it for a while, will you?"

"Well, you better make a move before someone else snaps him up if he's as gorgeous as you say." Nancy paused as a young couple strolled past hand in hand. "Wouldn't it put the longing on you? Anyway, do you ever see any of the lads you went out with before?"

"A couple from around here, but they were only a flash in the pan." Dorothy paused. "Well, actually I did spot this fella from Arklow in Gorey one time but he didn't see me. Thankfully. It's funny how you can fancy someone for so long and think this might be it and then find yourself dodging them after you realise that you actually had a narrow escape. Much as it pains me to say it, but my mother was right."

"Yeah, she wasn't exactly in love with him either, if I remember rightly. *'A bit fond of the drink, that lad.'* I can still hear her."

"*'That lad would drink it off a sore leg,'*" Dorothy mimicked her mother. "Lovely image that. Unfortunately, she was right. I ignored it for long enough, but the time came when I'd had enough. It was me or the drink."

"And you lost."

"End of story. But, I'd say I won, if you know what I mean. Anyway, enough about me. Tell me all about your romances, Nancy."

"Nothing to tell. Maisie put paid to that."

"Hardly her fault now, is it? You did that all by yourself."

"Ah, I'm only joking. I wouldn't be without her, but it certainly limits your chances." Nancy shrugged. "So, tell me, how's the job in the hotel going?"

"Yeah, it's working out grand. I like it, but I still miss Dublin, even though it's been years. And, seeing you, I miss that too. But sure what could I do when they closed the orphanage? It felt like the time to come home then, although I'm not sure. Although I suppose living-in at the hotel part of the week is better than staying at home all the time. I don't suppose my mother would disagree. She only has to put up with me on my days off." Dorothy laughed. "There might be a murder otherwise."

"Hers or yours?"

"Probably a double one."

"Well, back to the hotel. Any more juicy stories there . . . you'd a few good ones last year . . . and you know I'm no gossip."

Chapter 28

No-one had been more pleased than Nancy when Dorothy told her she was going to Blackpool with Brendan for a few days.

"Things are moving fast then with the Kerryman, Dorothy? I thought you said you were only pals? And here a few months later you're off to England with him?" Nancy's excited voice on the telephone was rushed. "Tell me all! We've only three minutes on the call, so you'd better be quick."

"They're not moving that fast, Nancy, don't get excited. There are four of us going to Blackpool to see the Illuminations. One of the girls in the hotel has organised it, she has an aunt over there who recommended it, says they're beautiful."

"Forget about the aunt – will you be sharing a room with himself?"

"Indeed I will not, you bold thing! What do you think I am, a harlot like yourself?" Dorothy laughed. "No, it'll be all about the dancing and the sightseeing. We're going for three days. I need to spread my wings. You've always told me I'm getting too set in my ways down here, and you the city girl that you are."

"Well, don't do anything I wouldn't do."

"Nancy, there's not a lot you wouldn't do."

The hotel had closed for a week in October for renovations, so they were all free. The timing of the trip to Blackpool had been perfect. They'd never have envisaged a world war waiting in the wings, much less that all the lights in Britain would be extinguished. Yes, they'd only just caught the bright spectacle in time.

She could still see the elegant ornate walls and ceilings and the chandeliers and hear the band as they'd glided around the dance floor of the Blackpool Tower Ballroom each evening and wishing she had one of those beautiful ball gowns that some of the expert dancers wore. A far cry from the ballrooms of Courtown or even Dublin. The magic of it all had never left her.

Their bed-and-breakfast lodgings were on a side-road, just off the seafront, near enough to be able to have an evening stroll and admire the Illuminations before arriving at the ballroom for their evening's entertainment.

The landlady was from Clare and delighted to have their little group staying.

"I don't usually do meals any more, except breakfast but, seeing as you and I share Clare links, Dorothy, I'll make an exception." She smiled at them. "Five o'clock then. How does bacon and cabbage for this evening sound?"

"Sounds great to me." Brendan rubbed his hands. "I'll look forward to that."

"We're privileged, thank you, Mrs. Kelly, that would be lovely." Dorothy turned to the other three as the landlady moved away. "Now, none of you better be late. Only for me you wouldn't be getting fed at all. Remember, five sharp, no later."

"Indeed, Your Ladyship." Brendan grinned at her as the other two bowed in her direction, their hands in the praying position. "Much appreciated."

"I mean it." Dorothy stood up. "Now who's coming to the amusements? I want to try out those fruit machines. We only have a couple of days to do everything."

"I'm coming with you. You never know, maybe we'll make our fortune?" Brendan pulled back her chair. "Come on, Dorothy, no time to waste. We'll see you two back here at five. On the dot, remember!" He winked at them.

The golden glow of Blackpool carried her through the winter. It was late spring before the unease began to set in. Decision time was looming and it wasn't helped by the pressure she felt coming, not just Brendan, but from casual onlookers.

One in particular.

"Are you not married yet?"

Every time she met him or passed the roadside bench where he usually sat, on the way into the village, his comments had been a constant low-level irritant for years. A miserable old bachelor, the greasy collar of his dirty brown coat turned up, sitting there on the bench, watching the world go by, he couldn't resist the taunt.

"No, I'm waiting 'til you get married first." She'd tried that to shut him up, but he wasn't to be silenced and ignoring his comment only seemed to encourage him more.

"Not talking to anyone today, Dorothy?"

The very sight of him in the distance put her in a bad mood, anticipating his smart remarks. Often felt like suggesting that if he had the odd bath maybe he'd find a woman willing to marry him, something to wipe the smirk off his grimy pocked face.

He was annoying enough, but when Maude started dropping hints it got to her.

"Would you ever drop it, Mother, you're as bad as that auld Wally eejit, him sitting there at the crossroads!" she snapped. "If I decide to get married, you'll be the first to know – now will you ever cut it out!"

"I was only saying." Maude raised her eyebrows. "Brendan mightn't be prepared to wait around if you keep dithering. You'd need to make up your mind. He's a nice fellow and you're not getting any younger."

"Do you think I need reminding? Now, just drop it."

It had been after the May Bush Dance that decision time had come, prompted, not just by Maude's prodding, but by her own instinct. She knew she couldn't sit on it any longer. It wasn't fair on Brendan. He'd been pushing her for months to make a decision.

Once the May Bush Queen had been crowned, the crowd began to disperse. A chill had crept into the breeze and the clouds were gathering overhead as the outdoor dancing finished. They picked up their bicycles from where they lay propped against the ditch.

She noticed that Brendan seemed reluctant to mount and just began pushing his along.

"Look, Dorothy, I need to know where I stand. Where we're going."

She was tempted to say "Home" and make a joke of it, but this was something she couldn't just kick down the road. It had to be dealt with.

"I know, Brendan, I know." She paused. "I just don't know where to begin."

"What do you mean – 'begin'? It's a simple enough question. Are you going to marry me or not?" He sounded exasperated. "I can't go on like this. I have to have an answer. I'm really not prepared to wait any longer."

"It's not as simple as you think, Brendan."

She was going to have to tell him. For a moment she considered stopping and sitting down on the ditch to reveal the bad news. No, it might be better to keep moving along in case he took a notion to just mount his bike and ride away once she'd told him and that would be the end of it.

"What I'm going to tell you, Brendan, is awful and I doubt you'll want to marry me once you've heard it."

"Nothing can be that awful, Dorothy."

"Oh, believe me it can." She kept her eyes cast down on the road as she pushed her bicycle. "Something happened years ago. I've not told anyone this, so you've got to promise me you won't repeat it. My family don't know. It's very complicated."

"I can't promise anything until you tell me."

"No, Brendan, you have to promise. No matter what happens once I tell you, you've to promise never to mention it to anyone."

"Okay, okay, I promise."

"I know, you've always wondered why . . . well, physically . . . why I'm always a bit . . . how can I say it . . . buttoned up." She paused. "There's a reason. It's not that I don't love you or anything, because I do, and if I were to marry anyone it would be you."

"I don't like the sound of this, Dorothy. What do you mean, a reason?" He looked baffled. "Despite our age, I've always been prepared to wait. I've never pushed you now, have I, Dorothy?"

"You haven't, and that was always a relief to me, but what you don't know is that I mightn't be able to change, even if we were married." She paused. "And I want you to know it's not anything to do with you."

"I don't understand. What are you saying? Are you afraid of having a baby or something?"

"No, that's not it. Look, there's no easy way to say this . . . look, Brendan, I can't say it."

"You can't stop now, Dorothy. What are you trying to say, just spit it out."

"I was raped."

"What?" He stopped his bicycle and stared at her. "What are you saying? When did this happen?"

"A long time ago. I was very young." Dorothy could feel the wobble coming into her voice, but she knew, now that she'd started, she had to get to the end.

"Who . . .?"

"You don't know him, it happened down in Clare, when I was living there with my Aunt Catherine. Looking after her children." She looked at Brendan. "You have to promise me, you're not to repeat a word of this. The family don't know. The only one I've ever told is my friend Nancy."

"What did you do about it? Surely you must have told someone at the time."

"I couldn't. No-one would have believed me."

"Of course they would. You should have told someone."

"It gets worse, Brendan. I couldn't tell anyone because it was someone in the family who did it to me." She looked at him. "It was my aunt's husband. He destroyed my life."

"Jesus Christ, they need to be told! You should have told your aunt at least and reported him to the police."

"Can you not see what it would have done to the entire family? I couldn't do it to them."

"So you let him away with it. Simple as that. He got away scot-free!"

"You sound like you're blaming me, Brendan. I was seventeen, I had no idea how to handle it. And who would have believed me anyway? And then I discovered I was pregnant." She began to sob.

"Pregnant! Sorry, sorry, Dorothy. I'm not blaming you, but it galls me to think that bastard got away with it." He lay the bike against the hedgerow and held her by the shoulders. "Don't cry, don't cry! How have you kept it to yourself all these years? And the baby?"

"That's why I went to Dublin. Nancy helped me. The baby went to a family, but I've no details. It broke my heart, as you can imagine. And not being able to talk to anyone about it was just awful. And to this day I wonder about her."

"I can just imagine." He shook his head slowly. "Jesus, that's an awful lot to take in."

"I know, Brendan. She's nearly fourteen now and never a day goes by without me thinking about her. Even still." Dorothy paused. "But, now can you see why I'm a bit distant . . . well, with the physical side of things? And, to be honest, I don't think that's going to change. I can't. I think he's destroyed that part of me."

Brendan stood silently for a while.

She waited.

"That's why I can't marry you, Brendan," she said at last, "and I'm sorry if you think I've wasted your time." She waited for a response and finding none coming, she continued. "I hope you don't think that, because we did have good times, didn't we? But maybe I should have told you all this sooner."

"Maybe you should have, Dorothy, maybe you should. You could have trusted me with it, you know."

He picked up his bike and they walked on.

CATHERINE

Chapter 29

County Clare
1919

Mary had married young. The first of the brood to leave home, Catherine missed her. The daughter who most reminded her of her younger self. The better parts, but tougher, less inclined to let people get away with things.

She wished she hadn't let it slide. Only herself to blame for that. After the whole Dorothy thing, she'd had the upper hand for a while. Should have held on to it, but it went against her nature, and gradually over time, without her hardly noticing it, she'd let him slip back into his old ways, as she had slipped into hers. And, by the time she realised, it all seemed too much of an effort to stoke herself up to that level again in order to do anything about it.

It pleased her that Mary seemed to miss their regular chats as much as she did. It had become a ritual, now she was living in the town, that Catherine would drop in each week when she went there to do the grocery shopping with Thomas. He bought his tobacco supply and made a trip to the library to exchange his books after which they would return to Mary's house for a cup of tea and soda bread before making the journey back home.

"Well, our business here is done." Thomas stood up from the table. "Are you right, Kate?"

She recognised the underlying message. The highlight of her week being cut short when he decided.

"The horses are leaving now."

The self-satisfied look on his face irritated her, the way he appeared to take pleasure in the fact that he held the reins. Always held them. He'd make the same joke of it each week, as he stood over her with his coat on, supping the last of his tea.

"Sure, what's your rush? Mother isn't finished her tea yet, and neither am I. Will you for heaven's sake just sit down!" Mary's firm voice didn't always secure a few more minutes.

"Time waits for no man. Time is money. Things to do. Places to go. Come on, Kate, knock it back there."

Rather than leave behind a bad atmosphere in Mary's kitchen, Catherine complied as usual.

"Do you always have to do that, Thomas?" She waited until they were out of earshot.

"What do you mean, woman? Do what?"

"Oh, don't pretend you don't know. Rushing me out of there. We only see our daughter once a week. Could you not spare half an hour without causing a scene?"

"There was no scene. Unless you want to make one of it." Thomas gave the pony a whack of the stick.

She knew when to withdraw. One word too many from her and he'd refuse to call to Mary's with her the next week, like he did before when she wouldn't let it go. He was too cute to link the two incidents and give her cause for argument. He'd just find an excuse.

"Sure, didn't I call to her during the week when I went to the Mart. I delivered the eggs to her, remember?"

"Well, I didn't see her. That visit wasn't intended to be instead of today. I only asked you to drop them off as you were passing."

EILEEN

Chapter 30

"I'm behind with the work."

Eileen had heard it all before. She stood in the hallway listening to the conversation filtering out from the kitchen. No point in intervening until he'd made his excuse. Make it awkward for him to come up with a second one.

She walked into the kitchen and looked him straight in the eye. "I'll go in with Mother and we can do the shopping and call in on Mary. You can stay here and catch up with whatever jobs you want. No need for you to come at all if you're busy. Do you want us to drop back your library books or anything?"

Annoyed at being out-manoeuvred, he threw her an acid look. "I'll decide who goes. Not you."

It was exchanges like this that would have taught her mother a lesson. When to hold back. But Eileen wasn't one to pay heed. He mightn't recognise it, but his daughter had one of his own traits. A similar stubbornness laced with a lack of fear. Something she wished her mother possessed. Eileen knew that in one thing she differed from her father. She only used it when absolutely necessary. Her fiery spirit was an asset. It helped her to keep going until she bested him.

Escape from his grip was the only route out if she wasn't to be worn down like her mother. Eileen could see that. Her only regret when she made her decision to go was leaving her mother alone to take the full brunt of Thomas's control. Her gentle mother whose energies had been put into her children and now she was about to miss out on the life of another of her daughters. With Mary and Tommy married, no longer living under his roof, she was going to be left with young John, who was no match for his father. Harsh as it might sound, she had to live her own life and leave her mother to the life she had chosen. Even if, when she made that choice, she hadn't realised what she was letting herself in for.

Not looking forward to breaking the news, Eileen already had her ticket booked and go she must. It had been hard not to discuss it before she'd made her decision, but she feared that her mother might try and talk her out of it and she couldn't allow that happen. Not if she wanted a life. Knowing there would be little opportunity for her mother to visit her once she departed, the journey by ship being so long, made it all the more difficult. With a trip to town such a palaver, there was no way that Thomas would entertain a voyage for her mother to visit America. That was for sure.

She had already written to Aunt Johanna in Boston to confirm her arrival date. Telling her father was another matter. She could just imagine his face and how he would forbid her to go without his permission. But he had no rights in her life. Not anymore. The thought of telling him bought on a little quiver of nervousness, but she was ready for him.

"You lived your life the way you wanted, didn't you?" She eyeballed him out in the yard, confident that her mother was well out of earshot. "Yes, we all know, you lived it just the way you wanted. But I can assure you, you'll not live mine for me."

She stared him out. The freedom of realising she was no longer under his control surprised even herself. Like being buried in a pit and the lid being whipped off to reveal infinity. No longer confined by limits. Not his limits anyway.

"Well, I hope it keeps fine for you over there in the U.S of A." Thomas pulled the sprong from the manure heap and recommenced filling the barrow. "I thought you were going to marry that nurse fella from the lunatic asylum?"

"Don't speak about him like that. His name is Seamus. As well you know." Eileen fumed. No point in entering to a debate with him. Best to keep this short. "I have no plans for marriage."

"Have you told him that?"

"Don't worry, he knows. No need for you to concern yourself."

"Well, you needn't be coming back here looking for a home if it all goes wrong."

His final threat, trailing away as he muttered it under his breath, confirmed to her that he knew he was beaten. If he'd forced the issue she would have give him a stronger hint that his grubby little secret might surface. That's if she stayed at home. No, she'd save that one. Only if she had to would she use it.

CATHERINE

Chapter 31

Although it had never been mentioned between them, Catherine knew that Mary Ann suspected. Suspected that Thomas, her handsome husband was a street angel and a house devil. She didn't know quite how her mother knew, but she did. But then her mother was always astute, not quick to judge someone, but could get the measure of them fairly sharply. But out of some misguided sense of loyalty she'd never mentioned anything. Kept her opinions to herself.

Although she'd never said anything to him, the only one who really knew what her husband was like beneath the exterior was Cornelius. And that was from his own experience, long before she'd even met Thomas. Knowing how discreet her brother-in-law was, he wouldn't let his left hand know what his right hand was doing, she was certain that he'd never have drawn breath on his opinion of Thomas. Not to her mother anyway, but when she thought about it he'd probably discussed it with Maude. Maybe she'd said something to Mary Ann. Maybe not said anything directly but, knowing her sister, she'd most probably have hinted at it, dropped enough clues to ensure their mother was aware of the situation.

It was clear that Mary Ann knew. It was in subtle little things, like the differing ways she related to her sons-in-law. Despite his reserve, Cornelius always got a warm welcome on his occasional visits. Ramrod straight, behind the handlebar moustache there was an honesty and a dependability that exuded from him, something to be admired and Mary Ann always seemed to get a bit of banter going between them.

"Ah, he's a bit of a stiff auld poker is Cornelius, but you can always rely on him." The way she'd accompany it with a grin confirmed her fondness for him. Always having checked first that Maude wasn't within hearing when making the pronouncement during one of their annual visits.

There were never any such comments made about Thomas, never a mention of him at all.

"Oh, it's yourself." The slight indifference in her mother's voice when he'd appear at the door. The big smile on his face in an effort to charm her was wasted. At least in recent years. It hadn't taken long for her to get a handle on him, so it only worked for a short time before Mary Ann cut through the fake flattery.

Catherine had noted how, over the years, Mary Ann had become expert at deflecting any banter he might direct at her. Didn't like the slight mocking tone that was contained in it. Always polite to him but never warm. Would rarely ask after him in the way she would about Cornelius. The enquiries were always about the children and how they were doing, her animated face confirming her delight in them.

She'd often wondered if Dorothy had confided anything to Mary Ann, but that awful period didn't seem to have altered Mary Ann's attitude towards him, so probably not. She was still cool with him, but no cooler than she had been before. She gained a little comfort from the belief that her mother most likely had no idea. No need for her too to have carried the suspicion that he might have been an abuser.

The knowledge that her mother understood her marital difficulties, without ever mentioning it, had been a comfort over the years. It might have been better to have been honest with her, but then again knowing Mary Ann's belief – *'Once you've made your bed you have to lie on it'*, maybe it had best been left unconfirmed.

That was what she missed now that she was gone. That silent understanding and support. Missed it more now that Eileen had decided to go on her adventure. To America. How she'd have loved to have her mother here now to talk to her about how she coped with so many of hers having emigrating. The wonder now of how she'd never complained. Allowed them all to live out their dreams with no obstacles placed in their way. And to think that Hugh had gone so soon after their father was buried. She wished she had some of her mother's strength now.

"I'm going to miss you, Eileen. What am I going to do without my lovely girl?" She tossed her daughter's curls in an effort to stop herself breaking down. "You'll write, won't you?"

"Of course I will, Mother. What do you take me for? A cold heartless daughter who'll instantly forget her mother as soon as my ship sails?"

"But you'll write every week, won't you?"

"I promise. I promise, Ma. How many times do I have to tell you?" She rolled her eyes to heaven. "Unless I meet some handsome hunk of a Yank as soon as I get to Aunt Johanna's and then I mightn't have time. Ah, you know the way it is!"

"Oh, you'll be lucky!" Catherine laughed. "You'd better make time. Anyway, she doesn't keep Yanks. It's only the raw Irish lads she takes in as lodgers. The fellas with the carroty tops and sticky-out ears and there's plenty of that type around here, so you won't be interested in them."

"Well, I'm always optimistic." Eileen grinned. "Anyway, I'm a bit of a carroty-head myself."

"Burnished copper, I'd call it."

"But then you're biased, Ma. Anyway, maybe you'll come over and visit?"

"You'd better get yourself a good job then and send me over the money. I doubt that your father would be happy to finance such a trip."

"You're right, he wouldn't." She paused. "We'll see what I can do although maybe you shouldn't hold your breath."

"Go on. Up those stairs and get finished with your packing." Patting her daughter on the shoulder, she propelled her towards the open door. "Your father will be at the door in an hour and giving out if you're not ready."

"Oh, I know what he's like. Itching to get rid of me." She laughed as she headed up the stairs.

With her daughter in her bedroom putting the final touches to her impending departure, Catherine busied herself cleaning around the already spotless kitchen, thoughts of how different things might have been had Eileen married locally. She'd had several chances but the only one that seemed like a possibility had been the doctor's son Seamus Power. A lovely young man. A disappointment to his father, preferring to train as a psychiatric nurse and work in the Ennis Asylum than follow his father into a branch of surgery. It was clear he was mad about Eileen and she him but, somehow, he'd failed to get her to agree to marry. She'd only had one conversation with her daughter about it before leaving it be.

"I'm not ready, Mother." Eileen hadn't tried to hide the irritation in her voice. "Everyone around here seemed to assume that marriage is every girl's ambition. Well, maybe someday, but I want to live a bit first."

"I'm only saying. He's a lovely man."

"I know. He is lovely, Mother. If I was interested in marrying it would be Seamus, but not now."

"Well, if you delay too long he may well be snapped up before you've done your 'living' bit."

"I'll have to take my chances with that then."

She remembered Eileen standing up from the table, as if afraid that if this conversation continued in the direction it was headed, she might say something she'd regret. It was something in her glance that Catherine had picked up, something she may have considered her mother might not want to hear. Something that in her close observations of a certain marriage might have done nothing to encourage her to follow that path.

"I'm off out to meet Seamus now and I'll be leaving him in no doubt that I'm happy for him to feel free to get on with his life when I go, and not be waiting for me. So don't you be giving him any false hope whenever you bump into him after I'm gone, Mother."

She'd held it together until Eileen had departed before giving in to her tears. No one to understand her loneliness, just as there must have been no one to share her mother's when Hugh went off.

"Sure, you still have Mary and the lads, Mother." Eileen had tried to be brave when the last farewell was imminent. "And John is still living with you here in the house."

"Yes, but it's not the same," Catherine had sobbed. "Mary has her own family to keep her busy and sure the lads are the lads. You know how they are. They wouldn't understand. No, I'm really going to miss you, Eileen."

"Well, are you right there, Eileen? Have you everything?' Thomas stood in the door, blocking out the sunlight. "Come on now. No point in dragging this out."

Catherine watched as he picked up the suitcases. It was the way he turned abruptly out the door that told her she was on her own now. No matter how much he was going to miss their daughter there was no chance he'd share it with her.

DOROTHY

Chapter 32

County Wexford
1923

The wind whipped through the trees outside as the rain lashed down. Gazing out through the window, Dorothy could see them swaying with a force unusual for early May. Only yesterday she'd noticed their young leaves had taken on a tiredness after the long dry spell. This morning, with the overnight rain having refreshed them, they were once again showing their bright green spring attire and every so often a strong gust had them dancing with a renewed vigour.

Once she'd recovered from the shock of hearing of Brendan's death she found herself thinking a lot about him. She was glad her mother was having a lie-on in bed. Didn't want it pointed out – the futility of pondering the 'what might have beens'.

You made your decision. You let him slip through your fingers, so there's no point in whinging about it now. A bit late for that. Not that Maude had said anything much, but she could just imagine her thoughts.

"I don't wish to discuss it, Mother." She'd shut down the conversation immediately, once she'd broken the news that herself and Brendan would no longer be going out. There was no chance she was going to be drawn into any explanations about the matter.

He hadn't dumped her immediately. They'd allowed it to dribble along for a while after her revelation, but she could feel the change. He'd said it was more the lack of trust on her part, rather than what had happened to her, but she wasn't sure and she couldn't blame him. They'd parted amicably and had the occasional walk during their break from work, but they both knew it was over. Despite everything, she still retained the fondness and gazing out the window, couldn't help allowing her mind drift over a future that might have been, had Thomas not put paid to that by screwing her up.

The details of what exactly had happened to Brendan were scanty. She was aware that while they'd shared the same aspirations for the country, they hadn't agreed on the method by which they could be achieved and had agreed to differ. It hadn't been difficult to shelve their opposing views as political debate only came to the fore around the time of the Easter Rising in 1916, by which time they had gone their separate ways.

So much unrest during the Civil War meant that reports of what had happened to him were confused. The manager of the hotel had only heard the news second-hand and understood that he'd been killed by falling masonry in Dublin, wasn't sure if it was during or following damage left after a battle. He couldn't say whether Brendan had been involved in the fighting or simply a civilian going about his business on his way to or from work in the Dublin hotel that he'd moved to. She wasn't sure she wanted it confirmed that he'd taken up arms, but she had her suspicions.

Remembering Blackpool brought back bitter-sweet memories. It was only recently she'd wondered about that decision she'd made so long ago and wondered if it had been the right one. It was at her father's graveside, looking across at Bridie and MJ her husband and the way he looked after her in her grief, that she felt so alone. It would have been nice to have had someone like Brendan there to support her. But that ship had sailed a long time ago.

EILEEN

Chapter 33

Boston 1920

From the very beginning, Aunt Johanna's was a home that felt right. The smell of her home-baked bread and scones, made fresh most mornings, wafting up the stairs, lured her down for breakfast. That and the smell of the weekend rashers frying on the pan. The Sacred Heart picture on the wall, with the red lamp glowing below it on the shelf, and the faded Saint Brigid's cross pinned to the back of the door had amused her when she first arrived.

"You can take the woman out of the bog but you can't take the bog out of the woman. Isn't that right, Aunt Jo?"

"What are you on about, child?"

"Holy Catholic Ireland is alive and well in the United States of America, I see." Eileen nodded her head in the direction of the various hints of their homeland that dotted the kitchen. As soon as she'd said it, she wished she'd kept her mouth shut. Maybe her aunt would take offence.

"It is." Johanna laughed. "I'd had to display reminders here to keep the lot of you youngsters that I've housed over the years in check. Remind you of your roots, lest you lose the run of yourselves while you're staying in my house. I don't want to be responsible for that and have you all turning into heathens."

"Can I give you a hand there, Aunt Jo?"

"No, you're grand. Just sit yourself down and you can pour out the tea there." She placed a dish of rashers and tomatoes on the table and turned to scoop up the fried eggs onto two plates. "Here you are. Get that into you and help yourself to the other stuff."

"Oh, this looks very tasty." Eileen took two rashers and a tomato.

"Do you know, I didn't realise how much I missed female company in the house until you arrived." Johanna reached for the milk jug and topped up her cup. "Over the years I've got used to the girls having left home, but it's lovely now to have another woman in the house. I don't think I've had one staying here since your cousin Bridie. And that was a long time ago. Always lads since, and you know yourself, they're grand, but they're not the same."

"Well, I'm sure you must have had enough to do with all those comings and goings over the years." Eileen laughed. "No shortage of lodgers. You couldn't have had much time to be lonely."

"Oh, they've been keeping me busy alright, but it's been an all-male house for so long, apart from myself, I suppose I'd just got used to it." Johanna sat down. "You're a breath of fresh air, the missing piece of a jigsaw. Slotting together just grand now."

"I hope the lads didn't mind bundling in together to give me a bedroom?" Eileen looked across at her aunt. "I feel like the cuckoo in the nest."

"Don't you worry, child – sure they've got the big bedroom between them now." Johanna laughed. "And anyway, it won't be for long. Charlie is getting married in a few weeks, so Liam will have the room to himself after that. Sure he'll think you'll be able to introduce him to lots of lovely young women. I heard them talking about taking you to the dances, but you needn't think that's just for your benefit."

1926

Johanna wasn't happy at the idea of Eileen stepping out with a divorced man. It was one of the lads mentioned it first. The divorced bit. She'd said nothing. Waited until Eileen eventually shared this piece of information, just as she knew she would in time.

"Not a good idea, Eileen. It usually only ends up one way. In disappointment." Johanna picked up her knitting from the basket beside her armchair. "If he can't make a go of it the first time, well, maybe he's just not a suitable candidate for marriage."

"I'm only going out with him, Aunt Jo. Not marrying him." Eileen laughed. "You're jumping ahead a bit, don't you think?"

"I'm only just saying." Johanna started a row of the scarf. "Just be careful."

After registering her disapproval she kept her counsel, hoping that in time the romance would run its course. She wasn't wrong. It was shortly after herself and Hugh returned from their trip to Ireland that it did run its course.

Over the years, Eileen invited Ron home for tea on a few occasions and Johanna was suitably polite. She didn't do any special baking like she did for the girlfriends of the lads, and Eileen knew why.

She kept the visits to a minimum, just enough to show she was serious, and hoped Aunt Jo would come around in time, seduced, as she herself was, by his charm.

It had taken years for Eileen to realise that despite his protests to the contrary, Ron had no intention of telling his family about her. They'd slipped by so fast she'd hardly noticed. He loved her, that she believed, and that knowledge had been enough to keep her going, that and the good times they had together.

"What would you like to do for your thirtieth?" he'd asked one evening as they left the cinema. "Let's do something special."

"That's not for a few months yet. Let me have a think about it."

It was the approach to her birthday that focused her. Soon she'd no longer be able to call herself 'a girl'. A big milestone that. And what exactly had she done with her life? The big adventures she had envisaged when she left home – what had happened to them? Where had they taken her? Trips to various States to see the sights, New York, Niagara Falls and the beautiful autumnal colours of New Hampshire. They'd had lovely times together, there was no denying that, but these highlights had masked the stagnation that controlled her life. The inaction of a man. A man who hadn't enough gumption to overcome his weakness. A sudden understanding of her mother's life, albeit controlled in a different way. How easily and subtly it could happen.

The forthcoming birthday was an awakening, making her wonder how he had managed to go so far as divorce, when his Irish Catholic upbringing seemed to have had such a stranglehold on him. The difficulty he seemed to have in moving on with his life and putting down firm anchors to build a new one. Oh, he talked about it, but that was as far as it went. Doing something about it openly was a different story. What was there to stop him?

"I don't want to upset anyone."

Even he had to know the excuse had worn thin.

"But you don't mind upsetting me?" She was aware of becoming a nag, so often had they had variations of this conversation. "You're years gone from the family home. I just don't know what's so difficult about letting them know you've moved on!"

"I know, but it's easy for you. You don't have to consider anyone else."

"What exactly is it you're afraid of? Do they disapprove of me? Not want you to have a new relationship?" She continued prodding. "I thought I got on fairly okay anytime our paths have crossed. They didn't seem to have a problem with me."

"It's not that."

"Well then, what is it, because I sure as hell have no idea what's paralysing you. Unless you don't love me. Is that what it is?"

"No, that's not the problem. I do. Love you, that is."

"So is it their approval you want? Or you don't want to deal with any consequences if they don't?" She didn't even try to hide the irritation that had entered her voice. "This is worse than pulling teeth. What's wrong with you? Can you not give me a reason? They're American, after all. Hardly bothered by the usual Irish parochial concerns. What the neighbours might think is not something that is likely to bother any of them."

"I don't know what to say to you."

His predictable feeble retreat from all questioning. No change there. Even to him it must sound weak. It was weak. But what irritated her most was how strong a stone wall it was. And he stuck to it. The conversation never went any further. Each time he avoided dealing with the situation he'd have a reason, according to himself. An excuse, according to her. Confrontation always saw him play the silent card, something she often wondered if he was aware of doing. The subtle technique to put her in the role of the nagging wife. Something she was not. Neither wife, nor nagging. No, she didn't think it was deliberate. He wasn't conniving. Just spineless. The *drip, drip, drip* of so many watered-down excuses had the inevitable consequences. A gradual eroding of her respect, as the weakness of the man beneath the excuses emerged.

It was during this slow process of inaction that the telegram from Ireland arrived, and telegrams only ever meant one thing. Bad news. A certain flutter of excitement always accompanied the dread of opening a telegram.

The increased pounding under her ribs caused her fingers to tremble as she split it open. Her mother was ill. How serious it didn't say. It was the order to come home that worried her.

"But she was alright when you were there only a couple of months ago, Aunt Jo, wasn't she?" Eileen looked at her aunt for reassurance. "You didn't detect anything, did you?"

"No, she was fine. She didn't mention anything was the matter." Johanna patted her niece's back. "No need to panic yet. You just go and organise your passage and I'll iron these clothes for you and you can start packing."

Chapter 34

County Clare

By the time she arrived in Clare her mother was already a week in the grave.

"Why didn't you let me know she was so ill?"

"Didn't you get the telegram?" Her father looked at her with a face that told her he considered he had done his duty.

"She'd been ill for weeks and you never told me."

"What was the point? What help could you be over there in the United States of America with your big job?"

His ability to put everyone else in the wrong clearly hadn't left him.

"I'm a waitress in a café. I'd have come home."

"And what were you going to do when you got here? You could hardly have stopped her dying now, could you?"

"Did it not occur to you that I might have liked to see her before she died? To talk to her? To say goodbye?"

"Well, maybe you should have thought about that when you

took yourself off. Any of us could have died while you were over there enjoying yourself."

"Pity it had to be her then." The force of the words as they burst out shocked even herself. She looked at her father in dismay.

"What the hell do you mean by . . . ?" Thomas's mouth began to droop slightly at one corner and Eileen watched in horror as he started to crumple to the ground. Like a cardboard box folding down on one side, all happening in slow motion.

Frozen for a few seconds, she managed to react, rushing forward just in time to ease the fall, so that he hit the floor gently. She recognised the stroke, had seen it happen once before in the restaurant. A man's face collapsing as he tried to speak, making no sense, before his son caught him as he slid off the chair.

She wiped the glob of porridge from his chin and waited for him to swallow before feeding him the next spoonful. His green eyes followed her every movement, so she kept her expression neutral. Always a struggle, but her Catholic upbringing forced her to make the effort. The bit of kindness. Show a bit of compassion, even if she didn't feel like it.

"Jesus said, '*Do unto others as you would have them do unto you*'." She could still hear the nun's voice. It always sounded easy when you were a child. Not something you'd ever question. Add a few years and the reality soon puts you to the test.

If he'd been a stranger she'd have had no difficulty. Could have managed it with warmth in her eyes and the occasional smile. But for her father she hated having to do things for him. Personal things. The feeding bit was probably the easiest. She couldn't even contemplate the washing. His clothes, yes, but her brothers could deal with his physical hygiene. Take turns with that. Not something she could or would ever engage in. Not with what she knew.

The urge was always there, the impulse to shout out what she really felt. She managed to keep it under control, but sometimes she had visions of herself shoving her face close up to his and spitting it out straight into the middle of his dial.

"You made our lives a bloody misery. The way you treated Mam. The way you tried to control us!"

Possibly the only thing that stopped her was that she had more of her mother's genes in her than she realised. More of his and she might have done it. Had she inherited his qualities it would probably have meant that she wouldn't now be in this position. She'd just have left him there on his own to rot.

She hadn't always felt like this about him. She remembered a time when she'd loved her father, enjoyed doing things with him. He'd made learning new things fun. Growing vegetables and crops. Barley with the beards. The all-seeing eyes of the potato. He was comical sometimes, made them laugh. That fun had stopped around the time when Dorothy was minding them, but Eileen didn't tie it up with that. Not back then. Didn't know what had happened nor why, or that it had anything to do with him. So, he still remained 'her daddy'.

Bestowing upon himself the full title, Constable with the Royal Irish Constabulary, he would always emerge the hero of each tale.

"Tell me 'bout when you were a constal, Daddy?" With the curiosity of a child, Eileen couldn't hear enough of his stories. "You were the best policeman in Ireland, weren't you, Daddy?"

"Oh, not just in Ireland. In the world, child, in the world."

Too young to recognise groundwork being laid for control of their lives, Eileen idolised him. Daddies always knew best and their childhood discipline didn't appear to be anything out of the ordinary. He'd never beaten them, not like some of her school friends whose fathers took the leather belt to them. No, he'd just make a run at them and maybe give a light swipe on the back of their legs with his hand. Nothing that hurt, just a warning. Big, handsome and strong, that was her memory of that time, even if sometimes she had been a little afraid of him. It was more the tone of his voice and the way his face went hard sometimes, and the way that his will was always the ruling one, even when her mother suggested something else. That was the bit, the control, she'd failed to understand back then.

His exercise of power took on a different face that only emerged as they got older. At least that was how she remembered it. Maybe it had been there always, but they'd been too young to recognise it. More evident when they were of an age to challenge him, when they wanted to do things and go places with their friends. As they began to question things it became clear there was no room for anyone else's opinion. Only one way to do things. His way.

"No one knows how to do anything right 'cept you, Daddy." Her own childish words, the innocence in them long forgotten. A very different tone when coming from the mouth of a teenager, especially with the little addition. "Is that the way it's to be then? No-one else is entitled to a view, I suppose?"

It hadn't been just adventure that she'd longed for. It had been that, but even more so it had been escape. Far away from the hypocrisy. The two-facedness of it all, while all the time strutting his stuff as the perfect pillar of the community.

He had forbidden most things. No knitting on a Sunday. No servile work allowed the Lord's Day. Except when it suited him to have them carry out chores for him. No going out dancing for his daughters until he decided they were old enough.

"Where's the harm in it, Thomas?" their mother had tried to intervene. "Sure they're old enough and they'll only be young once."

"I'll decide when they're old enough."

She'd seen the sharp look he'd shot at her mother.

When they eventually won the battle, the freedom was only allowed until midnight on a Saturday night, when he would wait for them outside the ballroom and walk them home. His stranglehold quenched all possibilities for fun and diversion. What made it worse was that his rigid regime only applied to the members of his family, not to his own life. No, he could do as he pleased. What he'd not known was that his daughter had become aware of his 'other' life.

It was around this time that she understood the brief snatches overheard through the walls down through the years: '. . . *womanising . . . no respect . . . the children might hear . . . keep your voice down.*' It made sense now, but at the time, while she didn't know exactly what was happening, her instinct told her it wasn't good. She'd burrowed under the eiderdown and pressed her fingers into her ears until the wax stuck to the tips. No matter how she tried to wipe the words from her memory, they stuck with a stubbornness she didn't quite understand.

By the time she got the real picture it was too late. Any effort on her part to intervene between them was met with a '*This is none of your business. It's between your mother and me.*' The damage was done. What she had witnessed had been the slow dismantling, brick by brick, of her mother's spirit. With no wish to make things worse, she watched helpless, as the heart to defy him seeped out of her mother. It was all too late when she realised that he had broken Catherine as effectively as if he had taken a sledgehammer to her, even though he'd never laid a hand on her. Her mother's only defence appeared to have been to ignore him and concentrate on showing the children as much love as she could, in the hope that it might help cushion his harshness. Eileen could see now how this must have been the only weapon left to her and she had used it to the best of her capabilities.

From the moment she understood just what his 'other' life was and that he had gone so far as to taint their family life with it, she was fearful that in a moment of anger she might allow it all to spill out. This fear of revelation had not been to protect him, but to spare her mother the grief of realising that her daughter knew.

She had once tried to draw up the subject of what might have happened to Dorothy, but the momentary flash of distress that she caught, before the expression on Catherine's face blocked her out, told her there was to be no opening up that wound.

As she fed him now, she tried to remember the good parts. Otherwise, she might be tempted to shove the spoon down his throat.

Chapter 35

The rough clay on the recently dug grave had dried out to a pale yellowish-grey after the dry spell. The late afternoon sunshine fell soft on the surrounding headstones lending an air of peace to the area.

After they had cleared the withered flowers from the grave and taken them to the bin, Eileen sat herself on the kerb stone of an adjacent grave, pen and paper in her hand.

"What year was she born?"

"Well, she wasn't 70, I think she was 69." Mary did a quick calculation. "Or maybe it was 68, I'm not sure."

"We can check it later. Her baptismal certificate is probably in the box at home. Or we can look in the back of that Bible she had. She always made notes of dates there." Eileen stood up. "Why are we doing this anyway? There's no headstone up yet. They won't put one up for months, not until the ground has settled."

"Well, I want to work it all out now while you're still here. Before you go back to America. The lads are useless at this sort of stuff. They never seem to be able to remember anything."

"I doubt that I'll have much choice now, will I?" Eileen rolled her eyes.

"What do you mean, choice about what?" Mary looked at her sister. "What? You mean you'd think of staying here?"

"Don't look so relieved." Eileen grinned at her. "I know you. You were afraid to ask me but hoping I'd say that, weren't you?"

"Of course I was, but I could hardly ask you to give up your life over there now, could I?" Her smile faded as she raised her eyebrows. "But are you really serious? You'd stay and look after him?"

"I'll give it a try. For a while anyway and see how it goes. But I'm warning you, if I feel the urge to murder him coming over me I'll be gone, before I do something I might regret." Eileen laughed. "Well, maybe something I mightn't regret. But it'll be over to you then, big sister, because I won't be serving time for him." She heaved herself upright. "And just so we're clear, I don't intend doing it alone, or full time. I'll want my days off, so you and the lads can work that one out between yourselves. Now, come on, let's see how they did it on other headstones."

They wandered off in different directions, stepping cautiously around the kerbings, careful not to trip on any hidden edges, many half concealed by the long grass that surrounded the older, long-forgotten ones.

"It's awful difficult to read some of them, they're so worn."

"Here, over here, Eileen. This is a more recent one. Look!" Mary waited until her sister had picked her way over. "The first person seems to need more space, that includes the address – the others that follow then only need two lines." Mary moved along the row, checking the inscription on the adjoining gravestones. "That seems to be the way on most of them."

"Some of them don't put the address. I think we should. Otherwise she could be anyone. There's an awful lot of O'Briens." Eileen wrote a few notes. "At least he agreed to have her buried here, near Granny and the rest of them. Let me just check how the Knocknageeha crowd did it." She stepped over a few of the graves. "Ah, yeah, they've the address on it. Funny how you forget these things, or don't even notice them. Anyway, how did you manage to persuade him?"

"Persuade him of what?"

"To allow her be buried here in the Abbey."

"With difficulty, I can assure you. But the lads weighed in and he was forced to back down, otherwise she'd have been on her own in that bleak place where his folks are buried." Mary paused. "I don't know why he was even pushing that, because he never had a good word to say about them. He just kept saying there was room in that grave."

"Oh, knowing him, he probably didn't want to have to pay for a new plot. At least she's among her own here. And strange as it might sound, it's lovely, look at the view – not that it'll be of much interest to her now." Eileen folded the piece of paper and slipped it into her pocket. "Why did none of you tell me she was so ill?"

"Daddy didn't want us to tell you. In case you worried."

"But there *was* something to worry about. She was dying!"

"I know. But we didn't realise that at the time. He made light of her illness." Mary thought for a moment. "In fairness to him, I don't think he did it deliberately. Keeping it from us. She wasn't sick for long. At least we didn't notice, but there had been a gradual slowing down of her heart. I don't think he even wanted to admit it to himself."

"Yeah, I know. Aunt Jo said she didn't see any signs when she was over on her visit – said Mam was fine. But I think she was as worried as I was when I got the telegram." She gazed down at the grave.

"But you're right, Eileen, we should have told you. At least that she was ill. But the way it was, we weren't expecting her to go, well, certainly not quite so quickly. I thought you'd have plenty of time to get back."

"But I was left out of it completely. You even went ahead with the funeral and you knew I was on my way." A tear of frustration trickled out of the corner of Eileen's eye.

"He wouldn't let us wait." Mary's eyes filled. "You know what he's like. I did try. You know the way he is when he gets a thing into his head. The boys tried too, but he was having none of it. Even the priest tried to persuade him. But he'd listen to no-one. Insisted on rushing ahead."

"You should just have ignored him, Mary, and contacted me earlier anyway."

"I know that now. I'm sorry, Eileen. I should have."

The misery on Mary's face stopped her from saying anything more. The same look she remembered on her mother's when she knew she should have intervened between Thomas and the children.

"That's why I want you to be in on the inscription for the headstone. He's hardly in a position to object now." Mary gave a weak smile.

"It's like it hasn't happened. I can't believe I'll never see her again." Eileen looked at the freshly dug earth. "I can't even cry. As if my head hasn't taken it in. Like it's just a bad dream and I'm going to wake up from it."

"I'm sorry." Mary put her hand on Eileen's shoulder and rocked her gently.

"I feel I've missed out. You're all at a different stage and it's as if I'm just joining you for the afters. Like something I wasn't part of, and now I can't catch up."

Even as she said it Eileen realised that she could never catch up, even if she spent the rest of her life trying to bridge the gap. Everyone had moved on from that motionless time after death, that stillness that follows after the worst has happened. She remembered it after her grandmother died, that interval when the earth seems to stop revolving in the way it normally does, after the last breath is drawn and the calm descends. The therapeutic healing of the wake was denied her, the slowed pace that settles alongside the busyness of the funeral arrangements. Plans jettisoned, no longer important, everyone involved in the sharing of memories. All except her. Her father had seen to that.

Mary picked a couple of stray dead flowers that had fallen from the bundle they'd discarded while Eileen stood at the foot of the grave making no move to help her. She gazed at the dried earth their clearing had exposed, glad when Mary took the remaining strays off in the direction of the heap of dead vegetation over in the corner behind the last row of graves. She wanted to be alone for a while, to wallow in the emptiness engulfing her.

She'd have been happy to come home to look after her mother for however long that might have been. At least that was what she thought she was returning for. Hadn't really gone beyond that. Left now with the feeling that she had been tricked. The limbo she found herself in scared her. Nothing to go back to in America. Only now was that becoming clear. She couldn't face the thought of returning. The prospect of trying to pick up the few strands that remained of her life again over there tired her. The motivation to start up afresh was gone. She might meet a new man if she returned. More chance there than here at home. But was that what she really wanted? The thought of putting work into a new relationship depleted her energy further. She was so tired. And it wasn't just the travelling. All she could see as she looked back at her experience to date – a general disappointment with the species. Nothing to return to in America. Looking after her father had never entered her head. Even if she'd had a plan, that would definitely never have formed any part of it.

She glanced over at Mary and was relieved to see her chatting to a woman washing down a headstone. By her relaxed stance, leaning against the edge of the granite monument, Eileen knew that Mary was in no hurry to get back to her now that she'd agreed to stay.

Over the following days she tossed possibilities around in her head and waited for one of the others to suggest options, but the silence had been deafening. Obvious that they were all waiting for her to make the offer. She knew Mary would already have discussed it with them, so knowing she was planning on staying made it all too easy for them to see her as the obvious solution.

She'd spent the days considering and had hopped from just accepting her fate to thinking that she just couldn't do it. And what if she chose the latter? Maybe one of the others would be forced to offer. But unlike her, they, apart from John, had spouses and children. She could hardly inflict their father on them and John had enough on his plate with the farm work. He'd never have time to look after an invalid, especially a demanding one.

Putting him into the County Home was an option. A tempting one. Doing so might not be quite so simple, maybe raising even more problems. As no-one had mentioned an alternative solution she had no idea if they'd thought about it, or how they might react if she were to suggest it. The problem if she did manage to put her father in, was that living in a community where they would undoubtedly think her callous, would corrode what remained of her own life.

"*He's up there in the County Home.*" She could already hear the neighbours' comments. Had heard the disparaging remarks about other families in the past. "*Wouldn't you think one of them would have looked after him at home?*" She could write the script. "*Would you look at her. Back up there in the home-place, free as a bird, and leaving her father to rot in the County Home. What sort of a daughter is she at all?*"

It would be hard to live with that in the background. So for the moment, it looked like she'd have to step into the breach, temporarily anyway, until she had a better plan.

In a twist of fate she could recognise that, despite her every effort, he still controlled her.

THOMAS

Chapter 36

The tartan rug had slipped and was threatening to fall to the floor. He'd have to call her if that happened. Not something he wanted to do. With his good hand he caught the corner and adjusted it, pulling it up further over his knees and tucking it securely between the arm and the cushion of the armchair. She'd left the kitchen door open so he could see John at work out in the yard. Every so often the dog would wander in and sit for a few minutes by his chair, looking up, hoping for a pat on the head. He seemed to know which side to position himself, as if sure of getting a rub of the good hand behind the ears. After a minute of stroking he stopped, knowing that if he paused long enough, the dog would stand up and lay his chin on his knee, hoping to prolong the contact. He preferred it that way. Less of a stretch. His good arm was inclined to tire easily these days, probably from overuse, not that he was doing anything much now. It had probably just got lazy but, still, it had to do the work of two.

"Atta boy." He rubbed the silky head and watched the brown eyes close in ecstasy, opening only when he stopped. The words were sometimes a bit of a jumble, he was aware of that, had to be, the way the muscles in his mouth and tongue didn't always do what he wanted, but it didn't seem to affect the dog's pleasure. The pleading look from the dog's eyes was all the communication needed between them for him to recommence the stroking.

His mind wandered back, dipping in and out of his life, sometimes idling over inconsequential details. He'd blanked out most of his childhood. That had been easy enough to achieve with a busy life and adopting an attitude, a belief, that there was no profit in looking backwards, especially when there was nothing to be gained. With all the physical activities that had kept him going no longer available to him, nothing to do now but sit here and be waited on, snatches sometimes came back, but always with bits missing. Never able to remember the whole incident. He wasn't sure if it was the stroke or if it was the result of the blotting out of the past that had done it. There'd never been any need to dwell on them. They were all dead. And probably just as well. The fragments that came back now were just chippings, like the stray slivers of wood that might shoot out from the fall of an axe. Hard to make sense of them, dots that never joined up.

"*I'll show you who's boss!*"

It was a shout he heard often. Could still hear it, the harsh tone of his father, but not remember any of the detail of the occasions when it was used. No recollection of what had occurred that set off the roar, but the intention was always clear.

"*Would you leave the lad alone? He's not doing a bit of harm.*"

Harder to recall the tone of his mother's voice.

"I'm telling you, woman! Chastise the child or he'll chastise you later!"

He didn't understand what the words meant, not until he was about thirteen or so, but he could still hear the breathy voice in his ears, as vivid as if the words had just been spoken. His body numbed beyond feeling, he had no memory of the pain of the slash of the lash, just the visual picture of it travelling through the air, before his mother intervened and put an end to the whipping. The fury in her face, a gift to him, as she wrestled the thin willow rods from his father, whose pocked face, ruddy with sweat, was frozen in surprise at her sudden attack.

"I swear if you do that again I'll kill you!" She held the rods, one hand at each end, flexing them, as if ready to launch a beating.

The slack mouth of his father suddenly tightened. He could remember the string of saliva that hung in a foam from his lip. Like a rabid dog.

"If you had your way you'd have him growing up soft!" With a wicked glare at her he spat on the ground before turning and stomping off around the corner of the barn.

Sometimes it came back to him like that. Other times it melted into another scene where he could see his father turn and slink off like a beaten cur who knew his reign of terror was over. He didn't know which was the true version. All he knew was that when his mother died, the beatings recommenced more fiercely.

The night the lamb died was when he made his decision. Or rather the next day when he had to break the news to his father.

"There was nothing I could do. It was half dead when it came out."

"You should have called me when the ewe was struggling."

"I did. I went up and called you but you were so drunk you must have fallen asleep again, because you never came, so I had to do it myself."

"God Almighty, accusing me, is it? My fault now is it that you couldn't even deliver a live animal? How did I raise such a useless son?"

"I'm not the useless one here. I could hardly leave the ewe to go and wake you again, now could I?"

"*I'm your father! Don't you speak to me like that, you little pup!*"

It was when his father turned to grab the brush leaning against the kitchen wall that he made his split-second decision and ran from the room. This was never going to happen again.

He knew where the stash was kept. The money from the beasts his father had sold. Under the mattress, as if it wasn't the most obvious place that a burglar might search. He might as well have nailed a sign to the gate.

He was surprised there was so much. It was separated into three paper bags, two of them grease-strained and soiled, as if he'd taken the money out with grubby hands and counted it before putting it back into its hiding place. To remain there until he, himself, wanted it. When his mother had been alive, she must have had some way of wheedling a few notes from him but it escaped him as to how she might have managed that. Maybe she just helped herself to the odd one now and again without him noticing. The food would be down to nearly nothing before he'd part with a note to restock the cupboard.

Now, it gave him pleasure to help himself to enough notes to see himself through until he got sorted. When he had counted them, he paused. Maybe a little more, just in case. Counting out a few more notes he put the remaining money back into two of the bags. The empty one would be evidence enough to torment his father. A certain pleasure in this little act of revenge. Knowing he'd taken only what was due to him for his unpaid work and the little extra for the suffering he'd had to endure, he shoved the grimy parcels back in their hiding place.

A few things into a bag and then he was off.

As soon as he'd buried his father and the paperwork was done, he sold the place. Couldn't bear to pick up the reins and take over. There was a certain satisfaction in the knowledge that there was no-one else to run it other than himself and he'd no intention of doing that. The farm that his father had always boasted about down in the pub – *'The best farm of land in the county . . .'* He had no idea how the neighbours mimicked him behind his back.

He was the last man to close the gates and all his father's own fault. This retribution should have him turning over in his grave. A fair penalty. That the farm had been part of his father's heritage made it easy to walk away and leave the past behind. He wasn't sure what he'd have done had it been his mother's.

He'd left no note for his father when he left. Let him wonder. It wouldn't have been long before he'd heard from the neighbours where his son had gone. A few years working with his mother's brother, helping out on his uncle's farm, enough to keep a roof over his head, while he did his training with the Constabulary. Better to have a second string to your bow. The uncle's arthritis had him fairly crocked and while the hired farm hand was able to keep the place ticking over, just about, he wasn't getting any younger either. By the time he'd finished the police training, Thomas found himself using all his off-duty time helping out, but there were no other relatives and he had the future in mind. Lots of hard work now, a down-payment for his future, a thought that made it easy to just get on with it. Eventually it would pay off. And the uncle was grand – easy-going and appreciative of the extra labour. When the uncle died, he'd fallen on his feet – as he'd presumed. Inheriting the place meant that he was able to leave the Constabulary behind. A farm of land and a house without the same ugly memories. A man of property now, the future was his. Nobody was ever going to exert control over him again. Not a parent, nor a boss. He could do whatever he wanted with his life.

For someone who believed in never looking backwards, now that he'd nothing else to occupy him, the strength to push back the stray thoughts that had begun to torment him seemed to have deserted him.

He could now see something of his mother in Catherine. Although a much more timid version, the way Catherine had stood up to him when he tried to control things was similar. Especially as the children got older. Maybe he'd treated her badly. Must have had that bit of his father in him. Could have been nicer. A bit kinder. His own mother had defended him but then she went and died and he only a young chap. Left him to the mercies of a tyrant. But that wasn't Catherine's fault. Too late now to regret that. Anyway, it hadn't been all bad. Everything had been okay until the children got to an age when they talked back to him, hadn't it?

There were times when he could settle with that, but not for very long. The whole Dorothy thing kept pushing itself to the fore, smothering the good thoughts of how it used to be with the children when they were small. That had been a big mistake. Didn't know what had come over him, but he'd had a few drinks on him at the time. Things sort of went off the rails after that. In for a penny, in for a pound. What would have been the point in trying to win back any respect after that? Catherine had made it clear what she thought of him. There was no marital action after that. She didn't put him out of the bed, but told him it was only to spare the children knowing, to stop them asking questions. As far as he knew she'd told no-one but always the threat of revealing it was there. But then there was always the worry as to what Dorothy might say. That had never gone away. Didn't know if he could have trusted that one. Anyway, any shenanigans after that he'd kept well outside the family.

EILEEN

Chapter 37

She didn't know it then but the problem was to be more temporary than she could have expected. She busied herself working through the house, room by room. It was clear that her mother mustn't have been feeling well for quite some time. None of the freshness that she remembered remained in the house. Every room had a tiredness, a dullness about it. Not just the passage of time, rendering it old-fashioned, no, it had a general uncared-for atmosphere. Funny, Aunt Johanna hadn't mentioned that, although maybe she hadn't called to the house. Probably only met up with Catherine in Art and Ellen's. The light covering of dust on the rooms that were rarely used now and a griminess on the windows and on the surfaces of those rooms that were, showed the lack of her mother's touch.

"Sorry about the state of the place, Eileen." John looked at her, shamefaced.

"Oh, typical. Men!" She made light of it. "I'll soon have it back in shape. But you're going to have to smarten yourself up, John.

See those shoeboxes over there? That's all the paperwork you've left all over the place. I don't know anything about it, looks like it's mostly farming stuff, so you're going to have to get your head stuck into it and sort it out."

"Yeah. It just all got on top of me and you know the Da. He never believed in any of that 'nonsense' as he called it."

"Well, you can make a start on it this evening." She softened. "Times have changed, John. You and Tommy are making those decisions now, and he's not exactly in a position to complain. I'll give you a hand to sort the backlog."

"Thanks, Eileen. I'm sure this isn't what you came home for."

"You're dead right it's not. But the paperwork will be the easiest part. I'm good at that."

For the first few weeks of being cooped up with her father she kept a tight rein on her impatience, although if she were honest she'd have to admit that he'd become more docile. Not the man she'd been accustomed to.

The sharpness had gone out of his green eyes. That seemed to have faded into a vulnerability, the way he looked at her sometimes as she helped him. She no longer had to feed him. Now that he'd got back a little use of one arm, she'd made him feed himself after she'd cut up the meat. He'd bucked at this when she first introduced the change and it had taken a while for him to get the hang of it. But despite the protests, she persevered, and didn't react when, in the early days, he'd throw down the fork in frustration if the food fell off it. She just calmly handed him a clean one. She fought against the traces of humanity she felt seeping back into her bones, anxious that the anger at his having excluded her from the recent events might disappear too quickly. She couldn't allow that to happen, not before it had had time to disperse at her own pace. He wasn't going to control that. Knowing she was being childish, she couldn't help herself because it wasn't just that, there was all the rest as well. Not so easily jettisoned. Not a lot of time available to ponder over those grudges now, with all the busyness of tending to his daily needs and giving Tommy and John a hand at keeping the place going. Now that they were down one, they must be missing his input to the farm. She had to give him that. He'd always been a worker.

The doctor had told her that now that it had happened once, it would be more likely that he could have another stroke. It was something that could easily occur again. And he wasn't wrong, although she hadn't expected it to be so soon. She was glad it happened when John was minding him that morning while she went to town.

The note on the kitchen table when she returned, telling her they had gone to the hospital alarmed her. The mention of the ambulance meant it was serious. She went out to the yard to search for Tommy but there was no answer to her calls. She tried to calm herself by considering that he might be up the fields, but with the evidence of abandoned machinery and the dog hanging around the front door she knew he too was gone.

By the time she got there it was too late. And she was relieved. The two brothers met her in the hallway of the hospital. A massive stroke this time. John had left him seated in the chair at home when he went out to the field. When he got back he found him on the floor. At first they thought he may have tried to stand up and simply fell, but later when the stroke had been confirmed, it seemed more likely that it might have been the force of it that caused him to lurch forward.

It wasn't just having avoided that violent end at home that was responsible for the relief. It was having missed her father's final moments in the hospital. Only home a couple of months. Everything had all happened too quickly. She wouldn't have known how to react. She knew she couldn't have held his hand or kissed him. Unsure if she could even have shown any empathy or felt anything. More likely she'd have been able to do nothing other than just stand there like a stone. There hadn't been enough time to sort out her feelings about him. One look at the faces of her brothers told her that their experience of him must have been different, or maybe they just didn't know as much as she did.

The relief of a reprieve from the future months and years that had loomed ahead came after his funeral. The freedom to stay or go.

She decided to stay.

He'd not been much more than a lad when she left for America, only half baked, so it had come as a nice surprise to discover the adult her brother now was.

John proved easy to live with. Like their mother. Did his own thing and, not being one to pull against the tide, he was easily led when she wanted to update things around the house. Never an objection from him and the fact that he was handy with his hands whenever she wanted shelves or cupboards built was a bonus.

Big into sport, and with not much of a social life built up yet for herself, she sometimes went along to see himself and Tommy play a hurling match on a Sunday afternoon. It was there she bumped into Seamus again.

He'd called over to the house when she first arrived home from Boston to express his condolences on the death of her mother. His warm hug after Thomas's funeral felt good and she could see from the overly long way he held her gaze that he still had feelings for her.

"What are you doing on the side-lines, Seamus? Not like you."

"Ah, the story of my life. Always on the side-lines."

"I doubt that somehow." She ignored the less than subtle insinuation.

"Anyway, what has you here? One of their best players. Or that's what you always told me anyway?" She laughed.

"Oh, still am." He grinned. "A knee injury, so I've been out of action a few weeks now. I'm hoping to get back playing next month."

"So there's nobody in his life then?" She quizzed her brother later as she prepared the tea.

"Not recently, as far as I know. But you needn't think he's been pining away all these years. No, he's been busy enough in that area." John smirked at her. "So you might be still interested then?"

"I was only asking." She glanced up from the loaf of bread she had started cutting. "I'll kill you if you say anything to him."

"Oh, you needn't worry." John grinned. "He's been asking me about you too."

"Has he now?" She was pleased. "And what was he asking?"

"Asked me about your love life in America.."

"Be very careful now, I said I'd kill you." She waved the knife at him. "What did you tell him? Now, John, what exactly did you say?"

"I'm only joking. He didn't ask me that." He laughed. "I just knew that would get you. No, he just hinted at it. Just half checking that there was no-one. Skirted around it. I think he was wondering if you'd go out with him. So I said I'd ask you." He looked at her. "Well, would you, or wouldn't you? What'll I tell him?"

"Well, you can tell him that if he's not man enough to ask me himself the answer is . . . a big *'NO'*."

"So you would then, am I right?" He raised an eyebrow. "I'll tell him so."

"Tell him what you like. I can hardly stop you." She handed him the plate of bread. "Here, take that over to the table and I'll make the tea."

DOROTHY

Chapter 38

County Wexford
1932

The years had softened Maude. The scratchiness between mother and daughter had reduced, not suddenly, but gradually over the years since Cornelius died. Dorothy often wondered if it was the acceptance that her daughter seemed destined to be 'an old maid' as her mother had so eloquently put it, that had her draw in her horns and view the potential companionship in a different light. Someone to go places with, to do things with.

After Brendan, she'd managed to keep any potential suitors at arm's length, having made the mistake of breaking the man's heart, something that wasn't going to happen again. Lots of dancing partners, but dates outside of group activities were a thing of the past. Except for Henry.

"Mother, don't even think about it. It won't be happening." Dorothy could see the kernel of a hope settling in her mother's mind. "He's invited me to his sister's wedding. That's all."

"Well, you know what they say . . . *Going to a wedding is the makings of another'."*

"Stop it, Mother." Dorothy shot a look across the ironing board. "You're stuck with me for life, so get used to it."

"Well, he must have left the priesthood for something. That wasn't an easy thing to do. Did he ever tell you why?"

"It just wasn't for him, but you can stop poking around, Mother, because I can assure you he doesn't have designs on me." Dorothy gave a final press on the blouse before putting the iron down on the hearth. "There, that's all the ironing done."

"It can't have been easy for him though."

"You can't let it go, can you? Look, I'll take you out of your misery. There is nothing romantic going on between myself and Henry. He just likes a companion to do things with. And so do I, so there, Mother, forget anything more, because it won't be happening." She picked up the bundle of clothes and headed up the stairs.

It no longer bothered her, the occasional developing twinkle in her mother's eye. Once she'd hit forty, she'd closed the door permanently on any possibility of marriage or children. Something about that milestone gave her comfort. Not that she'd any doubt as to what the future might hold for her, it was more that the occasional vague uncertainty as to whether she'd made the right decision no longer crept into her mind. She had settled into her life now.

It hadn't rained for weeks and the sun baking the earth had yellowed the grassy route of the pilgrim pathway as they wandered around the island. She was glad that Maude didn't start up a chatter, but seemed happy to just wander along with her own thoughts, leaving herself and Henry to theirs and to enjoy drinking in the view.

A number of swans glided along the lake, adding to the sense of peace and solitude that surrounded them. Henry had suggested they go on a weekday and she could see why now.

He'd cemented his intentions, or lack of them, when he asked Dorothy if her mother would like to join them on a trip to Our Lady's Island that week. She was pleased that the suggestion had come from him. A chance to permanently wipe any residual trace of hope from Maude's head.

"But the pilgrimage isn't until August, Dorothy?" Maude, pleased at the invitation, but puzzled.

"I know, but he says it's much nicer when there are no crowds around." Dorothy looked at her mother. "We can pack a picnic and make a day of it." She paused. "Well, what'll I tell him? You'll come, won't you?"

"I will. Tell him I'd love to." Maude smiled at the thought. "I've only ever been there when there were crowds, so it'll be nice to see a different view of it."

"D'yeh know, Henry, I never knew the half of it. You're a great guide, even if the Cromwellian story was horrific. To burn down the church and to think he wasn't even satisfied with that but he had to massacre all the poor people as well?" Maude shook her head slowly. "What a savage! Can you just imagine those poor people, and they only looking for sanctuary on the island and he couldn't even let them have that."

"Tough times, Maude. I'll show you the Mass rock later, where they used to say the Masses." He picked up another sandwich. "This is a banquet fit for a king. The pair of you did a great job on the picnic."

"The least we could do, Henry, and you doing all the driving." Maude smiled across at him.

They sat in silence under the shade of the tree for a while eating. Dorothy lay back on the rug and looked up into the green canopy overhead, the sun's rays filtering through as she rested.

A faint breeze rustled the leaves.

"D'ye know, I think I can hear the voices of those Druid women from long ago."

"What are you on about, Dorothy?" Maude looked down at her daughter, her face screwed into a query.

"Listen. Listen to the leaves, it's like they're whispering." She paused. "Wouldn't you wonder what they're saying? Still there, those women, a thousand years on."

"Fanciful, you were always fanciful, Dorothy." Maude laughed and looked towards Henry. "Gets notions, that one."

It was one of the last memories she had of her mother.

"Thank you very much, Henry, that was delightful. I'd only ever been here when there were crowds. It was a totally different experience today. Just lovely. I'll remember it forever." There was a happy look on Maude's face as Henry dropped them home after their day out.

It was a great comfort that her final memory of her mother

wasn't of the pair of them scrapping over some trivial way of doing things at home. The end was sudden, but peaceful. A heart attack. Never a complaint leading up to it. Just a case of not waking up one morning when Dorothy took her up the usual cup of tea before her mother rose.

The brothers had taken on the job of organising the funeral, until she'd pulled herself together enough to sort out the domestic bit.

"I don't know what's wrong with me, Bridie. I can't seem to get myself together, to know where to begin."

Her sister, uncharacteristically the leader, had been the one to coax her into action.

"It's the shock, Dorothy. You were the one that found her, and it wasn't as though it was expected. She was as fit as a flea." Bridie tore off a sheet of paper and began making a list. "You're expecting too much of yourself – it only happened yesterday. But, come on, we'll make a start on it and leave Fonsie and the lads to sort out the rest of the stuff."

Within a couple of years, Henry too was gone. Had been offered a teaching job in Dublin which he took. Relations had improved with his family, following the years of shame they had attached to his leaving the priesthood.

"They've buried the hatchet, Dorothy. Time I went home, before it's too late. They're not getting any younger and, seeing that they want to welcome their only son back into the fold, it would be churlish not to meet them halfway on it."

In those early days, she missed him more than she realised she might, but the odd letter updating her on his news kept her in touch. The annual visit to stay with Nancy in Dublin always included an afternoon tea in a nice hotel of his choosing. Just what she needed, a nice companionable friendship, nothing more. No matter what Nancy might have preferred for her.

EILEEN

Chapter 39

County Wexford
1936

It was Dorothy who'd suggested that they holiday in Wexford for a change.

"It's years since you've been over, Eileen. Time you paid us a visit. At this stage you must have seen everything on that west coast that's worth seeing. It's not the only place worth visiting, let me tell you. We have the best beaches in the country here in Wexford. The sunny southeast. None of that drizzly rain that you're so used to over there in your side of the country. So how about it?"

"Not a chance, Dorothy. You couldn't match our side of the country."

"How would you know, Eileen? Sure, you never visit us. I'm the one who always goes over to you, and lovely and all as it is you need to come over here and I'll show you seasides! You've only ever seen Courtown, but there's miles and miles of a strand that stretches twenty miles, from Cahore southwards to Curracloe – nearly to Wexford town. Now beat that!"

"Well, maybe. We'll see."

Since Maude died, Dorothy had often invited them over to visit but somehow they'd never got around to making the journey. A niggle of guilt when she thought about it. The last few years must have been lonely enough for her cousin.

"Well, what's wrong with this year? I know it's late in the season, but why not make the most to the Indian summer?" Dorothy had pressed her. "Might be the last chance you get. It's not as though Monica is at school yet. Sure, she's not starting school until next year."

"How about we do it, Seamus?" She put it to him that evening. "Take the children over to Wexford for a holiday? Make the most of the good weather before the autumn really sets in." She knew he'd go along with whatever suggestion she made. "You've still a week's holiday to use up and God knows the winter will be long enough. I feel bad that we haven't been over to visit Dorothy. She always comes here to us. I think she misses her mother, even though she and Aunt Maude had a scratchy enough relationship."

"Wherever you like." Nodding behind his newspaper, happy enough that she'd do the organising and be content to follow. "Wexford sounds good to me. We can check out those nice beaches she's always boasting about. See how they measure up."

She watched him play in the waves with the children. As they splashed water up on him, he feigned terror and ran through the surf away from them. She admired the way he never seemed to tire of their childish games.

Second time around was better. And how easily, in her search for adventure, she'd have missed it. But then again she hadn't been ready that first time. The most useful thing she'd harvested from sowing her wild oats was a better level of maturity and a recognition that they didn't come any better than Seamus. Fortunate for her that his flame had never quenched and it hadn't taken long for hers to reignite.

"Far be it from me to give you a swelled head but, do you know, I often wonder something." She smiled up at him, shading her eyes from the sun as he walked up to where she was sunbathing on the rug.

"And what would that be now?"

"I often wonder how were you not snapped up all the years I was away? A fine cut of a man like yourself." She grinned.

"Oh, I came close to it. Numerous times. Just so *you* don't get a big head. Ah sure, they don't know what they missed." He shook himself over her. "Here, that'll cool you down."

"Would you get away. You're like a big dog." She laughed.

"Anyway, I've told you before, so what has you wondering about that after all these years?"

"I was just watching you there in the water with Monica and James. You're a great father. And you're not a bad husband either. I just feel lucky, I suppose. But spool back there a bit. Numerous times? Discuss."

"Ah well, maybe a bit of an exaggeration." He grinned.

"But seriously, Seamus, did you ever think about marrying?" She searched his face.

"Didn't I marry you?"

"Ah, you know what I mean. Like before I came back." She paused. "What if I hadn't come back?"

"I did think about it. Lots of times. Although, seriously, just once." He paused. "She was lovely. Down from Dublin on holiday and we were involved for a while, but she wasn't interested in a life in Clare and I didn't fancy moving to the city. It just sort of fizzled out. A long-distance relationship. It wouldn't have worked. I told you all that before."

"Yeah, I know, but sometimes I need reminding how lucky I am." Eileen propped herself up on her arms and looked down at the children still playing at the water's edge.

Seamus picked at the threads on the rug. "I don't know if I should tell you this . . ." He paused. "I didn't tell you this before, but she did write to me. Shortly after you came home. Out of the blue. Wondering if we could meet up again."

"And did you?"

"We did, but it didn't feel right. For me, anyway. You were there lurking somewhere at the back of my mind. Even if you hadn't come home I couldn't do that to her." He gave her a playful punch. "But then you were back here, so I had hopes. She did write again, shortly before we got married so I wrote back and told her about you and that was the end of it."

"Well, maybe then that was one of the good things my father did for me. Forcing me to stay and look after him. Otherwise I might have gone back to the States before I had the chance to recognise your worth." She stood up, scanning the beach for the children. "Where are that pair? Where have they got to? You're supposed to be watching them."

"I thought they were your children too?" His words were lost on her as she'd already started to run towards the water's edge.

"Come out of the water now, children! Before you shrivel up altogether. You know you weren't supposed to go back into the water without me or your daddy with you."

"Ah, Ma, just a few more minutes!"

She watched as Monica grabbed James' hand as a wave threatened to suck him under.

"No, out now, before one of you drowns. The tide is coming in." She beckoned firmly. "We're going to have the picnic now." As she knew it would, the mention of food did the trick.

"The brothers are heading off to the hurling match this afternoon. It's the county final down in Wexford Park. I've asked Seamus if he'd like to go with them and he jumped at the chance," Dorothy announced after the children had left the breakfast table.

"Oh, I bet he did. I think he's had enough of building sandcastles at this stage." Eileen could see from the look on Dorothy's face that she had a plan for themselves. "You're up to something?"

"I am. But first I wanted to get rid of the lads for the day, all of them." Dorothy grinned. "You, me, Monica and James are going to dine out for a change. A meal in the Taravie Hotel it is."

"Now there's a plan. I like your thinking, Dorothy."

"You'll be able to see my workplace. I'll just let the boys know they needn't come home here looking for a dinner this evening because there won't be one. The staff have gone on strike."

"Well, I'll break that bad news to Seamus and get a few bob from him to finance our banquet, and in the meantime maybe you'd round up the children, Dorothy, while I clear up here."

The two women sat on the bench, looking out towards the sea. The children had begged to be allowed to play along the harbour wall, but Eileen, knowing it would have Dorothy's nerves jangling, resisted their pleading.

"I said no. It's too dangerous. What if you fell in?"

"We're not going to fall in. I promise. I'll hold onto James' hand. Please?" Monica smiled, using all the charm she could dredge up. "Please, please, please?"

"You can't make a promise like that. You're not going to fall in on purpose, are you? No, the pair of you can go down onto the sand and play, when you've finished your ice creams. Where we can see you."

"Okay." The resigned note in her voice suggested she knew when she was beaten. "Come on, James. Let's go down and sit on the rocks."

He shoved the last of his ice cream into his mouth before reaching out a sticky hand for the safety of his sister's grasp.

The women sat in relaxed silence for a while.

"Do you think poor Bridie even remembers me?" Eileen said then. "Sometimes I have my doubts, she's so quiet."

"Ah, she does, Eileen. It's just that she's gone very quiet in herself – there's nothing wrong with her brain or her memory. But then you've got to remember she was in America when you were small so she wouldn't have had the chance to know you as a child like I did."

"I never thought about it like that, Dorothy. I suppose I really only met her as an adult and not often enough to have built up a relationship, like I have with you."

"I'd say that's it, but you're right, she has gone quiet. She's like that with everyone, but I know by the way she smiles when you call over how pleased she is to see you. You must see that. She often takes out postcards people have sent her over the years and she's shown me ones you sent her from the holidays over the years. She loves getting them. It's just that she's off in a world of her own a lot of the time."

"Yeah, she seems to be. I got a shock at first because the Bridie I remember was so different. But then, that was when Mickie Joe was around."

"Ah, she's content enough in herself now, although you wouldn't always get too much chat out of her, not like before. Although she enjoys your children. Seems to chat away no problem to them. And they loved going over to her the other day and helping her with baking the scones."

"Well, I think '*help*' might be stretching it a bit, Dorothy."

"It did Bridie good though, a bit of young company. But remember, it's a long time since you've seen her, Eileen, and a lot has happened." Dorothy shook her head. "She never really recovered after Mickey Joe's death. She'd had a hard life up to that, but that was the finish of her when he died. An awful thing to happen. Buried under the snow like that and we didn't know until it thawed and he was found. Poor Bridie. D'ye know, I don't think we knew the half of it."

"What do you mean, Dorothy – I thought he was lovely by all accounts?"

"Oh, he was, Eileen. One of the best. No, her life was good with him. I never saw her happier, but before that, her first husband Joseph getting drowned. They were very young and she only a month or so married. Ah no, poor Bridie had it tough." She gazed into the distance, remembering.

"I don't think she had it easy in America either. Did she ever talk about it?"

"Not a lot. Just things in general, like the places she saw and working in Uncle Hugh's shop and living with Aunt Johanna. But now you mention it, she never told us much." She looked at Eileen. "What makes you say that?"

"Nothing really, just a few things Aunt Johanna hinted at."

"Like what?"

"Well, I don't think the marriage to that fellow Seán was too happy. And losing her daughter." Eileen glanced at Dorothy, unsure if she'd said too much. "Aunt Johanna never elaborated, but I just gleaned that life over there was harsh on Bridie and maybe that's why she came home."

"Yes, probably that's why she never wanted to talk about it. Ah, she deserved the years of happiness she had with MJ, especially after America. She never told us half the hardship she'd had over there. Ah sure, I suppose we all have our little secrets." Dorothy stood up from the bench. "Come on, we'd better check on those children."

Chapter 40

"A pity she'd never married and had children of her own. She'd have made a lovely mother." Eileen watched them out through the window – the children going off over the fields, hand in hand with Dorothy.

"Who are you talking about, Eileen?" Seamus took his boots off on the mat and, picking up the bucket, walked across the floor in his stocking feet and emptied the potatoes into the sink.

"Oh, Seamus, you might have rinsed them out in the yard first! You've brought half a field of clay in with you." She scooped them from the sink and tipped them back into the bucket. "Here, take that out and run the water over the spuds outside." She passed the bucket back to him. "Dorothy. I was talking about Dorothy. Look at the way Monica's face is turned up, drinking in her every word. It reminds me of the days when she came over to Clare to mind us when we were kids. How I couldn't get enough of her and her stories."

She pondered over it as Seamus disappeared out the door. Golden days. That was until Dorothy did the sudden flit.

In the years that followed, Dorothy had always stayed with Mary Ann and when she'd come over for Catherine's funeral she'd stayed with Art and Ellen.

As she stood there looking out the window, it came back to her. The innocent chance remark from Aunt Ellen, when she'd come back from America, a conversation that firmly stamped out any lingering doubts she might have had.

"Art, did you notice the coldness between Dorothy and Thomas at Catherine's funeral?"

"No, I noticed nothing." Art looked across at his wife in puzzlement.

"Oh, men, you never notice anything!" Ellen rolled her eyes and turned to Eileen. "I thought it was odd the way she'd hugged us all, but Thomas got nothing more than an icy nod. And then, at the 'afters' Dorothy helped out with the catering. I was watching and I noticed that she never went towards him with the plate of sandwiches." Ellen paused. "Of course, you weren't there, Eileen. That was terrible. Imagine that, missing your own mother's funeral. That must have been awful for you."

"Ah, woman, you're imagining things!" Art glanced over at her, a warning in his eyes.

"No, I'm not. I definitely detected something. Not that I'd be too keen on Thomas myself." Ellen put her hand to her mouth and the colour rose up her neck. "Oh God, I'm sorry, Eileen. I'd forgotten for a minute there that he's your father."

"Don't worry about it, Ellen. I know Dorothy's not too keen on him either." Eileen nodded.

Not a subject to broach with Dorothy. Best to leave sleeping dogs lie. Nothing good would come of it. Of that she was certain.

A pattern had developed. There had been no planning. After that first time on the Wexford holiday, it all just seemed to fall into place each summer. Dorothy made an annual visit westwards to Clare and every second year Eileen and Seamus took the children on a visit to the east coast.

From the start, Dorothy insisted they stay in the farmhouse, although Eileen felt that it might be too much of an invasion to have four of them crowding her out.

"Why don't we rent a place nearby?"

"Indeed you will not. Sure, there's only Fonsie and myself here, and knowing my brother he'll be glad to have someone other than me to talk to. It's nice for him to have a man staying for a change."

"It's not Seamus I've my doubts about. The pair of them get on well. It's the children. I know Fonsie is easy-going, but he wouldn't be used to that. They might drive him mad."

"Not at all, sure he's as relaxed as they come. If he was any more laidback, sure he'd be dead. No, you'll all stay here, Eileen."

1945

It surprised Eileen that even as her children became teenagers they still wanted to go over to Dorothy's for holidays and loved when she came to Clare. The year they'd had a trip to Killarney planned the children had objected to going with them.

"We don't want going off with you two old fogies! What would we be like with our mammy and daddy? Bored stiff, that's what." Monica smiled but the firm set of her jaw confirmed she meant business. "We'll only go if Dorothy comes too." She looked at her mother. "Well? Are you waiting for me to write to her or will you?"

"Okay, okay. It's well I don't take offence easily. I'll ask her." She grinned. "What age do you think Dorothy is then? She's much older than your old fogie parents."

"Yeah, but she's fun." Monica dodged the tea towel that Eileen swung at her.

"Get off with you! You're not too old for me to take the wooden spoon to you." She laughed as Monica took the writing pad from the dresser drawer.

"Now where is that pen?" She slapped the pad down on the table and looked around. "Ah, here it is. Now get to it, Mother!"

The *'holidays with Dorothy'* as they were always referred to, formed part of family lore, especially the Galway and Kerry ones.

"Are you sure Seamus doesn't mind me tagging along every year, Eileen?"

"Not at all, Dorothy. Don't you know he loves you? And it's not exactly as if you're getting in the way of any romance. I think we've passed that stage."

"I wouldn't like to feel I'm butting in on your family time though."

"I can assure you he prefers a bit of adult conversation. It beats taking 'lip' all day from two bolshie teenagers. No, he loves you joining us, you can be sure of that In fact, he's always the first one to ask if you're coming."

"Maybe he's hoping you'll say I'm not?" She laughed.

"Oh no, Dorothy, the memory of that wet week in Dingle has never left him." Eileen smiled over at her cousin. "I think there would definitely have been murders had you not been there. Remember that one?"

The rain had never let up except for the occasional unexpected blast of sunshine when the mist lifted and they could at last see the landscape, if only for a few minutes. Dorothy had bought them plastic raincoats and took them all out of the rented house a few times. The promise of fish and chips for tea at the end of their hike was enough to lure the children. Eileen had been grateful for her insistence. Otherwise they'd only have a wet week of misery and whinging to look back on, with herself and Seamus getting increasingly irritated with their squabbling.

When it came to the farmhouse holiday in Spiddal she wasn't sure if Dorothy would be bothered, but the children seemed keen on the idea.

"Well, living on a farm, sure she could have gone into that business herself."

"Well, ask her." Monica was insistent. "I'm sure she's well capable of telling you if she's not interested."

Eileen was surprised by Dorothy's enthusiasm.

"Of course I'd love to join you. Won't it be nice to spend a week on a farm and not having to feed calves or lambs or be cooking a dinner for the lads! I'll be able to sit back and watch someone else do it." Dorothy laughed. "Tell me, what part of that would I not like? Oh, you can count me in. That's if it's alright with you lot."

DOROTHY

Chapter 41

1953

The monthly pre-arranged telephone call to her niece in Clare was something Dorothy looked forward to. As she rode the two miles along the road to the post office, a gentle breeze puffed at the fresh green leaves of the hedgerows and blew down some of the white blossom of the blackthorns onto the roadside. Here and there she could see early signs of the flowers of the chestnut trees forming. Not long now and they would blossom into creamy candelabra to delight walkers who strolled along one of her favourite routes during the season.

As she cycled, she gathered the bits and pieces of news in her head so she wouldn't waste any of the few minutes of the phone call trying to recall the happenings of the last few weeks. When there was a lot of scattered news, she'd sometimes make a list and take it with her just so she wouldn't forget, but not a lot had happened recently, so there hadn't been any need. She hoped Eileen had more news for her.

She stood well back from the telephone box when she arrived, not wanting the man inside to think she might be listening to his conversation. He was the full of the box, a stained brown overcoat straining over his ample backside as he leaned forward onto the wooden ledge. She hoped it wouldn't break off with the weight of him. A farmer from a few miles out the road, she only knew him to nod to. The bike leaning against the wall of the post office was his. She recognised it. She'd sometimes seen him riding to the village, the tattered wicker basket strapped to the front handlebars of the bike, which was a few sizes too small for his generous torso. They exchanged nods as he exited the telephone box and he held the door open for her.

"Sorry for keeping you, missus."

"No problem at all. Sure you have to take the time to say what you have to say." She smiled at him.

Eileen picked up the phone immediately, as Dorothy knew she would. Same day, same time each month.

"She's pregnant, Dorothy!" Eileen blurted it out. No preamble. It all just shot out as soon as the operator had connected them. "She told us yesterday."

"Hold on there, Eileen, calm down. Who? Who are you talking about?" Dorothy knew it could only be about Monica, otherwise there wouldn't have been such panic in Eileen's voice.

"Monica, my daughter Monica, who else?" Eileen sounded annoyed.

Dorothy felt an old familiar churning inside her and, leaning back against the wall of the telephone box, took a breath. She glanced outside. Thankfully, no-one waiting to make a call. She didn't need an observer.

"Eileen, Eileen, stop now for a moment." Another big breath to quell an anxiety that could only be rising from some far distant familiar past. "Let's just take a minute, nothing is going to happen immediately."

"But Dorothy, this is a disaster, she's not even finished her teacher training."

"No, Eileen, you're wrong. A disaster is if she were dead, and she's not, now is she?" As she uttered the words, the sense of them calmed her. She paused.

"I suppose you're right, Dorothy, but you've no idea of the shock she gave us."

She could hear the slowing down of her niece at the other end of the phone. Little did Eileen know. "Am I right in thinking Martin's the father?"

"He is, of course. I could kill him. I could kill them both." Eileen voice rose.

"That wouldn't really help now, Eileen, would it?" Dorothy tried to lighten things and was relieved to hear the makings of a chuckle at the other end.

"I suppose you're right, Dorothy, but what are we going to do? She's messed up her future."

"Well, it's not a question of what *you* are going to do, Eileen, it's what *they* are going to do. But what *you're* not going to do, Eileen, is panic."

"I know you're right, Dorothy, but the upset of it? I'm not the better of it."

"I know it's a shock and something you'd rather not have happened, but it'll all work out in the end, you'll see. But you might need to let them think through their options themselves." Dorothy paused. "Like I say, nothing will happen quickly, so no need for you and Seamus to go wading in there with your size sevens. At least Martin is no fly-by-night, and sure weren't they planning on getting married anyway when she was finished her studies and had some teaching experience under her belt?"

"Well, she's going to have more than teaching under her belt now."

"Look, Eileen, just give them a bit of time to work it out themselves."

By the time the operator began making her presence known to indicate the end of the time, she'd managed to calm her niece sufficiently to ensure that the wrong thing to say or do might be avoided, in the short term anyway.

On the way home there was plenty to think about. It brought her right back to those days of panic. She could sympathise with Monica. Had every idea of the terror that would have taken over her life when she missed her period, but her grandniece could calm down now that she'd told her mother and father, and Martin, his. For her, that was the worst part over and Eileen and Seamus would come to terms with it, she knew that, once they'd got a grip on themselves and got over the 'what will the neighbours think' bit. Monica would never know what it'd be like with more than just that worry to deal with. The additional horror of knowing that the resulting child would not be coming from a loving relationship and never being able to tell anyone about it.

At seventy now, what would it really matter if someone knew, if her secret was to be discovered? She wondered if she should confide in Eileen. Might make her feel better about Monica's situation. Show her that it wasn't as complicated as she might imagine.

She dismounted at the bottom of the hill leading to home. Strolling along, pushing the bike, with a balmy sun shining on her back, it seemed like a possibility, that maybe this would be the time to share it.

That notion didn't last long. Thinking about it over the cup of tea when she got home, she knew it could never happen. When the other ingredients of her own dilemma came back into her head, she knew that. It could never happen, could never be shared. No lovely Martin in her situation, ensuring a happy ending.

Chapter 42

1958

By the time the new Butlin's Mosney Holiday Camp had opened and grown in popularity in County Meath, Monica had a husband, a toddler and a baby.

"How would you feel like joining us for something different this year, Dorothy?" Eileen looked at her cousin. "I have to warn you, it's very different. Three generations of us joining forces for the holiday. Not something we've tried yet, so I hope it'll work. Keep us young anyway. What do you think?"

Dorothy knew it had been Monica who'd hatched up the plan and had put her mother up to checking it out.

"Sounds like a good idea, Eileen. I've heard it's a great place. All the entertainment laid on." She paused. "Eileen, how would you feel if I took Bridie along?" Dorothy sounded unsure. "We'd get a separate chalet, of course."

"I think that would be a great idea. The change will do her good."

"I don't know if she'll agree to come, but I'll try and persuade her." Dorothy was relieved. "I think she might. She enjoyed the trips to Clare when she came with me. Herself and Ellen got on great. What with Art dying so soon after Mickie Joe, it took a lot of persuading and it was a long time before I was able to drag her along after that, but I managed to get her there in the end."

It was the first time she'd suggested it. The idea of the independence, of not all being under the one roof was what made her think it might be a good opportunity. She'd seen an article and photographs in the newspaper about the holiday camp and it looked great. And what made it even more attractive was all the different activities that were available. She could take Bridie off to try them out without interfering with the holiday plans of the others. She might like the Bingo and watching the ballroom dancing. It might even get her dancing again. She remembered her mother boasting about Bridie's popularity on the dance floor in her young days.

"I hope that one doesn't have her head turned in the wrong direction. They tell me the lads in the Hall are always around her, like bees at a honey pot." Maude's admonition to hide her boast. "Always up on the floor."

"The girls always say she's the best dancer in the parish, Mother, that's why." Dorothy envied her sister, not being old enough then to go to the dances with them. "Why do you always have to take the good out of everything?."

And then there were the sessions later, when she'd watched Bridie try to teach Mickie Joe the Charleston at home.

"Ah, Bridie, you're wasting your time. I'm a waltz man, just about able for the *one-two-three, one-two-three*. I'll never get the hang of this kicking-up-my-heels thing. I'm too old for this lark."

"Ah, MJ, you're not that ancient. Yet. It's too early to give up, it'll come. Look, even Dorothy's mastering it."

"What d'ya mean, *even* Dorothy? I'm a natural, I'll have you know, sister!"

How the three of them had laughed! She'd love to have that Bridie back again.

The bright blue sky of the morning, with only the odd fluffy cloud drifting by was exactly as the weather forecaster on the radio had predicted.

Fonsie lifted the two suitcases up onto the train at the station in Gorey. "Will you manage them from here yourselves? I don't want to be carried all the way to Dublin, if this train takes off with me still on it." He smiled at them.

"Thanks, Fonsie, we'll manage from here."

"Well, enjoy yourselves, girls, and say hello to Eileen and the clan for me."

"Will do. Thanks again, Fonsie." Dorothy smiled at him. "You won't forget to pick us up next Saturday, sure you won't?"

"I'll try to remember." He laughed. "Off with yous now." He stepped back as the stationmaster, working his way along the row of carriages, arrived to close the door.

"Here, Bridie, this one is empty." Dorothy peered in through the glass panel of the cabin door before opening it. "We'll be able to sit by the window and see everything." Picking up her case she raised it up, managing to slide it onto the overhead rack. "Here, pass me in your luggage and I'll put it up for you."

Bridie manoeuvred her case in through the door and slid it along the floor towards her sister.

"Good heavens, Bridie, what in the name of God have you got in the case?" Dorothy looked at her sister in amazement as she lifted it. "There's no way I'll be able to heave that up onto the rack."

"Well, I brought a few books, I thought we might be needing them. And then there's my walking shoes. Probably that's what's making it so heavy."

"Whatever about the walking shoes, I don't think we'll have much time for reading, Bridie, not where we're going. Not from what I hear about this place anyway." Dorothy grinned at her. "We'll shove it over to the side for the moment and ask the ticket collector to put it up for us when he comes around." She took off her jacket and sat down. "Here, spread your jacket over the rest of your seat, Bridie. I'll do the same. Might put people off coming in to join us. In case it gets crowded."

"I suppose it'd be nice to have the space to ourselves." Bridie folded her jacket and laid it carefully the length of the bench seat before sitting down opposite her sister. She rubbed the upholstery, smoothing its velvety surface. "This feels new, like it's been done up recently."

"You're right, it does." Dorothy examined it. "Last time I was on the train to Dublin it was a bit shabby. They must be upgrading them." She looked around the carriage, admiring it with new eyes. "I love the wood. Gives a lovely rich feel, a bit of luxury. Wouldn't like the job of polishing it though."

"Ah, I'm looking forward to this." Bridie settled herself against the padded back of her seat as the whistle blew and they were on their way.

"Good. So am I." Dorothy looked out the window as the train began its chugging out of the station. "Look, Bridie, there's Fonsie, he's still there waving at us. My God, he's getting to look like our da. Like mother used to say *'the wispy old head on him'*. I hadn't noticed him getting old. Go on, give him a wave!"

After that, they travelled in silence for a while, admiring the passing countryside, perfectly placed as they were to watch the sea views all along east coast as they travelled northwards.

The door opened.

"Tickets please, ladies."

Dorothy had heard him approaching with his call to each cabin along the carriage and had them ready.

"Return, I see." He punched the tickets before handing them back. "Keep them safe, ladies, don't lose them."

"We've a favour to ask." Dorothy smiled at him. "She's brought the kitchen sink with her and we can't lift the case up onto the rack. If you wouldn't mind?"

"No, problem at all. Mind your head there." In one movement he swung the case up and onto the rack.

"Thanks a million."

"Not a bother. Enjoy your trip, ladies."

Chapter 43

They had already checked in to one of the adjoining chalets by the time the others arrived and already heard a few announcements over the Tannoy about the afternoon activities and the little boy lost who was waiting at the information office for someone to claim him.

"That Redcoat said we couldn't miss it. It's the building with the pink walls." Dorothy pointed. "Oh, that must be it over there. All those people queueing outside."

They could tell it was oxtail soup on the menu, as the recognisable smell wafted out through the blue-framed windows of the dining hall. As they joined the tail end of the queue they peered into what seemed like a huge space, lines of tables and chairs in strict formation inside and waiters and waitresses running up and down the rows serving those already seated.

"Have you ever seen anything like it, Bridie, the size of it? We'd better not get lost in there on the first day of our holiday." Dorothy laughed. "Can you imagine the announcement! *'Two grey-haired women. When last seen they were both wearing navy cardigans.'*"

After the dinner they went for a walk around the camp to explore, wandering up and down the colourful rows of chalets.

"Isn't it so pretty, Bridie? The lovely roses on the archways and the yellows and pinks and blues of the different rows of bungalows."

"It is surely. Just lovely." Bridie stopped and turned around to survey her surroundings. "It's just beautiful. I've never seen anything like it. I can't put my finger on it but there's something magical about it. Don't you feel it, Dorothy?"

Dorothy hadn't expected much discussion, and was surprised that she got such a lengthy response. Lengthy by Bridie's standards. Eileen was right. Already this holiday seemed to be just the thing to bring some cheer into her sister's life. Something totally new with no associations with the past.

"Well, whatever about that dining hall, there's no way we can get lost here. Look, Bridie, they've letters as well as numbers along the rows." She was cautious as to how she put it. Wasn't sure if her sister had noticed the system. Already she'd heard the callouts for lost people, so she needed to be sure.

"D29." Bridie, eyebrows raised, smiled at her sister before turning at the next rose-covered arch.

"Okay, okay. I know you're not thick. Or daft." Dorothy grinned. She needn't have worried. "Just checking you noticed. Remember what mother used to say? That you were the beautiful one, but I was always the sharpest. Not sure she meant it as a compliment though."

Eileen and the others were travelling from Clare by car and so hadn't had the experience of being picked up with their luggage by the Butlins Express train from the station. It had been a delight, toot-tooting along as it wended its way through the camp, passing the groups of waving children. It reminded Dorothy of the Noddy book she'd just bought for Monica's young May. She watched Bridie waving back, a big smile on her face and she couldn't wait to take Monica's children for a spin on it and show them the pictures of Noddy's Toyland train.

"Here's your programme for the week." Dorothy handed them each a booklet. "It has all the organised events listed, day by day. I've been leafing through it. We won't have a minute to spare, there is so much to do. And look, there are shows on most nights in the theatre and plays in the playhouse. I think we're going to have to set up a babysitting rota, Eileen, so Monica and Martin can get out a few nights."

"That mightn't be necessary, Dorothy. I heard that they have nurses that go around at night, up and down the rows of chalets, and they'll announce if there is a child crying." Eileen paused a moment. "Although maybe you're right, I'm not sure that Monica would be happy with that system. She's a bit over-protective."

"Don't think I can't hear you, Mother!"

Dorothy and Eileen sat in their deckchairs and watched as Monica positioned herself on the low wall that surrounded the tiered fountain, keeping an eye on her daughter. May had insisted on sitting under the shelter of the lowest tier, splashing about in the shallow water.

"*Mammy, Mammy, look at me! I'm getting wet under here!*"

The child delighting in every spray that came in her direction whenever a light breeze whipped up made them laugh.

"Look at her! She loves it. This is a great place for kids." Eileen rocked the pram beside her, the sleeping Conor oblivious to the shrieks of children in the swimming pool. "Where's Bridie? Is she having a nap?"

"Indeed, she's not. This holiday has been great for her." Dorothy beamed. "I can't believe the change. She's off at the dance lesson in the ballroom. Not that she needs any, she could be giving the classes herself, but she was happy to go on her own. Didn't seem to need me with her."

"Maybe she's met a fella. Has that occurred to you? Maybe that's why she didn't want you to go with her." Eileen laughed.

"Perish the thought, Eileen. I know she's put a fair few through her hands in her lifetime, but we don't need any complications."

"Ah, Dorothy, that's the auld spinster in you talking. You wouldn't deny her a bit of pleasure, surely?" Eileen laughed.

"Well, let's just say, it's not exactly the sort of change I'd be hoping for her."

The child in the buggy gave a groan. Eileen glanced in at him but he just seemed to be changing his position.

"And this little fellow asleep through it all. We'll have to enter young Conor here into the Bonny Baby competition."

"Well, I've one here for you, Eileen." Dorothy passed over the programme. "The Glamorous Granny competition. Take a look."

"Oh, I'm not ready for that, Dorothy."

"Which bit? The glamour or the granny?"

"The *granny* bit!"

"Well, I've news for you. You *are* one. There's no easy way of putting it." Dorothy laughed at the horror on Eileen's face. "And you already qualify on the glamour front. I'll check out if you need an entry form."

"You'll not do any such thing! There's no way I'm going to parade myself up there on a stage. Granny indeed! Don't ever use that word about me again."

"You're still a granny, whether you like it or not." Dorothy grinned. "You need to start taking it on board. And enjoy it."

"Where has the time gone to?" Eileen shook her head slowly. "One minute I'm a granddaughter and next it seems I'm a granny?"

"I don't know why you're so surprised. Didn't anyone ever tell you, that's how life goes." Dorothy paused, her smile fading. "That's if you're lucky."

"When you look at them now, Eileen, how do you feel about the panic of the unexpected pregnancy?"

"Oh, I never think about it, Dorothy. I never thanked you for the way you handled me at the time. I was in a right state and sure look at them now? I wouldn't be without the grandchildren and sure Monica and Martin are as happy as a couple could be." Eileen paused and looked at her aunt. "And, do you know, I'm going to tell you something, something I'm ashamed to admit to now."

"And what's that?" Dorothy had a fair idea what was coming.

"I thought of encouraging her to have the child adopted."

"And did you say it to her?"

"Oh, God, no. Thankfully I kept the thought to myself – well, I discussed it with Seamus and he stopped me." She looked at Dorothy. "Can you imagine what sort of relationship I'd have with my daughter had I voiced that idea?"

"Well, not the one you have now, that's for sure."

"Yeah. Seamus took it better, much calmer than myself, but at least he managed to make me put a zip on it, me and my big mouth."

"Wise man, your husband."

Dorothy lay back in the deckchair and closed her eyes. A faint urge to divulge her own daughter made a gentle nudge at her. No, not a good idea. Smother the urge. The complications would change everything.

EILEEN

Chapter 44

County Wexford
1960

They all thought it would have been Bridie who went first, so it came as a shock when the phone call came from Fonsie with the news that Dorothy had had a massive heart attack. Having just come in after collecting the eggs from the henhouse, she'd been waiting in the kitchen for the lads to arrive for the breakfast after milking the cows. Two eggs had already been broken onto a saucer and sitting there waiting to be put onto the frying pan. Another four were in the bowl beside it, next in line for cracking. They found her in the armchair, peaceful as can be, but with a blue tinge around her lips.

"She must have felt it coming on. The way she got herself to the chair. The rashers were still in the Aga and they weren't burnt so she can't have been there too long."

"Well, that's a comfort, Fonsie, although I still can't believe it." Eileen was shocked, although with a slight relief that she hadn't had the coronary out in the fields or on the beach where she mightn't have been found so quickly. "You're really going to miss her. We're all going to miss her. Look, Fonsie, myself and Seamus will come over tomorrow and if it's okay we'll stay for a few days after the funeral in case you need a hand with things. Would that be okay with you?"

"Oh, Eileen, if you'd stay on that would be great. With all the comings and goings over the last two days I can't even think, but one thing I know is that when it all stops it's going to feel quare lonely here in the house. Yeah, I'd really like it if you and Seamus stayed a few days afterwards."

"She was great company, Fonsie, wasn't she?" Eileen paused. "And for you she must have been like an extra farmer."

"I don't know what I'm going to do, Eileen. She'd do the work of three men." Fonsie hesitated, as he looked shamefaced at his cousin. "That sounds awful. I don't mean it that way. We got on great. So it's not just the farm work I'll miss her for."

"Oh, Dorothy would appreciate that one, Fonsie." Eileen smiled. "And how has Bridie been taking it?"

"Ah, not good. She's missing her very badly. Coming over here more and just sitting in the chair, the tears running down her face a lot of the time."

"I'll call over to her later. You're going to be busy and so with us staying on after the funeral, it might help Bridie to have another woman around for a while. I know the wives of the Cornelius and Arthur are great, but they've enough to be doing and it's no job for you lads to sort through Dorothy's things. I'll give Bridie a hand with that."

"That'd be great. I'm at a loss to know what to do. I was never much good at helping her around the house, other than making sure she had enough firing in and keeping the hedges trimmed to her liking and the gravel scuffled. It was my mother, when she was alive did most of the house stuff and then Dorothy, she took over after that."

"We're really going to miss her. She was always great on the holidays. Not just with Monica and James when they were small but with the grandchildren in more recent years. She just had a great way with them."

"Yeah, she was always good with the youngsters, the nieces and nephews around here too." Fonsie paused. "I know I'm a right auld bachelor, but Dorothy should have got married. She'd have been more suited to having her own family instead of staying on here looking after an auld curmudgeon like me."

"She had her own life as well, Fonsie, and it was a good one. The job in the hotel, although I know she'd gone from there for a good while, but she'd lots of friends. Anyway, Fonsie, I'm sure you weren't that difficult. She wouldn't have stayed if you had been. Not the Dorothy I know . . . knew. Oh, God, it's hard to say that. It doesn't even sound right."

"Ah no, I'm not that bad, but I don't think I ever let her know how much I appreciated her help." He sighed. "And it's too late now."

They sat quietly for a while until Fonsie broke the silence.

"I'm really glad you're here, Eileen."

"So am I. So am I."

"I was dreading having to go through Dorothy's things. The stuff up in her room. Clothes and stuff."

"You needn't worry about it, Fonsie, I'll do that with Bridie, but are you sure it's not a bit soon?"

"Maybe it is, but seeing that you're here I think it's for the best. I daresay you won't be visiting much now that she's gone."

"Well, I'm sure we'll be back, but I'll talk to Bridie in the meantime and we'll get a start on it." The note of sadness in his voice broke her heart but she knew it was true.

"Thanks, Eileen. I didn't really want to ask Bridie myself. You know yourself. She's had enough of death."

She walked into the neat bedroom and sat on the side of the bed. As she stroked the pink candlewick bedspread and listened to the silence that fell around her, a large hole seemed to open up inside her. She could still get the faint trace of the 4711 eau-de-cologne, Dorothy's favourite, in the air. Hard to imagine that she would never see her cousin again, never share another holiday or hear her laughter as she played with the children. The tears spilled over as the size of the hollow space registered, leaving her empty and bereft.

"Oh Dorothy, where have you gone on us?" Eileen looked around the room slowly, noticing detail she'd never concentrated on before. All the signs still there. The grey hairs caught in the hairbrush, the pink lipstick, the same one that Eileen suspected had been on the go for years, only worn on holidays or when she'd been working in the hotel or at the weekend dances in Courtown. She'd taken Eileen and Seamus there on a couple of occasions years ago when they managed to talk Fonsie into staying at home and keeping an eye on the sleeping children for a few hours. Eileen remembered being surprised at the fact that Dorothy seemed to know most of the other dancers there and was never short of a partner.

"And why wouldn't I know everyone? Do you think I don't have a life when you're not here?" Dorothy had teased her. "Do you think I'm a nun?"

"Ah no, that's not what I meant . . . "

"Stop right there now, Eileen. Don't go digging a deeper hole for yourself." Dorothy smiled. "You might be surprised . . . "

At times she had wondered, but then Dorothy had never come across as a sad sort of person. Unlike her sister. Undoubtedly she did have a good life, now that she thought about it. The wide circle of friends that she'd introduced them to on their trips to Wexford over the years had confirmed that.

She stood up. Best to get on with the job, but where to start? She'd involve Bridie later.

Opening the wardrobe, a waft of lavender escaped, strong enough to suggest it might be fresh from this summer's blooms. She smiled at the conversations they'd had about Maude and her mothballs.

"Oh, I hate the smell of those things." Dorothy turned up her nose. "My mother always insists on using them, and I keep telling her she's stinking out the chapel on a Sunday with the smell of them. Do you think she'd switch to lavender? Not a bit of it. *'They might smell nice, but they'll not keep the moths away.'* Would you really be worried and the clothes about fifty years old anyway?"

Eileen ran her hand along the rack of clothes, a mixture of dresses, skirts and blouses. She picked up the black skirt and white blouse, her work uniform. Washed, pressed and ready to go again, even though she'd left that life behind several years before, apart from the odd special event in the hotel when they'd call on her. Well, she definitely wouldn't be needing that any more.

Eileen considered lifting the clothes out on the bed and sorting them. No, maybe that should be left until last. She'll wait until later or maybe tomorrow and get Bridie over and see which of the outfits she might want, and which ones to keep for the sisters-in-law. In the meantime a start on the drawers, one at a time, might be less daunting.

She pulled open the top drawer and revealed a selection of underwear and nightdresses. She fingered the lace trim on the soft cotton flower-sprigged fabric of a nightgown that still had that new feel. Very pretty, but clearly never worn. She smiled at the thought of Dorothy saving it for a special occasion. She'd have laughed at it herself. Ever hopeful.

She worked her way down through the drawers of stockings, socks, silk scarves and cardigans, feeling like she had no right to be going through another's private things. But it had to be done by someone and maybe it was best that she was that one.

The bottom drawer held a selection of items, put there most probably because they wouldn't have been in regular use. Gloves, two winter scarves and a couple of woollen hats that didn't look like something Dorothy might wear, except for frosty winter morning feeding the calves. An old wooden jewellery box with ornamental inlay work on the lid sat to one side. Eileen wondered about its origin as she ran her hand over the satiny patina. Clearly much older than Dorothy, she'd never seen it before – she pondered if it might have been handed down the generations. She sat on the side of the bed and opened it. Inside she found a few pairs of earrings she'd seen on Dorothy and a glittery headband that looked like it was from her 'flapper' days along with a couple of long pearl necklaces. A wedding ring that possibly belonged to Aunt Maude had fallen to the bottom of the box with a pair of rosary beads. A few badges and medals that clearly belonged to Uncle Cornelius from his Constabulary days were enclosed in a small navy velvet bag. She'd ask Fonsie about those later.

Going back to the chest of drawers she bent down to replace the jewellery box and saw something that had been sitting underneath it. A flat parcel, wrapped in several sheets of yellowed tissue paper that had crisped with age. Laying the jewellery box on top of the chest, she reached in. The tissue fell away as she lifted it out and exposed a white knitted matinee coat. Eileen held it up and admired the intricate lacy pattern around the yoke. She wondered who Dorothy might have knitted it for. As far as she knew there hadn't been any new babies in the extended family for quite some time. Well, not until Monica's children came along, or since, and she remembered the outfits that Dorothy had knitted for them. But now, with the pink satin ribbon threaded through holes around the neck, she was able to discount Monica's young Conor and anyway he was a bit old for matinee coats at this stage. Maybe this was one she'd made and forgotten to give it to whoever it had been intended for. But then why the yellowed tissue, clearly not recent? She laid it on the bed. Time enough to work that out later.

Realising she'd made no progress, she just put everything back in the drawers – maybe best to leave those for when Bridie came over. What next? Perhaps the bookcase.

She picked up a book that lay horizontal, slotted in on top of a row of canvas hardbacks, obviously too large for the height of the shelf. Its red-leather cover was brittle with age, one corner scuffed, another peeling away from its glue, revealing thick cardboard underneath. Puzzled as she leafed through it, she admired the sketches, some of which looked familiar. It took a few minutes before she saw the identification written with the New Jersey address, probably in case it was ever lost – Aunt Maria's diary, the journal Dorothy had told her about. She'd forgotten its existence. It was all so long ago and now here it was.

She heard Fonsie on the stairs. "Fonsie, come in here for a minute! Look what I found!" She held out the diary. "Look! Aunt Maria's diary."

"D'yeh know, I remember seeing that years ago, Eileen. Lord, that brings back memories. I'd forgotten all about it. Poor Maria! Part of history now."

"Would you mind if I borrowed it? For Monica. She's always very interested in hearing family stories and she's started working on the family tree recently and this might add to her research."

"You can have it, Eileen, but let me have a glance through it before you take it back to Clare with you." He held out his hand. "I'll return it to you tomorrow and you can give it to Monica for safe keeping. There's no point in me holding onto it, with neither chick nor child to follow on after me. I'd be happy that it will go to a good home where it'll be passed on to future generations."

"Thanks, Fonsie, Monica will be delighted with that. I know she'll treasure it."

Chapter 45

County Clare
1976

Eileen was perusing a bundle of photographs. Monica had been pestering her to try and cast her memory back to identify some of the faces and, after breakfast when Martin had left for work, she'd got stuck into the job. They'd sorted most of the photos in the boxes, but these last ones were still a frustrating mystery. She'd been wishing that whoever took them had put the names and dates on the back. She was no wiser now than the last time she'd tried.

She liked to get a few small jobs done each morning. At least one chore completed. That and a read of the newspaper and the crossword at least half done before a short walk. She was inclined to put off the walk as long as she could. The legs were still sore, particularly the right one, but Monica always saw to it that she got the exercise in before the lunch.

"It could be raining this afternoon, Mother. The longer you put it off the harder it'll be. I know it's difficult but you are making progress, even if you don't see it yourself. I do. So go on, do a lap of the green while I'm getting the salad ready."

These markers gave a comforting rhythm to her life, simple stuff that others would deem dull, but it suited her now that for the moment she wasn't as mobile as she'd have liked.

Yesterday's job had been polishing the silverware. She suspected that Monica only kept it because it had a history behind it, most having come from Mary Ann's. As far as she knew it had been passed down from Mary Ann's mother which would make Monica at least the fifth generation into whose care it had passed.

"I suppose I need to earn my keep," she joked as Monica set her up at the table, spreading out a newspaper to protect the wood surface. She'd already equipped her with the necessities, a soft cloth and silver polish and an old soft toothbrush to get into the crevices. The items for cleaning were all lined up in a row. The candlesticks had been a wedding present, as had the ornate silver basket that Monica used to hold fruit. The teapot, sugar bowl and milk jug were the inherited items. She could never understand their function. In her lifetime they'd never been used for the purpose for which they'd been designed.

"Why don't you ever use them, Granny?" she remembered asking Mary Ann when as a child she'd polished them for her in the old farmhouse.

"Ah, child, sure they're only ornaments. Can you imagine the taste of the tea out of that yoke? And as for the milk? No, I'd never put it in that jug, sure it'd be tainted. Dust collectors, that's all they are."

And here she was again, polishing them. The full circle.

She'd got into the habit of setting herself targets. Something to justify her existence and give a sense of achievement, to satisfy her when she thought back over her day. She wished she could be the sort who was happy enough to just sit and be a passenger, content to be waited on and read her books and listen to the radio. Why did she always have to have this little niggle of guilt if she didn't contribute something? But then without some goal the days would probably just drift into one another and leave her with the sense that she was just *'waiting the call'*. She smiled at the memory of old Ned.

He'd lived in the cottage down the road from herself and Seamus. An almost blind man who fed all the stray cats in the neighbourhood once he rose from his bed at noon each day. His key was always left in the back door so that neighbours could have access. She used to check on him in the mornings, mostly at the same regular time, and the conversation always started the same way.

"How are you this morning, Ned?" She'd stand in the doorway of his bedroom and see him stretched out, lying on his back.

"Ah, just waiting the call, missus. Just waiting the call!" His own little joke.

The regular response was missing one day when she called his name. He just lay there on his back, his mouth open. The lack of an answer and the pallor frightened her, but just as she moved forward to check if he was cold, he turned to face her with a big guffaw.

"Did I get you there, Eileen? Did I nearly get you?"

Since she'd moved in with Monica and Martin she sometimes wondered if she was in the way. In the beginning anyway. Especially with the broken legs. It can't have been easy for her daughter having to deal with her crocked mother and a big lump of a teenage son who was still at home considering his future, as well as a full-time job in the pharmacy.

Seamus's death had devastated her. It had been hard during his long illness, watching him struggle as his muscles grew weaker, until he'd ended up in the wheelchair. It was awful to see the frustration in a normally tolerant man. She could see it was driving him mad, especially as the house wasn't built with a moving vehicle in mind. At least with the walking sticks he'd managed to potter about independently. Fortunately, or unfortunately, the wheelchair stage had only lasted a few months – he hadn't even got to mastering the turning of the corners from the hallway into the various rooms with any degree of skill before he died peacefully in his sleep.

If she'd got a penny for every time she had to endure *"Ah, sure time's a great healer!"* she'd be a rich woman. But she was lucky to have had him so long, seeing that she was a bit of a late starter in the marriage stakes.

She'd only been widowed a few years and the hole in her life beginning to close over when she'd had the fall that led to her staying with Monica and Martin. The neighbour's dog, a friendly old mutt but excitable, had tripped her as she left the house one morning and sent her crashing down the front steps at the hall door. Whatever about having broken one leg, when that healed she might have managed to continue living alone, but with both of them banjaxed, there was no way she could manage to hobble around on crutches. With little choice in the matter, at least in the immediate term, she had to go along with their plan, but the prospect of the loss of her independence worried her.

The weeks drifted into months, and the longer the legs took to heal the more concerned she got about the move back to her own two-storey house. In the end it was Martin who suggested he'd convert one of the spare rooms and garage into a 'granny flat' as he called it and that she might consider the possibility of moving into their bungalow to live permanently with them.

"That's very kind, Martin. It's not every man would welcome his mother-in-law to live with them."

"But you forget, Eileen, I'm not every man." He threw a mocking look at her. "I'm a rarity."

"Sure you're a saint, Martin!" She laughed. "Let me have a think about it. We wouldn't want you to be regretting it in a few months' time now, would we? This needs to be carefully worked out."

"Well, don't take too long or I might withdraw the offer."

After much tossing and turning over the proposal in her head, they agreed that if Eileen were to sell her house some of that money could be used to fund the conversion into a self-contained unit to their bungalow and no-one would be in anyone's way. Once they'd agreed to allow her to finance the project she felt happier about it. Not under so much of a compliment.

The sale of her own house went smoothly, despite the emotional wrench, and now with the work on the granny flat almost at an end and her legs working fairly well again, she was looking forward to moving into her new abode, her own independent quarters. While it was time to give her daughter and son-in-law their own space she'd a slight niggling worry that she'd miss the comings and goings in the main house.

"You needn't worry, Mother – I'd say Conor will be in and out to you, to get away from us. He likes discussing his options with you. Thinks you understand him better than we do," Monica reassured her. "Anyway, you're not barred from dropping in to us. And I hope we're not going to be barred from visiting you."

A caller to the house a couple of times a week was a treat while she was staying with them. All the better if they had a car and time to spare for a little outing. It didn't matter where to. Anywhere and everywhere was of interest to her. Just to have a jaunt and to get out from under her daughter's feet. Even if they were just going to the post office or to do a bit of grocery shopping. She wouldn't even need to get out of the car – well, for months after the fall there hadn't been any question of it. She'd be content to just sit there and wait while they were doing their business. Rolling down the window was enough to satisfy her, to be able to watch the world go by. She often felt guilty that Monica might feel it a burden to provide all the entertainment, so an outing like this would take some of that responsibility from her shoulders and she might pick up a bit of news to take home. Once she was more mobile again she'd be able to amble about on her own, but in the meantime she had to take advantage of the possibilities that any moving vehicle might present.

Thank God she still had good eyesight. Didn't know what she'd do if she couldn't read. Changing her library books was a big highlight. Twice a month Monica would drop her off and she'd spend a good hour selecting the reading matter for the next two weeks and have a chat with the librarian, an avid reader herself, who always had a tip on any new acquisitions. Sitting on the bench outside afterwards, waiting for her lift, sometimes added to the experience. The odd familiar face would join her and they'd catch up on the news around the locality.

"Sure maybe I'll come with you?" she'd say if she spotted Monica collecting the shopping bags from the hall stand. She'd ignore the eye-roll, knowing it was the one thing that Monica liked to do on her own. Stuck indoors, cabin fever could set in. She needed to get out, even if it meant putting up with her daughter's shuffling impatience as she stopped for a chat with an acquaintance in the vegetable aisle. That had to take precedence, even knowing that Monica was anxious to get the shopping done quickly and get home to put the dinner on. "Sure, why don't you get on with getting your stuff," she'd say, "and I'll wait here and mind the trolley and have my chat."

Getting old meant she was never in a hurry, certainly not in a hurry to arrive where she was headed anyway. Every opportunity was to be savoured – and, even if it caused a little irritation, she was prepared to risk that. A knock on the door was great, especially when it turned out to be someone new or news about something unusual. There was always the anticipation.

ANNE

Chapter 46

The green area that served as a sort of park for the local children to kick their ball formed an oval shape in the middle of the housing estate. Monica often wondered if the councilmen who'd sowed it originally had deliberately planted the trees in the exact positions that would later serve as goalposts for the local children. Great foresight if that had been the case, but no doubt they had children of their own.

It was being mown now by the council workmen. They never bothered with the strips of grass on the pavements outside the crescent of bungalows, although Monica was sure they were supposed to. She'd gone to the local shop for a bottle of milk and was walking back up the road when she'd overheard one of the regular workmen chastising the new lad on the team when he made a move to the grassy strip outside her house and began cutting it.

"Leave that. Let them do their own bit. No need to be giving them bad habits. Just concentrate on the park area."

She remembered a brief embarrassment in the shifty move as he spotted her turning into her driveway, knowing full well she'd overheard him. Not that she minded. She'd planned on taking out her lawnmower anyway.

"I'm back." She put the milk in the fridge. "Do you want a cuppa before I go out to cut the grass in the front garden?"

"Ah, no, love, it'll do when you've finished and we can have it together!" Eileen called back from the sunroom. "Time enough."

"Grand, I won't be long."

She paused before starting to run the mower over her strip at the kerbside outside the fence, tired after mowing the front lawn. She rested her arms on the handle of the mower and looked around. She noticed the bottle-green Morris Minor passing slowly on the road outside. The little orange arrow-like indicator still stuck out, like it was stuck or the driver had forgotten to cancel it. One of the older models of Morris Minor not often seen nowadays, perhaps it belonged to a vintage-car enthusiast. As the car veered left around the oval green parkland, the jerky driving of the grey-haired woman behind the wheel suggested that she had learned her skill long before any driving test had been introduced.

It was only when she rounded the green for the second time, as Monica finished mowing, that she became curious as to why the woman was driving so slowly. The indicator poked out again and the woman jerked to a halt a few yards away and several feet from the kerb, blocking the entrance to the house next door.

Monica, her curiosity further raised, wheeled the lawnmower into the driveway and picking up the yard brush went outside again. She began sweeping the grass clippings, in an effort to appear busy and not simply gawping.

She glanced at the woman as she exited the car and smiled.

"Excuse me. I wonder if you can help me?" the woman said.

Once outside the car, she looked a lot younger than her pose behind the steering wheel had suggested. She was smartly dressed in a black coat and blue silk scarf and Monica noticed her sprightly step as she approached.

"I'm sorry to disturb you, but I'm looking for a family called Barrett. I believe they live somewhere around here, but I don't know the number of the house." It came out in a bit of a rush as if she'd rehearsed it.

"Well, you've come to the right place. I'm Monica Barrett." Who in heaven's name is this, she wondered.

The woman brightened. "I can't believe I've struck lucky on my first enquiry! I thought I'd be going around all day searching. So you're Monica. Well, it's really your mother, Eileen, I'm looking for. I believe she's staying with you."

"She is, yes. She had a bad accident, so she's been staying with us."

"Would it be possible to speak to her?"

"Yes, of course." She hesitated. What could this woman possibly want with her mother? "Are you a friend of hers?"

"Oh, no, I've never met her. You see, I'm hoping she might be able to help me. I'd trying to track down a certain O'Brien." A hopeful look crossed her face. "If it wouldn't be too much trouble?"

Monica relaxed. Ancestry stuff most likely. Excellent. Maybe a new link in the family tree. "No trouble at all. But you'll need to move your car because you're blocking the next door's driveway and they won't be too happy if they come back." She pointed to the Morris

Minor. "You can park it here outside ours. It won't be in anyone's way."

She waited until the woman bumped her way to a halt against the kerb and got out.

"I'm sorry for intruding," she said. "Especially if your mother isn't well."

"Oh, she's much better now. It's no trouble."

The woman followed Monica into the drive and stood waiting for the invitation to enter the house.

"Come on in." Monica looked over her shoulder as she entered the hall. "And what led you here, to us?"

"Well, I'm afraid it's a long and complicated story."

Chapter 47

Dublin

It had been the dogged determination of her daughter that had brought her to this point. Left to herself, she wouldn't have had the courage to even try.

"Mam, you must. I know you want to, however much you say it's not important to know. I saw how getting involved in helping Angela with her adoption project for college had an effect on you."

"It did, I admit."

"And, I hate to say this but … you've already left it so late, it may be too late. We've got to do it now."

Valerie knocked on the door of a redbrick house in Dublin, an address that had turned up on a document they had procured from the nuns, was the first decent lead that they'd had.

On the doorstep, a woman called Maisie had recognised the name Dorothy when she asked.

"Oh, yes. My mother was friends with a Dorothy. I knew her too, but her name was Dorothy Redmond, not O'Brien. They were great friends for years. Come on in. She's gone a bit forgetful, but she should be able to fill in some of the blanks for you if it's the same Dorothy."

Heart racing, Valerie followed Maisie along the hallway.

Maisie raised her voice. "Hey, Nancy! I've brought a woman to talk to you about Dorothy!"

Anne was washing the dishes when she heard the hall door opening, followed by an excited shout.

"*Mam, Mam, you're not going to believe what I've got to tell you!*" Valerie came rushing down the hallway and stood in the doorway, arms outstretched, gripping the door frame. "*We've hit the jackpot! I've met your mother's friend!*"

"You're joking …" Anne stuck the sudsy plate in her hand in the rack and grabbed the kitchen towel to dry her hands.

"No! She's been living at that address all these years!" said Valerie, throwing her handbag on the table. "Nancy Dunne, that's her name, the friend. She has a bit of dementia, so her memory was hazy at times – but she knew all about your mother being pregnant and having to give you up. She was very vague about your father though – didn't seem to know. The name Redmond has entered the puzzle now, but I've got leads for you to follow! County Wexford and County Clare, here I come! Well, not me. God, I'd love to be able to go with you, but I can't get the time off.'

"Well, Wexford will have to wait. Have you forgotten I'm off to Clare in a fortnight with the Women's Club, so I might try following up there first."

"You go for it, Mam!" Valerie was delighted.

Chapter 48

County Clare

The woman followed Monica into the hall and halted, a hand on her chest, fingers splayed, as if to quiet her heart. "You see, I'm following up a lead that links this O'Brien relative to your mother's family."

"Oh, I see." So this was no casual enquiry. It might be a sensitive issue.

"My name is Anne Kirwan or at least it was."

"Well, the name Kirwan doesn't ring any bells with me, but come on in. My mother is in the sun room." With a jerk of her head, she beckoned the woman to follow her.

"She won't mind, will she?" Anne asked.

"Not at all. She loves visitors. Doesn't get out as much as she'd like to now. Broke her legs in that accident a while back and she's still recovering."

Anne waited in the hall, holding back as Monica went into the sun room.

"Mother, you have a visitor." Monica stepped aside to make room for Anne to pass. "Come in, Anne, come on in. Mother, this lady is Anne Kirwan. Anne, this is my mother Eileen."

Anne moved forward and extended her hand to the woman in the armchair.

"Hello, I'm sorry to disturb you . . . "

"Oh, don't worry, Anne, you're not disturbing me at all."

Eileen put the bundle of photographs she had been sorting onto the little table beside her chair and shook hands.

"Mother, Anne is looking for a certain O'Brien relative of hers who she thinks might possibly be related to your family."

"Well, Anne, there's nothing I like more than an interesting interruption. And this sounds like it might be one." Eileen smiled at her. "Why don't you take your coat off and sit down?" She turned to her daughter. "Will you make a pot of tea there, Monica? I'm sure Anne would like a cup and you must need one yourself after all your mowing."

Monica smiled at Anne and hurried out, anxious to get back as soon as possible in case she missed anything.

Anne took her coat off, hung it over the back of an armchair and sat down, placing her leather handbag at her feet. "You're very kind to give me your time, Eileen."

"Not at all. I've got all day and Monica here is an avid builder of the family tree. Maybe we can find this relative of yours."

"I hope so."

"Have you come far, Anne?"

"From Dublin."

"Oh, well, definitely you'll have more than tea then."

"No, no, I didn't come down from Dublin today. I'm staying in Lahinch. I'm down here in Clare for a few days with friends from my Women's Club."

"Lovely over there in Lahinch, isn't it? Are you staying in the hotel near the front?"

"I am. It's very comfortable."

"Very handy for the beach."

"Yes. Right beside it. Not that I swim or anything, but there are lovely views along the seafront there."

"Well now, tell me, who is this O'Brien you're looking for?" Eileen settled back in her chair and stretched out her legs, propping them up on the stool Monica had placed there for her.

"Well, I'm looking for my birth mother."

"Ah … I see."

Anne leaned down to where she had placed her handbag on the floor, opened the clasp and took out an envelope from which she removed old documents, their edges sepia with age.

"My birth and baptismal certificates."

She opened them out. The centre point of the folds had already torn, the edges of the tear fluffy with handling.

"I was christened Anne O'Brien but I was brought up by a family called Kirwan. I was always known as Anne Kirwan after, of course. Well, until I got married and became a Casey." She passed the certificates over to Eileen. "Mind – they're so delicate they're in danger of falling apart altogether."

"They certainly are."

"See here …" Leaning over, Anne pointed. "My mother's name was Dorothy O'Brien. Does that mean anything to you?"

Eileen's eyes clamped on the space headed **Mother's Name**. The paper shook in her hand when she saw the date of birth – 1901. She looked for the father's name: a blank.

"You'll have to let me have a think about that." The words came out slowly as she felt her brain shoot into reverse.

"Is something ringing a bell?" Anne said hopefully.

"I . . . I'm not sure." Eileen hesitated, hoping the shock didn't show on her face. She needed time to digest this. "I'm wondering what it was that led you here, to this particular house?"

"I first went to Ard na Gréine – your family home, I believe."

"And how did you know about Ard na Gréine?" Eileen was puzzled.

"It was Nancy Dunne who mentioned it – my mother's friend in Dublin. She couldn't remember what the link was, but said that Dorothy sometimes referred to it, and that it was near Ennis, so I followed up on that through the post office. According to Nancy, Dorothy's name was not O'Brien but she *was* somehow related to your family. She said Dorothy's name was Redmond. I would have put that down to her dementia – but, oddly, her daughter agreed with her." She paused and looked questioningly at Eileen who gave a little shake of her head. "So, as I was coming to Clare anyway, I went to Ard na Gréine – but when I got to the house there was nobody home. Luckily, a neighbour was passing by and told me your brother John lives there but that he was probably gone for the day. I told him I was trying to trace long-lost family and he told me where to find you, saying you were a great one for the family history."

Monica arrived in with the tea tray.

"Well, have the pair of you found a link?" Monica smiled down at Anne. "Have we some long-lost relative here?"

"Not quite, but we're working on it." Laying the certificates down carefully on top of the bundle of photographs, her hand trembling slightly, Eileen made room for the plate of biscuits that Monica handed her. She busied herself with the tea ritual and hoped Anne would put the rattle of the china teapot against the cups down to her age. "My memory isn't as good as it was."

In fact, nothing was wrong with her memory, and Eileen was relieved when her daughter just held out her hand to pass the teacup and saucer to Anne and didn't contradict her. But the quizzical look on Monica face told her she wasn't buying that excuse.

Eileen needed time to process the drama that was unfolding in her head.

"Well, Anne, tell me a little about yourself," she said.

"And what was it that made you want to check out your past? I mean now," said Monica. "Not that I'm saying you're old or anything." She laughed awkwardly. "I mean, why not when your parents were alive? Oh, sorry, maybe they are still alive? Oh, Lord, I'd better shut up! I'm digging a right hole for myself now."

Anne smiled. "Oh, I know I've left it a very late. Yes, my parents died years back. I did ask them about my birth mother but they had very little information other than what's on the certificates and the nuns' confirmation that my mother had come from a farming family, and was too young to look after me."

Eileen glanced at the papers balanced on top of the photographs again, hoping her daughter would keep the conversation going long enough for her to decide what to tell this woman.

"At the time I didn't really delve any further because I'd had a lovely life with them, the people who brought me up. They already had a son of their own, but they always treated me as if I was theirs too, so I was satisfied with that at the time." Anne gazed into the distance. "Yeah, I suppose that was it. What spurred me on recently was that my granddaughter, Angela, is doing research for a college project and part of it involves adoptions, so she wanted a real-life case to study. Although I wasn't officially adopted. It wasn't possible back then. But she picked me as her guinea pig for how it was in a pre-adoption period." Anne laughed. "So that's how my interest was renewed."

"And what did you find out?" Monica was intrigued.

"Well, I didn't have anything very useful to tell her. Nothing new anyway. Only about my life as I remembered it growing up knowing I was, well, I suppose you'd call it 'fostered'. My parents made no secret of it. They made me feel special and I was lucky to have had my mother up to ten years ago. She lived with me."

"And that's why you're here." Eileen put down the cup slowly and, looking across at her visitor, studied her face. "To find out where you came from."

Chapter 49

While they'd been drinking the tea, Eileen's eyes were drawn to the certificates and scenes from a long-ago time flashed before her, forming a picture that was not pretty. The tension that crept into the kitchen whenever her father entered and Dorothy was there. The muffled sounds upstairs. Dorothy crying. The way he wouldn't let any of the children accompany Dorothy out to the barn when a job was needing to be done. Like scratchy black-and-white silent film clips.

Dorothy's disappearance from their lives had not been talked about back then. At least not in their hearing. But with the instinct of children, they knew something had happened, just not something they were able to put words on. Not at the time anyway. It was only as they got older that Eileen fitted the pieces together, and all were scenes she'd tried to erase from her memory.

She remembered her father's handsome face and strong presence, always standing, showing his power as he towered over them when they were teenagers. She couldn't picture him sitting at their level, except at meals, but he must have sometimes. He'd never done anything to any of them, not that she knew of, but there was always a threat hovering, showing them just who was in charge.

Eileen knew it was a lot more than hovering threats with Dorothy. She understood why Dorothy, the person who loved minding them, the one they had such fun with, had turned into the girl who all of a sudden couldn't get away fast enough.

The womanising, that had come later. The fragmented rows that she'd overheard later between her parents had provided enough knowledge for her to lose all respect for him. Her mother had never drawn breath on it, but they all suspected he was far from being the perfect husband.

It had taken years to come to terms with it all. To settle on the probability that with Dorothy, unwanted attention had been the extent of it, and once she'd gone it was something that couldn't be changed. Nothing to do with her anymore. She'd thought she'd arrived at a place where she could leave it to rest. Accepted that it was something that her father would have to live with, in the unlikely event that it bothered him. And, later, after his death, leave him to rest. Whether in peace or not. But now it seemed that it was even worse than she'd ever imagined, much more serious than just unwelcome attention. She wondered if her mother had had any inkling.

Poor Dorothy. Long dead now. Eileen wondered why she had left this clue when she had kept her past so securely hidden all her life. The O'Brien name. Had anyone at all known? Anyone in Dorothy's own family over there in Wexford? Clearly her brother Fonsie had no clue. And Bridie had never said anything. But that in itself was no surprise – poor Bridie had enough of her own problems to contend with and none of her other siblings had ever mentioned anything.

Was the O'Brien surname on the certificate simply to give her secret daughter a link with the extended family if ever she chose to follow it up? Without revealing her own name? What was that about? Was it revenge? To expose his evil deeds? No, that was not the Dorothy she knew, that would be more like herself. Retribution wouldn't have been in her cousin's nature. Eileen wondered if it would have been simpler to have left a clue leading back to her Wexford Redmond roots. But who knew what had been in poor Dorothy's mind at the time? Maybe fear that her secret daughter would have landed on the doorstep of her grandparents Maude and Cornelius. Yes, that was most likely the reason for the O'Brien clue in the mixed-up head of a young Dorothy.

Now was the time to fill in the gaps. Dorothy's daughter deserved to know ... but not everything.

After the tea, Anne went to use the bathroom and Monica began to stack the tray.

Eileen leaned towards her daughter and said quietly, "There is something I need to tell Anne, Monica – but you need to hear it too. Just put the tray in the kitchen and come back."

Monica returned and sat, looking apprehensive, and soon they heard Anne's footsteps returning down the hallway.

Eileen watched as Anne resumed her seat. She drew a deep breath and said, "Anne, you've got the right O'Briens. There was a Dorothy. Now that I've seen the certificates and had a think about it, I think I can piece it all together."

"Oh, thank God!" Anne crossed her hands over her heart. "I was beginning to think I was on a wild goose chase, had it all wrong."

"No, you haven't. However, I'm afraid Dorothy died over fifteen years ago. A heart attack. It was very sudden." Eileen looked at Anne, a sadness in her voice. "I'm sure this is very disappointing for you, but I'll tell you what I know. She was my cousin, but older than us. What I can tell you is that she was a lovely person. The best sort. I was very close to her, even up to the time she died. And we all still miss her dreadfully. She looked after myself and my brothers and sister when we were children and she always came here to Clare every year on holiday. And later when I had my own children and grandchildren, we used to go over to visit her in Wexford. Up to the time she died." Eileen paused, unsure how much more of the truth she could tell this woman. "Nancy Dunne was right. Dorothy's name wasn't O'Brien. It was Redmond. Her mother and my mother were sisters. But your father was an O'Brien. Long dead now."

"Related to your O'Briens?"

"Oh, very distantly. If you go back far enough in Clare you'll find that every O'Brien has some link from long ago." Eileen rushed on, anxious not to leave a gap for too many questions. "But things didn't work out between them and she must have gone off to Dublin to have the baby. That was you. They weren't married, of course, but she gave you his name nevertheless." She paused, looking at Anne. "Well, in a sort of a way. As far as I know, she never told anyone she was pregnant. Unless she told her parents but, if so, they kept it secret all their lives. She left Wexford and went off to Dublin to work around that time. And she never said a word, as far as I know, even up to the time she died."

"And the name 'Anne'." Monica looked at Eileen. "Do you remember, Mother? Dorothy told us about her little sister Annie?"

"I do indeed. Oh, that was a sad story." Eileen shook her head.

"The poor child. Dorothy had a little sister, a beautiful little child with red curly hair. Apparently she was burnt in a fire when she was only a toddler. Dorothy was so sad about that, she was very fond of her. An awful tragedy."

"But do you not see the link, Mother?" Monica looked across at Anne. "She obviously called you Anne after her."

"What colour was your hair, Anne? Growing up?" Eileen asked.

"Red. Well, I liked to call it auburn. Sounded more glamorous."

"There you are. Runs in the family, although Dorothy herself had brown hair. Little Annie had the red curls." Eileen smiled. "And when Dorothy used to mind us, I always thought I was her favourite, because when I was small I had the same red hair and she used to say I was like her little sister Annie."

"Oh, that's so nice. That she might have called me after her. Sad, but really nice." Anne paused. "And what was he like? My father."

"How would I describe him?" Eileen hesitated, noting the way Anne leaned forward expectantly on her seat. This would have to be handled carefully. "Let me think. Well, I was young at the time so I didn't understand much. But thinking back, he was a lot older than Dorothy. But I suppose I'd have to be honest and say that he had a reputation for being . . . well, unreliable. Very handsome though and charming. But . . . unreliable, clearly." Eileen gave a weak smile. "Although I believe he was a hard worker. No shirker when it came to the farm."

"So he was a farmer?"

"He was indeed. And a good one at that." Eileen searched for the positives. "Yes, and very good-looking. You have his eyes. Green. That was him. I can't really tell you much more about him. He's dead a long, long time and like I said he was much older than Dorothy."

"Are there any of his family still around?" The look of anticipation on Anne's face worried Eileen. "Do they still live on the farm?"

"No, the farm has gone out of the family. Changed hands years ago. I was never really sure where it was." She hated lying, but it had to be done. "But leave that with me – I'll have to check around, but I think you might have to settle for us on the O'Brien side – myself, John and my older sister Mary. However distant." Safest now to move off the subject. "But the good news is that on Dorothy's side, the Redmonds, there would be nieces and nephews, her brothers' children and grandchildren."

"I'd be very interested in knowing about them." Anne's face lit up. "Are they still around?"

"Indeed they are. They're all over in Wexford. She had older twin brothers Cornelius and Arthur – they're long dead but they had families. Her brother Fonsie, he's gone too. A lovely fellow. Never married. But some of the other grandchildren still live in the homeplace. I can give you the details there, no problem, but I'd need to make contact with them first because I believe they won't know anything about this side of Dorothy's story. I know they'll be delighted and will want to meet you. But poor Dorothy! That must have been very lonely for her and she must have felt she couldn't share her sadness with anyone. What a shame that we didn't know! And she must have been sad because she was great with us children and with mine and the grandchildren also. It's a shame she never married."

"I have something else to show you." Anne reached down and rummaged in her handbag, taking out another envelope. "A picture of me as a baby."

Eileen took the faded photo from her.

"*Oh, my God! The matinee coat! I recognise it!*" Eileen gasped.

"There's absolutely no doubt now. Dorothy was definitely your mother. Who took the photo?"

"My parents. Around the time they got me." Anne looked puzzled. "If you didn't know anything about me, how do you recognise the matinee coat?"

"When I was going through Dorothy's things after she died and I found one similar. The only thing I can think of is that she must have knitted more than one from the same pattern and kept the one you'd worn when you were with her. There was a bit of a stain on the front of it and it was very old when I found it. It looked like it hadn't been washed, so that must tell you a lot. She clearly must have wanted to keep a bit of you. None of us could figure it out when I found it, but it all makes sense now."

"Isn't that so sad!" Monica's eyes welled up.

"Hold on a minute." Eileen heaved herself up from the chair with difficulty. "I'll be back. Just talk amongst yourselves there."

"Isn't it such a shame that you never got to meet her, Anne?" Monica shook her head slowly. "We had such lovely childhood memories of her. She came on holidays with us each year and I could talk to her. She was very soft and understanding." She grinned. "Unlike my mother."

"She sounds lovely."

"She was. Of that you can rest assured." Monica paused. "It's just such a shame you two never got to meet."

Monica talked on about her memories of Dorothy until Eileen appeared in the doorway.

"I have something for you, Anne," she said as she walked towards her, holding out a paper bag. "Here, open it."

She sat down heavily as Anne opened the bag.

"Oh, my God! I can't believe it." Anne gently eased out a little knitted matinee coat. "Exactly the same!"

"I'm afraid I threw out the tissue paper it was wrapped in. It had yellowed and crisped up but the coat is as white as when she knitted it."

Tears rolled down Anne's face as she held the precious garment up to her nose. "Thank you, oh, thank you so much! You've no idea what this means to me."

Eileen and Monica sat in silence until Anne had recovered enough to dry her tears.

"I have something else." Anne laid the coat on her knee and, opening the envelope again, took out a handwritten letter. "She wrote to me. My mother didn't give it to me until I was in my teens. Said it had been hidden inside the matinee coat – twin to this one – that she took me home in."

Eileen didn't need to look twice at the letter Anne passed to her. She instantly recognised the handwriting. The curlicued 'D'. Exactly the same as on the birthday cards that Dorothy continued to send them after she left.

She could feel her eyes welling up as she read the letter Dorothy had written to her beloved daughter.

My dearest Annie

I hope at some stage in your life this letter will be passed on to you. I cannot tell you how much my heart is broken at having to give you up. Please believe me when I tell you that if I could have cared for you and given you a good life nothing would have given me more pleasure, but that wasn't possible at the time. I did look after you for your first weeks and loved you so much. You were such a beautiful baby with little wisps of the red-gold hair that runs in my family, and you were so good. We had lots of cuddles together and I treasure every moment that I spent with you and I will never forget you.

I hope you have a very happy life and know how much I love you and hope you can forgive me for letting you go.

Love always

Your mother Dorothy

For the first time ever, Eileen wished he were still alive. Impossible though it was. He must have thought he'd escaped the consequences, but had he still been around, he'd have had to face the results of his actions.

She wondered if he knew. Might Dorothy have told him? Left him forever in fear of his secret being disclosed? Maybe it was what her father deserved. His 'other life', not over yet. She wondered how he'd deal with that.

She hoped she'd given Anne enough information to satisfy her about her father while wiping out the route to his existence sufficiently for her not to be tempted to follow up. Likely now that meeting up with Dorothy's Wexford family would occupy and content her.

But the bigger regret was that Dorothy was gone. Not here to share the wonder of her daughter, back to her after all this time.

THE END

Printed in Great Britain
by Amazon